PRAISE FOR

The Black Country

"Ripe with gory details . . . [Grecian] has a flair."
—*The New York Times Book Review*

"Devilishly dark . . . It isn't often that a mystery-thriller enthralls so completely . . . but as usual with Mr. Grecian, there is more to this tale than complex plotting . . . A displaced eye, a crumpled note, cryptic limericks and lost ribbons: Like our detective heroes, we follow these trails into the white-blinding snow to its brilliant and unexpected conclusion. Whether you read the tale in the dark night of winter or the haze of a summer sun, be prepared for the chill. The days are dark in Black Country." —*The Huffington Post*

"Grecian creates an eerie atmosphere from start to finish, and without giving anything away, the killer here is creepy and unexpected." —Bookreporter.com

"Startling and spooky . . . [A] bold melding of horror with historical elements." —*Publishers Weekly* (starred review)

"[Grecian] presents with fine precision the gray and gritty atmosphere of late-Victorian England." —*Kirkus Reviews*

The Yard

"Lusciously rich with detail, atmosphere, and history, and yet as fast paced as a locomotive, *The Yard* will keep you riveted from page one. It's truly a one- or two-sitting read."
—Jeffery Deaver, author of *Carte Blanche* and *The Bone Collector*

continued . . .

"Grecian has a talent for capturing gory details . . . extremely vivid (and strangely moving) . . . Bounding from the workhouse to the lunatic asylum to the stinking streets, [Grecian] does outstanding descriptive work on the mad and the maimed, the diseased and the demented . . . If Charles Dickens isn't somewhere clapping his hands for this one, Wilkie Collins surely is."

—*The New York Times Book Review*

"[A] mix of historical facts and vivid fictional creations. It's great fun . . . Grecian's debut is the promising start of a new series and should be one of the most acclaimed and popular mysteries of the year."

—*The Huffington Post*

"One can almost taste the grit of the city, smell the soot of the chimneys, and hear the clopping of horses' hooves as the hansoms rumble down cobbled streets. Alex Grecian builds his readers a world in Victorian London and populates it with good guys you'll want to root for and bad guys you'll want stopped at any cost. *The Yard* spans about three days, just the amount of time you'll need to race through this intriguing debut novel." —Bookreporter.com

"Grecian powerfully evokes both the physical, smog-ridden atmosphere of London in 1889 and its emotional analogs of anxiety and depression. His infusion of actual history adds to this thriller's credibility and punch. A deeply satisfying reconstruction of post-Ripper London."

—*Booklist*

"A brilliantly crafted debut novel with unforgettable characters. An utterly gripping tale perfectly evokes Victorian London and brings you right back to the depraved and traumatic days of Jack the Ripper." —Lisa Lutz, author of *The Spellman Files*

"This excellent murder mystery debut introduces a fascinating cast of characters. Grecian displays a flair for language as well as creating vivid (and occasionally gruesome) depictions of places and events."

—*Library Journal*

TITLES BY ALEX GRECIAN

The Yard

The Black Country

The Devil's Workshop

BERKLEY BOOKS

NEW YORK

THE
DEVIL'S
WORKSHOP

A NOVEL OF SCOTLAND YARD'S
MURDER SQUAD

ALEX GRECIAN

THE BERKLEY PUBLISHING GROUP
Published by the Penguin Group
Penguin Group (USA) LLC
375 Hudson Street, New York, New York 10014

USA • Canada • UK • Ireland • Australia • New Zealand • India • South Africa • China

penguin.com

A Penguin Random House Company

Berkley trade paperback ISBN: 978-0-425-27485-9

The Library of Congress has cataloged the G. P. Putnam's Sons hardcover edition as follows:

Grecian, Alex.
The Devil's Workshop / Alex Grecian.
p.   cm. — (Scotland Yard's Murder Squad; 3)
ISBN 978-0-399-16643-3
1. Police—England—London—Fiction.   2. Escaped prisoners—Fiction.   3. London
(England)—History—19th century—Fiction.   4. Mystery fiction.   5. Title.
PR6107 R426D48   2014   2013050430
823'.92—dc23

PUBLISHING HISTORY
G. P. Putnam's Sons hardcover edition / May 2014
Berkley trade paperback edition / April 2015

PRINTED IN THE UNITED STATES OF AMERICA

10   9   8   7   6   5   4   3   2   1

Cover photograph: Man/arch © Neil Denham/Trevillion Images.
Cover design by Sara Wood.

For my father

Push me down and shut my box,
And twist my arm about.
And listen to my merry tune.
I'll soon be coming out.

Push me down again, Dear Childe,
I'm safely hid away.
But I'm not gone; it won't be long
Till Jack comes out to play.

—Rupert Winthrop, "Jack in the Box," from
Londontown Rhymes for the Nursery (1893)

Karstphanomen | kärst • 'fän • o • men |
noun

1. A geological phenomenon of underground limestone formations that have selectively eroded and are consequently riddled with fissures, sink-holes, and cavities.

2. A secret society made up of prominent London citizens who believed that criminal punishment should more directly match the actions of the criminals themselves. The society operated throughout the Victorian era, but is thought to have disbanded by the early twentieth century.

—FROM *Fulton's Guide to Unfamiliar Words* (1923)

PROLOGUE

———❦———

LONDON
LATE APRIL 1890

The canvas hood covered his nose and eyes and ears, but there was a slit near the bottom of it for his mouth. He could hear muffled sounds, low voices when his captors entered his cell, direct questions when they were spoken close to his ear. When they asked him things, he could feel their hot breath through the canvas, on his cheek and on his scalp, and it raised goose bumps along his arms and the back of his neck, an almost sexual thrill. He could see floating halos of light whenever they brought a lantern into the room, a pale orange haze. They had cut off his long black beard where it curled out from under the edge of the hood. He had been proud of that beard, and the loss of it hurt him almost as much as the abuse his captors heaped on him. He could breathe through his nose, but inhaling caused the canvas to snug up against his face unless he kept his breath shallow. When he breathed through his mouth, through the hole in the canvas, his tongue dried out, and when he tried to swallow he felt an unpleasant clicking sensation at the back of his throat. They never gave him enough water. Food came once a day, barely enough to keep him alive. He couldn't smell it, could barely taste it. They fed him, poking chunks of bread through the slit in the hood and into his mouth. It was dry and hard, but he choked it down. They spooned broth through the slit and past his lips, spilling it onto the rough fabric and dripping it down his naked chest. The heat from it made his skin itch. He still tried to scratch himself, and tried to reach for those men when they came, but his wrists were chained to the wall behind him and his ankles were shackled. The irons bit into him, but the wounds had scabbed over and had bonded with the shackles so that they seemed to be a part of him now. It was this last detail that had convinced him they were never going to let him go. If they tried to remove those shackles, they'd have to rip them out of his skin. He accepted that they meant to keep him here, wherever this was, for the rest of his life. But he didn't want to die. Even here, in the dark and the silence, he still wanted to live. So he ate their bread and drank their broth and he sipped at the ladleful of water they gave him twice a day, and he tried not to think about his absent beard.

He didn't know how long he'd been there. A month? A year? More? The men came every day in shifts, sometimes one at a time, sometimes three or four at once. Always men; never a woman. He had long ago decided that he must be in a small room made of stone, no more than ten feet across and ten feet deep. The ceiling was low, not even six feet, but the shackles prevented him from standing anyway, and so it presented no great hardship for him. Some of the men who came had to stoop as they moved around him. He had learned to recognize the voices of all the men by now. He listened to the way they moved, to the pace of their shoes on the stone. He would know any of them if he met them in the street, even on the darkest of nights. Two of the men were familiar to him from his life before, when he had been a free man. He was sure of it. Something in their voices, something in the way they walked. They had pursued him and he had led them on a merry chase, but in the end he had been careless and they had captured him before he could finish his grand design, his nasty business.

And now they kept him in a box.

Sometimes, in the stillness, he found peace. He couldn't tell if his eyes were open or closed. The darkness was absolute. He sat without moving, partially suspended by the chains that held him fast. He was a spider, made helpless in its own web, unable to seek prey.

He was part of an old story, a story that spanned many centuries and many cultures. He was Loki chained in the Netherworld, Prometheus on the rock. He was a god and these men were mortals. They could hurt him, but they had not killed him yet. Perhaps they could not kill him. He was more than a man. He was an idea and was, therefore, immortal.

He heard them coming long before they reached his cell. Their hard-soled shoes struck the cobblestones and packed earth, and their footsteps rang out ahead of them. They stopped nearby, out there somewhere in front of him, and there was the faint splintery scrape of metal on metal before a door swung open on rusty hinges and they entered. There were two of them today.

He moved his tongue, tore it free from his teeth. It rasped against the roof of his mouth. He tried to muster some moisture, but there was none. He tried to laugh at the men, but the only sound he could make was a low dry rumble somewhere behind his sternum.

He heard the clunk of the ladle against the inside of a wooden bucket and then felt a welcome splash of water on his chin as the ladle was pressed against the hood and emptied in the general vicinity of his mouth. He gobbled at the air, at the meager stream of water, sucking in as much liquid as he could, but felt most of it dribble away. The canvas hood absorbed some of the water, and it spread upward through the fabric against his face. It was wonderfully cool.

The ladle was taken away and there was a long moment of silence. He knew what was coming and he tensed. His senses were hyper-vigilant, but he willed his muscles to relax. There was nothing he could do to prevent the coming trauma.

Far in the distance, beyond the confines of the cell, there came the hard, fast rapping of boots on stones. It came nearer and slowed, and he heard a man panting as he entered the cell.

"Exitus probatur." The man's voice was low and halting as he gasped for breath.

"Ergo acta probantur," said another voice, another man.

This was a greeting he had not heard before, and he presumed it must be something formal, a way in which his tormentors identified themselves to one another, or a part of some ritual. This man must have been late, missed some scheduled rendezvous with the others.

They rarely spoke when they were near him. How many of them were there? Where did they meet before they paid him their daily visits?

Now he heard the snap of a clasp, the creak of leather on leather. The one with the bag was here. He was the worst of them. Was he the one who had been late? Had he brought the bag or did he always leave it here in the cell?

"Use the iron?"

"No," one of the men said. "I told you. He didn't use it, we don't use it."

There was a grunt, a faint guttural protest from the other men, but no further argument.

Two metal instruments touched each other, a soft clink as the man took them from the bag. Silence again. Then a hand on the back of his head. The man with the bag grabbed his hair through the hood and yanked his chin up, exposing his throat. He felt metal against the stubble of his old beard and he closed his eyes. Then a blade dug in, deep, but not so deep that he would bleed to death there in the small stone cell. It was a careful cut, and he felt a brief flash of admiration for the skill involved before pain turned the insides of his eyelids red. A moment to let him recover, then the blade sunk in on the other side of his throat. Two cuts. He felt the tickle of blood running down his neck and pooling in the hollow of his collarbone.

They had cycled back to Chapman.

He had learned to recognize the rhythmic pattern of their violence. Every few days, he was being made to experience the pain of one of his victims, at least the victims these men were aware of. They only knew about five of the women, and so they rotated their torture, giving him the wounds of each of those five victims, one after another, then back

5

to the beginning. Again and again. They would hurt him and then go away and, when he had begun to heal, they would return and hurt him again. He took strength from the cycle. Ritual was life.

He knew what came next, but gasped anyway when he felt the scalpel enter his abdomen and slash sideways. He waited for his guts to spill out on the floor, but they didn't. They never did. The men knew what they were doing. They had cut just deep enough to hurt, to bleed, but not deep enough to kill. They were reenacting the injuries to Annie Chapman's body, but not going so far as he had. How could they? They didn't understand the drama. They were only mimics.

Blood ran down his thighs, and he heard it splash on the floor. What terrors would sprout from that blood, he wondered, if it took root in the earth?

His pulse pounded in his ears, and when it began to settle he could hear the men packing their evil bag and leaving. They swung the door shut again and he heard them lock it. They walked away down the tunnel, leaving him in silence once more.

Only when he was sure they were gone did he finally allow himself to scream. It was a waste of strength and energy, he knew, heard by no one except the rats and worms that surrounded him in the dark. But he screamed anyway. It wasn't a scream born of pain or helplessness or fear. It was pure anger.

Under the streets of London, Jack the Ripper screamed bloody murder.

1

Two men stood waiting beside three horses in the dark at the side of the railroad tracks. One of the men, the shorter one, moved nervously from foot to foot and blew into his cupped fists, despite the relative warmth of the spring night. The other man stood still and watched southward down the length of the rails.

They had arrived early and had to wait nearly a half hour before they first felt the track vibrate and began to hear a train in the distance, slowly moving closer. And then it was there, only a few yards away from them, huffing along, away from the city's center. With a shriek of metal, it braked in front of them and a stout man clambered down to greet them.

"*Exitus probatur,*" he said. *The end is justified.*

"Ergo acta *probantur,"* said one of the waiting men. *Therefore the means are justified.*

The train's enormous engine purred and grumbled behind them. An owl hooted and one of the horses snorted. The stout driver coughed and spoke to the other two in a low whisper.

"I'm having another thought about all this," he said. "It's too dangerous."

"Is it empty?"

"What?"

"Is the train empty? Are you the only one on it?"

"Yes, of course. Just me and Willie."

"Willie?"

"The fireman. He's in there feeding coal on the fire."

"We only brought one horse. We didn't know there would be two of you."

"It's fine. We'll ride together. But I'm trying to tell you we've been talking about it, Willie and me have, and we've changed our minds."

"Bit late for that," the short man said. "You've taken our money."

"You can have it back."

"You should do as you're told."

"I just don't feel right about it. Willie neither."

At last the taller man spoke. "The warders have been warned already and they've been paid to stay well away from the south wall. Nobody will be hurt except perhaps a prisoner or two." He used the tip of his cane to point at the driver. "Is it the well-being of convicted murderers that concerns you? The fate of men who are already waiting for execution?"

"Well, no," the stout man said. "I suppose not, but—"

"Such a man as that is no longer truly a man. His fate has been decided, no? This is what we say."

"Well, yes, but—"

"Then we're in agreement. You have ten minutes to convince Willie. Wait until we've got it sorted at the back of the train, and then get this thing moving again."

Without giving the driver a chance to respond, the tall man led his companion along the rails to the last carriage, the guard's van. He leaned down to peer at the coupling that held it in place. He looked up at the shorter man and smiled, his teeth glinting in the light of the moon. Then he knelt in the dirt and got to work. The other man ran up the line and began to work on another coupling there.

The train was fastened together with loose couplings, three heavy links of chain that allowed the individual carriages to get farther apart and then closer together as they moved, reacting to the speed of the train. The guard's van was weighted to keep the back end of the train taut, preventing the last few carriages from breaking their couplings and flying off the track at every sharp curve.

The tall man unfastened the last coupling, freeing the empty guard's van. The other man sawed halfway through a link in the coupling between two of the four rearmost cars. The birds and insects in the surrounding trees went silent at the sound of the saw as it *voosh-voosh*ed its way through twisted iron. Weakening the link was probably unnecessary, but the men had agreed to take no chances. Their mission this night was the culmination of months of planning.

When the link was sufficiently damaged, the man stepped away and tossed the saw far into the trees. He rejoined his companion, and they walked together to the front of the train. The driver shook his head, but didn't renew his argument. He climbed up into the engine and released the brake and the train began to roll forward. It picked up a little speed, wheels rolling smoothly over the rails. A moment later, the driver hopped down again. He stumbled forward but caught himself before he fell. He was followed by a thinner man who landed awkwardly, fell forward and rolled into the grass, but stood and nodded to the others to let them know he was unharmed.

The four men stood beside the rails and watched as the driverless train chugged away from them, gaining speed as it disappeared into the darkness. A soft plume of black smoke drifted up across the moon and then dissolved.

The stout driver quietly accepted the reins of a mottled bay. He and his fireman, Willie, heaved themselves up, turned the horse around, and followed the two other men toward the city.

THE LOCOMOTIVE ROCKED and bounced along the tracks, swaying from side to side and picking up speed as the last load of coal in its firebox burned away. The track approached the southwest corner of HM Prison Bridewell's outer wall, then curved sharply to the east, but there was no driver to slow the engine and ease it around the bend. The train had accelerated to forty miles an hour by the time the prison hove into view and the engine slammed through the curve, dragging ten carriages behind it. The loose couplings between them contracted and then quickly stretched taut as the carriages moved forward and back to accommodate the sudden turn. Seven carriages from the front, the middle link in the chain snapped where it had been weakened. The back of the train tilted, then slammed down onto the rails. A forward wheel jumped the track and, unmoored and empty, the final three carriages left the rails and powered down the embankment toward the prison walls as the front half of the train continued through the curve and away.

TWENTY MINUTES LATER, a few cautious prisoners left their ruined cells and began to explore. Among them, Griffin waved Napper back and squatted next to the warder's motionless body. He watched him for a long moment, looking for any sign of life. But there was none. The warder's head was split open and a large stone from the wall of the prison's south wing lay nearby, soiled with blood and matted hair. Griffin shook his head and clicked his tongue in disappointment. Napper misunderstood, taking the sound as an opening for conversation.

"Serves him right, says I," Napper said.

"Didn't ask what you say," Griffin said. "He wasn't supposed to be over here at all. The warders were warned."

"I'd've kilt 'im myself."

"Well, the wall saved you the trouble."

Prisoners were not allowed to speak. The walls of their cells were soundproofed, and when they were given exercise time, they were required to march silently abreast. Isolation was a part of the rehabilitation process. Griffin approved, despite feeling that rehabilitation was an impossible goal for most of the inmates of HM Prison Bridewell.

Griffin pulled the warder's jacket off. He removed his own bloodstained shirt and draped it over the warder's body, then put on the warder's blue jacket. Its sleeves were an inch too short for Griffin's arms and one shoulder was dotted with blood, but it was less conspicuous than his prison uniform, with its pattern of black darts on white canvas. He shrugged his shoulders up and stooped a bit and decided it looked passable in the dim light of the prison corridor. He snugged the warder's small cap down over his unkempt hair and kept his face to the wall as he walked, leaving the warder's body in the corner. Napper shut the door of his cell and followed a few yards behind Griffin, keeping to the shadows as best he could.

If it were possible to see Bridewell from above, it would look like the right half of a broken wheel, with four spokes radiating outward from a central hub. The rim of the half wheel was an outer wall that bordered a courtyard surrounding the prison. Each spoke was, in fact, a two-story double corridor, with cells spaced at equal intervals down the length of it. Each of the four spokes was meant to house a different class of criminal, all of them men. There was no exit at the end of any of these spoke-corridors, and a fire four years earlier had killed eleven prisoners, all of them driven by flames down the inescapable length of that wheel spoke. There had been no public outrage at the news of their deaths. The eleven prisoners had been convicted of murder or rape, and the prison had simply swept out the corridor, buried the remains, and quickly filled the vacant cells. Since the fire and the refurbishment of that spoke of the "wheel," less attention had been paid to where any particular prisoner was housed, and now murderers were kept with thieves and dippers were kept with male prostitutes. To leave the prison from one of the spokes, one was required to pass down the length of the corridor and through a heavy oaken door, banded with steel and locked from the other side. At that point, on any ordinary day, one gained access to the hub of the wheel and there were several doors to the prison yard from there, provided one was authorized to be moving around outside a cell.

At the moment, however, there were no warders in sight, except the dead man on the floor, and the prison was experiencing a brief bubble of calm that had settled in after the runaway train sheared off the southwest corner of the outer wall, plowed through six cells on the lower level of the south wing, and deposited itself, wheels still spinning, within the prison's hub, only two feet away from the next wing full of inmates. Rubble and the twisted mass of the train blocked the ruined walls of the cells. A massive cloud of dirt and smoke still swirled about, but had slowly begun to settle.

Griffin and Napper moved down the corridor to the far end, their feet sliding and crunching through grit. Griffin removed a chain from around his neck. Three keys dangled from the end of it, and he quickly selected the largest of them. He stuck it in the lock, turned it, and pulled the door open, scraping it against fallen rocks. Inside was a mangled corpse in dart-studded white cloth, only his lower extremities visible atop a fast-spreading pool of blood. Griffin left the cell and went back to the corridor, moved a few feet down, and tried the next door. He was conscious of the time he was taking and he concentrated on remaining calm. The train's carriages had sheared through the westernmost wall, beginning at the southern tip, killing everyone in those cells and collapsing the floor above as they went. The prisoners had been freed in their last seconds of life.

The prisoners on the other side of the corridor had fared better. Most of the cells on the ground floor were at least partially demolished, but much of the floor above was intact. Griffin could hear men beginning to move around up there, but there was nothing he could do about them. It would take too long to free them. He knew that there was very little time before authorities would arrive to restore order. Griffin eventually found three survivors on the ground floor, three who were on his list, and freed them. He motioned to each of them in turn, and they followed behind him along with Napper. When he had found everyone he could in that wing, Griffin doubled back to the door at the opposite end of the corridor. A man above him on the east side of the corridor began to shout, challenging Griffin to free him too. Others took up the chorus, but their voices were muted by the brown cloud of dust, and Griffin didn't even look at them. He had as many men as he could realistically take with him. All the men he wanted.

He took a deep breath and pushed against the door. It swung open a crack on its iron hinges, and Griffin saw Napper hug the wall. He smiled. At this point, the greatest danger to Napper and the others was not the warders.

The door cracked open and Napper scampered forward, pushed behind Griffin, suddenly brave and anxious to get out of the stifling corridor. Griffin shooed him back and sidled through the narrow opening.

The dimly lit hub was quiet. Without warders and prisoners moving through the space, the main room ahead of him seemed cavernous and long-since deserted. Griffin pulled the door open wider and, when the four other men were through, he shut the door and bolted it. The voices of screaming men in the ruined wing abruptly vanished, closed off by the enormous soundproof door.

Through a pile of loose stones at the base of the south wall of the hub, Griffin could see a wedge-shaped section of a locomotive carriage. If it had traveled through one more wall, it might have hit Griffin's cell in the next wing and killed him. He took a deep breath and looked around him at the other men.

One of them was tall and bald. He had a nervous air about him and would not meet Griffin's eyes. The bald man turned and moved away, and Griffin hissed at him to stay with the group. Any one of them who split off from the others was likely to be caught and returned to a cell. The bald man glared at him, or rather at his shoes, but rejoined the ranks, and Griffin motioned for them all to follow. Griffin could hear Napper and the others close behind him as they moved across the big room, navigating around evenly spaced wooden tables and chairs, scarred and blunted by years of use, and through another door at the far end.

He led them through a succession of smaller rooms and down a long corridor that circled the inside of the hub's outer wall. Above them, a gallery jutted out over the floor where a warder would usually be posted. Griffin wondered again about the dead warder they had encountered. Why had he not been warned?

They passed through another door, and Griffin shut it behind them. They were in a small room with an enclosure in the corner where Griffin remembered changing from his street clothes to the prison uniform. This was where new men were brought into the prison. They were now close to the world outside. Griffin had only been in the prison for two days, yet he was surprised by how much he already missed the outside world. He thought of horses and carriages and buildings with windows. He thought of flowers and trees, he thought of women. He looked at the others with him, and he knew that they were thinking of the same thing. They were all murderers, all sentenced to death for their crimes. There was a single door and a gate between the four of them and freedom. He wondered what they had planned for the days and nights ahead and concentrated on memorizing their faces so that he could identify them if they were separated later. He knew Napper, and the bald man's name was Cinderhouse. Of the others, one was tall and gaunt, his limbs and neck stretched long, his face lean and expressionless. He resembled a walking tree. His name, Griffin knew, was Hoffmann. He nodded at Griffin. The other man stayed in the gaunt man's shadow and scuttled along the wall as if hiding from everyone else in the room. Griffin had seen this smaller prisoner in the exercise yard. Some of the other inmates referred to him as "the Harvest Man," but Griffin had no idea what his real name might be.

He used the big key to unlock the door ahead of them, and Napper instantly bounded ahead, pushing the others aside in his hurry to get out. Griffin found himself forced against the door-jamb. He scowled at Napper's back, but held his tongue.

And then they were all outside in the fresh night air. Griffin looked up at a low scud of clouds drifting slowly through the deep dark blue. Beyond the clouds, he could see a scattering of stars and the hazy glow of a full moon. A drop of rain hit his cheek and he let it roll along his skin, savoring the coolness of it. He looked back at the prison, but the damage was out of his line of sight, around the curve of the hub. From here, there was no sign that the wall had come tumbling down.

Napper scampered ahead, staring up at those same stars, that same moon, those same clouds. Griffin's eyes narrowed and his breath quickened. His hands balled into fists, and he heard a low growl that he only gradually realized was coming from himself.

He felt eyes on him. He turned his gaze from the sky to the killers around him and realized that the tall gaunt man and the bald man were staring at him. Where had the Harvest Man gone? And why didn't he have a proper name? The gaunt man held a finger to his lips. The bald man shook his head slowly from side to side. Griffin nodded, annoyed, and motioned them forward across the dirt yard.

They moved over the grounds and to the gate in the high fence as the clouds opened up above them and it began to drizzle. The gate was abandoned, no warder in sight. Napper grabbed the bars of the gate in both hands. He pushed and it swung open, and they all followed him through to freedom.

Griffin stepped through the open gate into a wide brick plaza and squinted into the unseasonal fog. There was nobody outside the prison waiting for him, nobody in sight in any direction he looked, except the three remaining murderers. The night was silent and empty.

He watched the others disappear separately into the low-lying mist, none of them looking back or at one another. They were simply gone, marked here and there by pale afterimages against the dark sky. He felt a brief moment of panic, but squared his shoulders and made a quick decision. He fished inside the waistband of his trousers, found the hidden pocket sewn in the back, and pulled out a small chunk of blue chalk. He knelt and drew the number four on the damp bricks outside the prison gate, then an arrow that pointed away from the prison. He stood and filled his lungs with fresh air, decided to follow in the direction Napper had gone across the empty field to his right, and made himself disappear, too.

2

Detective Inspector Walter Day left Regent's Park Road and picked his way down the steps that led to the tow-path bordering the canal. The moon was bright and full and its light gleamed on the water, but did nothing to illuminate the ivy-covered rock wall beside him. The soles of his slippers slapped against the stones underfoot.

Day's wife, Claire, was under the mistaken impression that she hadn't been sleeping lately. In fact, she slept fitfully in short bursts that she later couldn't remember. She tossed and turned and snored and flung her limbs at him, trying to arrange herself comfortably around the mass of her belly. Day often snuck out of bed and went to the parlor, poured himself a brandy, and read until he fell asleep in his big leather chair. Tonight, the moon had beckoned. He had put on his trousers and slipped quietly out of the house, pulling his jacket on over his nightshirt.

His eyes felt bruised and gummy, improperly fitted into their sockets. He blinked, trying to clear them and bring the path into focus, but a soft fog hovered low above the canal. The night seemed filmy and immaterial. He trudged along, sniffing the wet air, passing slowly beneath bridges and low-hanging branches, heavy with dripping leaves, and watched as a long narrow houseboat passed him, unmoored and rudderless, drifting away in the opposite direction, until it disappeared around a bend.

He floated along beside the water and thought about his wife, thrashing about in their bed, generating heat. He felt powerless to help Claire or even to make her more comfortable. She was carrying all the weight of the pregnancy by herself. His helplessness made him anxious, made him want to run. At least as far as the towpath. A brief escape. Alone in the wee hours with the dark scent of canal water in his nose, he felt maybe a bit more free, a little less vulnerable.

He stopped and squinted up at the wall beside him, reached out and brushed his fingers against the cool black stones. Here beside the canal at two o'clock in the morning, with nothing to distract him from the inevitable, he saw that he had no control over his future, no control over Claire's life or the life of their coming child.

He looked away from the wall at the towpath ahead. A few yards ahead, he could see the bars of a gate gleaming faintly in the moonlight. There were no horses out this late to pull the boats through the water, so someone had closed the gates. He would have to turn back.

He stared at the tops of his slippers, watched them twist slowly around under him, and watched them begin the march along the path in the direction he had come, back up the steps, back to the road.

He paid no attention to the footpaths on either side of him and instead wandered up the middle of Regent's Park Road, thinking about the baby. That new Day on its way.

He stopped walking and took the slipper off his left foot, fished out a rock, and threw it as far as he could. He watched it disappear in the early-morning mist. He leaned against the trunk of a tree beside the path, steadying himself while he put his slipper back on, and looked up at the moon caught in the branches above. The tree had been there before Day was born and would no doubt be there long after he died. Black vines crept up the sides of it and tiny sprouts nudged through the bark, out into the night air. He wondered whether they would grow to be stout branches and nourish the tree. Or perhaps they were only offshoots of the vine, burrowing under and through the tree's bark, eventually choking it to death.

He balled up his fist and punched the tree trunk. Immediately, he regretted having done it. His knuckles hurt, and when he held his hand up and moved it in the moonlight he saw blood. He turned and rested his back against the unharmed tree and sank down along it to the ground, sat there. He bit his lip and plucked a blade of grass from the dirt between his legs, reached up and stabbed the moon with its tapered end.

Nine months had given him too long to think about things. His work had helped with that. He had buried himself in an overflowing caseload and ignored his nagging doubts about fatherhood. What did he know about being a father? His own father, Lord knows, had not set a wonderful example. Arthur Day had given Walter no clues as to how one went about the process of becoming a father. Everything—the entire life he saw ahead of him—was a complete mystery. If only things could remain unchanged. A happy life, a fulfilling job, a wonderful wife, and a tidy home.

But of course, it was too late for that.

He tore the blade of grass lengthwise. It separated easily along the grain, but it was useless now and dead. He dropped it back to the ground and felt sorry that he had killed it.

He may have slept then. He didn't know. His mouth tasted terrible. The moon, at least, appeared to be in the same place in the sky, so if he had slept, it hadn't been long. He pushed himself back up and patted the trunk of the tree and walked away from it, back up the lane.

He turned in at his gate by instinct and so did not immediately notice the young boy standing on his porch. When he did look up, he expected to see the familiar blue door at the top of the steps, but Claire was standing in the open doorway with a lantern held high. She pushed past the boy and came down the steps and set her hand lightly on his arm.

"Where were you?" she said. Her eyes were wide and searching, as if there might be a clue in the blunt planes of his face.

Day opened his mouth to answer and closed it again. He suddenly felt as though he had betrayed her. He had left her alone and had indulged in self-pity at a time when she needed him to be strong and, more than anything, to be there with her. He had acted as a child would act, and he shook his head at her now, unable to speak. He felt his face flushing with shame and was thankful that the lantern light was too weak for Claire to see him clearly.

"Inspector," the boy said. "Sir?"

Day looked up at him. "What is it, boy?"

"He's sent for you. Sir Edward has."

"At this time of night?"

"Sent for ever'body, sir. I mean ever'body there is. I had a time findin' you, too. They tol' me you was in Kentish Town, not out here. Posh!"

Day sighed. He didn't like to advertise the fact that he lived well beyond his means in Primrose Hill. The house was a gift from Claire's parents. "Tell me what's happened."

"They're out, sir. They're all out, the bad 'uns are. The whole prison's disappeared in a puff of smoke, and the bad 'uns are in the streets."

Day gripped Claire's arms and ushered her back up the porch steps and into the house, glancing about the whole while at the empty and now ominous lane that ran down along the wide-open park.

"Do you mean to say," Day said, "that someone has escaped from a prison?"

"More than one." The boy was excited, his small pale face lit up from inside. "A daring escape from Bridewell. A legion, a host, at least twelve or a hundred bloody murderers are on the loose."

"Twelve or a hundred? You've left yourself a wide margin."

The boy nodded. "It's all hands tonight. Sir Edward wants ever'body."

"Get in here, boy."

Day waited while the boy scampered past him into the house. He took one more look up and down the street, closed the blue door, and bolted it. On his way to the stairs, he pointed at a chair in the receiving room.

"Sit there," he said. "I won't be a moment. Got to put on some shoes."

"I can find my own way back to the Yard, sir."

"Not if what you say is true. You just wait for me and I'll make sure you arrive back there safely."

Without waiting for an answer, Day hurried up the stairs with his wife. As he ran, he let the slippers fall from his feet and clatter down the stairs behind him.

3

laire wasted no time, pulling out a suit from the wardrobe for him and hurrying to the dresser where he kept his cuffs and collars, studs and buttons in the top drawer. Her nightgown swirled around her as she moved, and he took a moment to appreciate her natural grace, even as uncomfortable as he knew she was.

"This isn't . . . Most of your collars are at the laundry," she said. "They won't be delivered until later today. This is the only one left, and you haven't worn it in ages. It's limp."

"I'm sure it'll be fine." Day quickly stripped to his underwear and began to dress himself.

"I'm setting out your special cufflinks. The ones Mr March gave you last Christmas."

"Those things? They're ridiculous. Like something from a penny novel, toys hidden here and there, completely defeating the regular purpose of a thing. And they're enormous! I'm sure the ordinary cufflinks will be fine."

Claire sat heavily on the edge of the bed and watched him button his shirt. She pulled her dressing gown tighter around her and retied the sash.

"Where did you go, Walter?"

"Nowhere. It was hot in here. I needed to get out of the house for a bit."

"To get away from me, you mean."

Day stopped looking for cufflinks. He picked up the box she had set out for him and went to the bed. He wanted to put an arm around his wife, to comfort her, but he felt suddenly awkward and so he busied himself fastening his shirtsleeves.

"I'm anxious, that's all it is."

"I know this isn't what you married." Claire looked down at her belly, swelling into her lap. "But Walter, I miss you when you're gone."

He smiled at her. "I was taking a walk. That's all it was. Couldn't sleep."

He straightened his cuffs and put an arm around her, and she settled against him. Then she straightened up and grabbed his hand.

"What's happened?"

"Oh, I skinned my knuckles on a tree. It's nothing."

"Walter?"

"Really. It's nothing. Don't be silly."

"I'll be as silly as I please." She kissed his hand. "Let's put an ointment on these scratches before they fester."

"I'll be fine."

"Put ointment on them anyway. Indulge me."

"I always indulge you. You are the smartest and prettiest and silliest person I know, and I have to keep you happy or you'll remember you might have married old Sam Whatsisname instead of me."

"That's true. Let's never forget good old Sam Whatsisname. So you didn't meet any prettier girls on the towpath tonight? Girls without giant bellies?"

"I prefer giant bellies. How did you know I walked along the towpath?"

"I'm sorry, Walter, but you smell like horse manure."

"That was a choice. I thought you might appreciate a new perfume."

"If only it *were* new. Horse manure has become your regular scent, you know."

"I'll step in different kinds of manure and get your opinion. We'll see what you prefer."

"Please do." She pulled back and looked at him, serious. "Oh, Walter, you are happy, aren't you? Or, at least, not too unhappy?"

"I am very happy every waking moment I spend with you."

"Me, too."

"I hate to leave you again, but I'll be back as soon as I possibly can." He rose and went to the bedroom door, paused with his hand on the knob. "You'll be all right?"

"We have at least two weeks before the baby's due, and I have

Fiona here if I need anything. Don't worry. Just be careful and come back to me today. I refuse to raise this baby by myself."

"Of course."

"And, Walter?"

"Yes."

"You might think about putting on your trousers before you leave."

Day looked down. He was bare-legged, in just his long woolen underpants and socks and garters.

"I thought I might give the other boys at the Yard a show."

"Let's save that for another day."

"Oh, very well."

Day rushed to put on his trousers, and Claire fetched braces for him. He gave her a quick kiss and dashed out of the bedroom to the stairs. He was reasonably certain he would have remembered his trousers on his own, but his thoughts were completely muddled. He only hoped that Claire hadn't seen the fear he was hiding from her.

4

Griffin caught up to Napper a quarter of a mile from Bridewell's walls. The convict was circling a terrace house at the end of a quiet street, its windows dark, its occupants slumbering.

Griffin stopped and drew a big chalk arrow on the stones at the mouth of the lane, then he melted into the shadows under the trees and crept forward. Napper didn't see him coming. Griffin was able to reach out and grab the other man's ear between his thumb and the knuckle of his index finger. He twisted hard and Napper yelped.

Napper tried to pull away, but Griffin kicked him hard in the back of his left knee. Napper pitched forward, and Griffin struggled to hold on to his ear. He heard a faint ripping sound and felt blood on his fingers. Napper screamed. Griffin clapped a hand over Napper's mouth and pulled him backward, Napper scrambling crablike to keep up, into the trees. A light went on above them, and Griffin heard a window scrape in its frame.

He let go of Napper's ear and got his elbow around his throat, applied slight pressure until the convict began to go limp.

He whispered in Napper's good ear. "Quiet now or I'll do you right here."

Griffin looked up and down the street and smiled. There, at the other end of the row of houses, was a small shack, painted green, with a prominent window in the front. It was a stand for cab drivers, a place for them to enjoy a quick spot of tea during the day when they were not allowed to leave their cabs unattended. Now it was dark and silent, shuttered for the night.

He put his mouth on Napper's ear again. "Shh. Very good. You're being very cooperative. Just a few minutes more, you useless perverted git."

Napper squirmed, testing Griffin's hold on him, but didn't try to answer or make any sound. Griffin tightened his arm around Napper's throat anyway, just a bit, to make the point clear.

Griffin waited until the light went out above them. He didn't hear the window close again and supposed the householder had decided to let in some air. Or was watching the street from the dark room. Griffin would have to be as quiet as possible so as not to rouse any more curiosity.

He jammed his arm under Napper's and brought it up so that his hand was against the back of Napper's neck. He pushed and Napper bent forward. With his other hand he caught Napper's good ear and pulled. Napper grunted and Griffin shushed him again.

He push-pulled Napper down the street, keeping to the shadows. Griffin paused outside the green shack, stared at it for a long moment, trying to figure out how to keep Napper quiescent while opening the shack. Napper stood patiently, agreeable as long as there was the threat of pain. Finally Griffin surrendered to the inevitable. In one swift move, he removed his hand from Napper's ear and pushed him forward as hard as he could into the corner of the shack's wall. There was a terrific thump and Napper went limp. Griffin looked around to see if any more lights would go on in the houses around them, then knelt and examined Napper. The convict was bleeding heavily from a scalp wound, but he was breathing.

Griffin stood back up and rubbed each of his shoulders in turn, easing out the kinks. It was no easy thing to move another person against his will, like a puppet. He took a deep breath and reached for the keys at the end of the chain around his neck. He chose one of the three keys and walked around the side of the shack to its back door. The key fit smoothly in the lock, as it did with most of the locks in London. He turned it and let himself in. The tiny space was empty, the supplies of tea and the little gas hot plate stowed away and covered with heavy canvas.

He went back and hoisted Napper's body under the armpits,

dragged him around the shack and inside. He checked again to be sure Napper was breathing, then used the canvas to tie him at the wrists and ankles. The cloth was thick and difficult to work with, and Griffin was sure he had them too tight around Napper's extremities. Napper would permanently lose the use of his hands and feet if the canvas wasn't loosened soon.

Napper began to stir, and Griffin bent over him and whispered close to his ear. "I've got a nice cell waiting for you down below, my friend. Just wait a wee bit in here and somebody'll be right along for you."

There was no response. Griffin didn't know if the prisoner had heard him. He smiled and shrugged and left the convict there on the floor of the little green shack. It really didn't matter whether Napper had heard him. Either way, the next hour in the darkness of the tea shop would leave him frightened and pliable. Griffin stepped back outside into the relative brightness of the night, the moon and stars shining down on him, the clean cool air that he appreciated so much more since he had been in Bridewell.

He locked the door behind him and went out into the street. He bent over the curb and fished his piece of blue chalk from the pocket sewn into his trousers. He drew the number one on the cobblestones and an arrow above that, pointing toward the cab drivers' tea shack. The chalk lines would be ignored by most passersby, but there were people who would be looking for that symbol, and they would remove Napper's body before the shack's proprietor arrived later on. With a little luck, that innocent man would never know how his odd little tea shop had been used in the night.

Griffin put the chalk back in his pocket, made sure his keys were out of sight beneath his shirt, and walked casually down the street and around the corner.

One down. Three to go.

5

Twenty-one of the best policemen in London stood at attention outside the office of the commissioner of police at 4 Whitehall Place. Ten of them were the elite inspectors of Scotland Yard's Murder Squad. Sir Edward Bradford looked at his notes and then up at his men. He set his notes down on the desk in front of him and ran his hand over his disheveled white beard. In his hurry to leave the house, he hadn't brushed it properly, but his wife had got up with him and brewed a quick pot of tea while he dressed. As she always did, she had pinned the empty left sleeve of his jacket up to the shoulder. Thanks to her, he felt a bit more awake and put together than he otherwise would have.

He cleared his throat and noted the time on the big clock at the back of the room. It was a quarter of four. He had acted quickly and was pleased that the entire Murder Squad, along with the best and brightest of his sergeants and constables, had already assembled, crowding the small area inside the railing that separated the murder room from the rest of the building. A few men jostled one another for space outside the railing, still within earshot of Sir Edward, and more police joined the swelling ranks every moment. There was much to be done, and Sir Edward was glad to have everybody and anybody he could muster.

"I apologize for calling you out at this hour," he said, "but most of you know the situation and understand why we're here. For those of you as yet unaware, several prisoners escaped this morning, barely two hours ago, from HM Prison Bridewell. We have limited information about those prisoners right now, and we'll find out more as the warden and his men sort out the mess there, but we must not waste time. Every one of the confirmed escapees is a murderer, and all of them were awaiting execution. They have little to lose at this point, and it is my great fear that they will take up their murderous ways again even before the sun comes up. We must make haste and catch them."

An older man at the back of the room raised his hand, and Sir Edward nodded at him. "Yes, Mr March?"

"How many prisoners have escaped, sir?"

Sir Edward saw Day's face light up at the sound of the familiar voice and watched the young inspector look around, trying to catch the eye of his former mentor. Inspector Adrian March had brought Day up from Devon and pushed for his promotion to detective. They had become good friends and frequent dinner companions, but had not worked together in many months.

"There is some question about that," Sir Edward said, "which I will explain in a moment. For those of you who have not yet met him, Mr March has kindly agreed to come out of retirement to help us today. He is something of an expert on the murderer's mind and may be able to lend a unique perspective. As might Mr Augustus McKraken, who has also joined us this morning. Both of them are highly decorated former inspectors, and I hope you will listen to whatever they have to say that might help us here."

The other men murmured their greetings and nodded their heads in the direction of the two retired inspectors. Both had been key investigators in the Jack the Ripper case. They had failed to capture that monster, but they remained well respected among their peers.

"As Mr March points out," Sir Edward said, "there is some confusion about how many men have escaped."

"How did they do it, sir?" Inspector Jimmy Tiffany was front and center, taking notes in a small cardboard tablet.

"A train derailed and destroyed the south wall of the prison."

Tiffany looked up from his notes, his eyes wide, as another wave of chatter ran through the room.

"Yes," Sir Edward said. "It beggars the imagination."

"Were any passengers hurt, sir?" This from Sergeant Nevil Hammersmith, who stood at the back of the room, towering over the other men nearby.

"There were no people on the train. Three cars split off and rolled down the hill, demolished the prison's outer wall, and traveled across the yard and through the walls of several cells. The rest of the train was found a mile away, abandoned but still on the tracks."

"And the driver?"

"There was no driver. There was no fireman. In fact, there was no record of that train leaving the depot in the first place."

"It went out on its own for a quick look round, did it?"

Sir Edward scowled at Inspector Michael Blacker, who he felt was generally too quick to make sport of things. Still, he was a good detective, and so Sir Edward tolerated the man's cheeky attitude. "Of course it could not have left the depot on its own, Mr Blacker. But that is a mystery for another day." He looked at Inspector Day, then looked back at Blacker. "Our first priority is to get these prisoners off the streets of London before they hurt someone. Very shortly now, men will be leaving their homes and traveling to work. At that point, these murderers may be able to blend in with other people, may be able to cause a great deal of chaos and damage before they are caught. We must get as many of them as we possibly can before daylight. We must contain this situation, and we must do so now."

Sir Edward realized he was talking through clenched teeth. His jaw hurt, and he paused long enough to take a deep breath. "Sergeant Kett? I don't see you. Would you raise your hand? Ah, there you are. Thank you."

Kett nodded, but remained expressionless, the lower half of his face obscured by an unkempt thicket that he usually groomed into the shape of a particularly impressive handlebar mustache. If his own beard were in better condition this morning, Sir Edward might have reprimanded the sergeant for his appearance.

"Everyone see Sergeant Kett? Good," Sir Edward said. "He has the names of some of the men who have escaped. The ones we know about, at least. We are still gathering information, but the warders at Bridewell seem to be somewhat confused about who is missing and who is not. Some men believed to have escaped may, in fact, still lie under the rubble of the south wall. There may be eight prisoners loose, there may be four prisoners loose. We need an exact number, but you men cannot wait for us to determine that number. Sergeant Kett will continue to gather information, and I want you to communicate with him constantly today. He will keep a list of who has been found by you, and he will do his best to add to that list as the prison tells us more, will you not, Sergeant?"

"I will."

"Good man. Everybody else we have is covering the train yards and the roads out of London. It is up to us to help contain and capture the prisoners before they can get far. All of you, talk to the sergeant briefly and get out there on the street. Kett will have temporary assignments for you, and he's got sketches of three of the men for you to look at. Memorize those sketches. I want a circle, beginning a mile out from Bridewell. I want half of you working your way toward the prison. Look under every shrub, overturn every rock, examine every windowpane of every home. Remain in pairs. Do not wander off on your own. We will keep runners moving back and forth so that you will have a steady stream of information. It should go without saying that these are dangerous prisoners and you need to be alert at all times. The rest of you do the same, but work your way from that mile mark outward, away from the prison. Obviously you'll have more ground to cover, so move quickly. Catch these men. Catch them before they can harm a single person."

He looked out at the sea of faces, all good men, all of them committed to keeping London safe. "Be very careful," he said. "I want every one of you back here by end of day unharmed." He slammed his hand against the desktop. "Now go!"

The crowd dispersed, gathering around Sergeant Kett for their assignments. Sir Edward saw that Kett was passing out lists of everything they knew about the prisoners and wondered how the sergeant had made time to create the lists. He caught Inspector Day's eye as the detective crossed the room.

"Mr Day, Mr Hammersmith, I'd like to see you both in my office, please."

Sir Edward gathered his notes and led the way to his small office at the back of the room. He allowed Day to open the door and preceded him through. He went around his desk and laid the notes on the blotter, but didn't sit.

"Please close the door."

Before Day could move, another man entered and closed the door behind him.

"Mr March?" Sir Edward said. "I don't recall asking for you."

Retired Detective Inspector Adrian March was a stout man with spectacles and muttonchops, his curly grey hair worn long enough to brush against the top of his collar. He carried a cane, but didn't appear to need it.

"If it's all the same, sir," March said, "I'd like to be paired up with the inspector." He nodded to indicate that he was talking about Day. "We make a good team."

"You did," Sir Edward said. "Mr Day also makes a good team with Sergeant Hammersmith. I plan to pair them."

"Then I'll be a third, if you don't mind. There to offer whatever assistance or advice I can. I'm afraid I don't know most of these other men and I'm not as fast on my feet as I once was. I'm familiar with Mr Day's strengths and know those qualities he may require of me."

Sir Edward sighed. "Very well. You're kind to volunteer your services at this ungodly hour. I can't very well order you about like a constable, can I? Please take a seat."

Adrian March smiled at Day and frowned at Hammersmith and sat down. Sir Edward wondered why March seemed displeased with Hammersmith, but then noticed that the sergeant had a long soup stain down the front of his shirt, which he had apparently tried to hide by buttoning his jacket all the way up. But he had mismatched the buttonholes, and his jacket skewed strangely across his rail-thin chest. He was tall and lean, with a narrow face and almost feminine features. His hair stuck straight up, uncombed, except for a mass of it at the front that had fallen into his eyes. Sir Edward was used to Hammersmith's slovenly appearance and realized he no longer even noticed the frequent stains and rips that the sergeant habitually sported. He sighed again. He was still unsure about whether he ought to have promoted Hammersmith to the rank of sergeant. In addition to his unkempt appearance, Hammersmith was unruly and impulsive. It was nearly impossible to keep him in line. But he brought qualities to his police work that many of the detectives did not. He was sensitive, caring, and brave, quick to leap into a fray if it would help the cause in any way.

"Mr Day, Mr Hammersmith, Mr March, while the others beat the bushes for the escapees, I would like you to investigate some discrepancies in the information we're receiving from the prison."

"Sir," Hammersmith said, "with respect, I feel I would be best suited to the search itself."

"And you may be, Sergeant," Sir Edward said. "But Inspector Day will require assistance and, as I said, you work very well together. I think each of you may see things at HM Prison Bridewell that the other would miss."

"But Mr March is here to help," Hammersmith said. "He can assist Mr Day."

"You make me weary, Mr Hammersmith. For the time being, you will remain with Mr Day. And Mr March. Perhaps the three of you together will uncover something faster than you might otherwise do and then . . . only then, Sergeant, will I reassign you to the manhunt. Do we understand each other?"

Hammersmith nodded, but his expression was black. Sir Edward was touched by the young man's devotion to justice. *Just wait*, he thought. *Be patient and try not to get yourself killed before you become the great policeman I know you could be.*

"The head warder claims that all the dead prisoners have

been accounted for and that four men have escaped," Sir Edward said. "But there is another man, a clerk on the prison staff, who claims there were five escapees. Both of these men seem to be absolutely unshakable in their convictions, and that worries me. It makes every bit of information coming out of that place suspect."

"I should think the head warder would have the best information," March said. "There must be four escapees."

"Perhaps," Sir Edward said. "But perhaps not. No one is infallible, and I want to know the truth. Were there four escapees? Five escapees? Perhaps there were twenty or thirty, for all we know. Find out for me. We can't catch four men and call the job done if there are five men on the loose."

"Yes, sir," Hammersmith said. His expression was grim. "And we'll be back in the manhunt within the hour." *Back in.* As if he had been called away from the hunt when it hadn't really started yet.

"I'm afraid I have one more task for you," Sir Edward said. He kept his eyes on Day so as to avoid Hammersmith's inevitable grimace. "I want to know why there's such confusion in the numbers. In the event of a catastrophe like this, it's my opinion we should have immediately been given all the facts we needed. Instead, there's a great deal of dithering going on at that prison. I worry there's mischief afoot."

"Mischief, sir?"

"Yes, Mr Day. It is, of course, possible that the confusion there tonight is perfectly natural. To be expected. But a train was deliberately derailed just outside the prison walls—"

"You really think the derailing was deliberate?" March said.

"Don't you? If it was an accident, why is there no record of that train being sent out? Why was the train empty? Why has no driver come forward?"

"Perhaps he was thrown clear," March said. "Or he might have walked back through the carriages and been in the end of it when it derailed. He could be lying under the rubble at the prison even now. In fact, that may account for the confusion there. The extra body of the train's driver."

Sir Edward stared at Adrian March for a long moment. Then he straightened his back and shook his head. "No," he said. "No, that train was deliberately tampered with. And I think someone at Bridewell knows about it, was a part of the scheme."

"Scheme?"

"Yes, scheme. Someone broke those prisoners out. Why?"

"Did he . . ." Day said. "Whoever did this, did he intend to free a specific individual? Or is it possible the train was the real target, do you think?"

"A very good question, Mr Day," Sir Edward said. "This had to have been very carefully planned, in my opinion, and it took a great deal of courage, a great deal of intelligence. I do not think wrecking an empty train was the goal."

"If we determine who has escaped, we may be able to lay our hands on the person who masterminded the thing."

"That is my thinking."

"Jimmy might be the better man for this," Day said. "He is more methodical than I tend to be."

Sir Edward smiled at him. Day was sticking up for his sergeant, trying to get them assigned to the manhunt in order to make Hammersmith happy. He admired the attempt almost as much as he was annoyed by it.

"Inspector Tiffany does not have the same knack for talking to people that you do, Mr Day. Nor does he leap to interesting conclusions the way that you do. Jimmy Tiffany's methodical practices are more useful to me in the pursuit of escaped prisoners."

Day tried one more tack. "This doesn't seem like it's a Murder Squad assignment, sir. Nobody's been murdered."

"Every convict currently outside those walls is a murderer. Murder has most certainly been committed. I just hope no fresh murders are being totted up by that lot while we sit here worrying about who ought to be catching them."

"My apologies, sir."

"Of course. Mr Day, there's one more thing you should know. One of the escaped men, one that has been confirmed for us, is named Cinderhouse."

Day's eyes went wide and he leaned forward in his chair. "The same?"

"Yes, the same man you and Sergeant Hammersmith apprehended last year."

It had only been a few months since the Yard's official tailor, the man who had fitted every policeman for his uniform, had revealed a secret taste for small children. Cinderhouse had murdered an inspector and, later, a constable in his efforts to evade capture. It had been Day's first case, the first case of the newly formed Murder Squad. Cinderhouse had killed Sergeant Hammersmith's closest friend and paid a threatening visit to Claire Day before finally being caught and brought to justice.

"He knows where I live." Day stood suddenly, almost knocking his chair over backward.

"Sit."

Day hesitated, and Hammersmith pushed himself back from the desk to stand beside him.

"We should check on Mrs Day," Hammersmith said. "She's pregnant and alone."

"Please," Sir Edward said. "Mr Hammersmith, would you sit back down, too?"

Both men reluctantly pushed their chairs back to their former positions and sat down.

"I share your concern," Sir Edward said. "You must trust me. I have given the situation some thought. There is no reason to think this man Cinderhouse will go to your home or try in any way to strike back at you or your family. He's no doubt trying to get as far away from London as he can right now."

"But sir—"

Sir Edward held up his finger to cut Hammersmith off. "But just in case," he said, "I have sent a constable to guard your home."

"Only one man?"

"He is all I can spare. But Constable Winthrop is a good lad. I chose him personally. A very large fellow, and very bright. Claire will be safe, I promise."

"Yes, sir."

"Now, you three get to the prison and find some answers for me. I'm certain we're being manipulated and I don't like it."

Day rose without a word and went to the door. He held it open for Hammersmith and nodded to Sir Edward before leaving. Adrian March lingered a moment, as if he wanted to say something privately to the commissioner, then he, too, rose and left the office. Day closed the door after them. The sudden silence was almost startling.

It was going to be a long day. Sir Edward hoped that every escaped prisoner would be back in a cell by nightfall. He only wished he knew how many they were supposed to be looking for. And why they had been set free in the first place.

6

Griffin had carried his keys right past the guards without being searched. A simple matter of money exchanging hands. One of the keys, a master for every cell in Bridewell, had been put to use in the escape. Another skeleton key had been used to open the cabby stand. Now he used the third key to unlock the back door of St John of God Church. He stopped inside the doorway and listened. All was quiet. He crept forward through what seemed to be a storage room full of shadows. Shapes that might have been piles of old curtains, extra pews, spools of braided cord, crates of books. Remembering his instructions, he stopped in the center of the room and knelt beside a threadbare rug. He pulled it aside and ran his fingertips over the floor. A seam ran perpendicular to the grooves in the smooth wood. He got his fingernails into the seam and pulled until one of his nails bent back. There was a flash of pain and he felt sudden moisture. He was bleeding. He wiped his fingers on the leg of his trousers and felt around his neck for the chain, raised it over his head and felt for the flat teeth of the largest key. He jammed them sideways into the seam and pried at the floor until he heard a soft pop and a square chunk of wood, roughly two by two feet, came loose. He smiled and lifted the wood up and out, set it next to him.

There were other ways to access the tunnels beneath the prison, but this was the fastest.

He put the chain, with its keys, back around his neck, tucked it under the front of the stolen warder's jacket, and sat on the edge of the opening in the floor. He could feel cold air wafting up at him, curling around his ankles and up under his trousers. He kicked his feet out and found a ledge three feet down in the dark. He tested it, then put his weight on the ledge and scooted forward. Held on to the lip of the opening and felt forward with one foot until he found another narrow ledge farther down. A staircase. He kept one hand on the cold wall and the other gripping the edge of the hole in the floor above him and moved cautiously down. The air grew colder and then warmer; the square of slightly brighter darkness above him shrank, then disappeared as he went around a shallow curve in the tunnel wall. He stumbled and nearly fell when he reached the bottom, expecting another stair and stepping down too hard on a stone floor.

He took a moment to catch his breath and remember the instructions he'd been given. There was, he'd been told, a lantern hanging from a hook on the right-hand side of the wall three or four feet from the bottom of the stairs. He ran his hand along the stones until his fingers encountered a hook, but there was nothing hanging from it. They had forgotten. Or they had left the lantern in the wrong place.

There had been far too many mistakes made tonight.

But of course, that was why there was a backup plan. That was why they needed Griffin.

There was no time to waste. He oriented himself and began walking, slowly, shuffling along so as not to trip over anything in his path, one hand always on the gritty wall beside him, until he saw a light far ahead.

Griffin slowed down and edged sideways along the tunnel, trying to be invisible. The silhouette of a man cast a blunt-edged shadow up and along the curved wall. Griffin's foot scuffed up against an old timber, and a pile of bricks tumbled down from the other end of it, scattering in the dirt. The man turned and held the lantern high. He was bald, and the harsh paraffin light made his skin look yellow. Cinderhouse. The escapee swung his head back and forth like a snake and squinted at Griffin.

"Your name is Griffin," he said.

Griffin sniffed and stepped out into the fuzzy pool of light. "It is," he said.

"You're following me?"

"No."

"Then you got the message, too," the bald man said. "Just like me. Telling us to hide down here."

"Yes." It wasn't entirely a lie. He had sent the message to the other prisoners, but had included himself.

The bald man nodded. "You came by the well?"

"The well?"

"You came down here through the old well?"

"I came down a staircase."

"A staircase?"

"Hidden beneath a church."

"Look!" The bald man held out his free hand. It was bleeding and covered with fresh blisters. "I hurt myself climbing down that well."

"There must be more than one way to get down here," Griffin said.

"Where are we?"

"I was going to ask you that."

"There are buildings down here. Have you seen?"

"No. It's dark."

The bald man nodded again. "This was hanging from a post." He held up the lantern so that its light spread out across the wall beside him. "I think we're in the old city."

Griffin looked up at the high-timbered ceiling, arched and weathered by long-ago rain. They were in a courtyard that had once been aboveground. Tunnels branched away from them in several directions, and Griffin almost smiled to think that those dark ominous mouths had once been sunny footpaths. London had sunk into the mud and had been rebuilt on top of itself.

Thousands of people had once walked down the road they now stood on, but it had been covered over and forgotten. The yellow lantern light revealed blank brick walls, yawning glassless windows, doors sagging on ancient wooden hinges.

"Yes," Griffin said, "I think we are."

They both jumped as a fox ran across the courtyard and disappeared down a dark tunnel, its orange tail a blur.

"Do you think people live down here?"

"I suppose it's possible."

"Listen," the bald man said. "Listen, we could stay down here. They'd never catch us."

"We?" Even in the dim glow of the lantern's light, Griffin could see the need in the bald man's eyes. This was not a person who did well on his own.

"Well, yes. We're right under their feet." The bald man chuckled, a rasping, uncertain sound. "They're right up there, looking for us. And they'll never find us. Not in a lifetime of searching."

"You think not?"

"No. I mean, what if they came down here? What then? Why, we'd simply move to a different spot and they'd pass right by us because we'd know the area down here and they wouldn't. It's a perfect maze. We'd be safe forever."

"I see," Griffin said. "And we could simply fetch ourselves down to the market on the corner for a loaf of bread and a fish pie, could we?"

"Well . . ." The bald man shook his head. "I didn't say it would be easy, did I?" He pouted. "We'd have to go above sometimes. Of course we would. Only once in a while, and only to get food and other necessities." He sniffed and looked around at the abandoned façades. "I'll bet if we were to clean one of those storefronts out, we'd find it a perfectly suitable place to live. After a time, we could even bring others. Have a little community of our own. Even a child or two running about in this courtyard. There's all the room in the world down here. And wouldn't a child just brighten the place right up?"

7

D etective Inspector Adrian March, late of Scotland Yard, stopped Day at the edge of the murder room, where the railing gave way to the entrance hall.

"Walter, my boy," he said, "so good to see you again. How is my favorite pupil?"

"I wish the circumstances were better," Day said. "Were you introduced to Sergeant Hammersmith?"

"I only just met him in Sir Edward's office."

Hammersmith smiled at March, but the retired inspector didn't smile back at him. His eyes traveled up and down Hammersmith's misbuttoned jacket and settled on a bloodstain halfway down his left sleeve.

"I'm frankly surprised the commissioner had nothing to say about your attire, Sergeant," March said.

As if on cue, Sir Edward's office door opened and he called out, "Hammersmith? Is Hammersmith gone yet?"

"I'm here."

"I'd like to see you."

"Yes, sir."

The sergeant turned to Day and grimaced. "Well, I suppose I know what that's about."

"Did you have no clean shirts today, Nevil?" Day said.

"I had one. I really did. Hanging up neat as you please in the closet, ready to put on in the morning."

"What happened to it?"

"It's still there, I imagine. It was hanging next to this one, and in the dark . . ."

"Nevil, you ought to have all your shirts washed at once. Then you won't have this sort of problem."

"But I can't wash the shirt I'm wearing on wash day."

"Don't hang that shirt back up," Day said.

"I might need it again."

"Then don't eat soup on wash day."

"Never again."

Hammersmith trudged back across the room and the office door closed behind him.

"Is he any good as a policeman?" March said.

"Nevil?" Day said. "He's better than I am, I fear. Absolutely relentless once he's on the scent."

"You're describing a dog," March said. "And I've seen many dogs that were better groomed."

"He's a good man."

"If you say he is, then he must be."

"He is."

"I see you're wearing the cufflinks I gave you. Tell me, have you kept up with your lock skills?"

"I've still got your old set of keys," Day said. He reached for the breast pocket of his jacket and came away empty-handed, a puzzled look on his face.

"Were you looking for this?" March held out a well-worn leather case.

"How did you . . . ?"

"You must be more aware of the people around you. I was easily able to lift this from your pocket."

"That's very good."

"I'll teach you how to do it."

"Did you look inside the case? I've added to it a bit. Two new picks and a handful of keys to fit some more recent locks."

"Really? You know there are ways to reduce the number of tools you've got to carry around. You could get by with just three keys and a pick or two," March said.

"You haven't lost your interest, then? Since leaving the Yard?"

"On the contrary, I've become even more keen. Do you know there's a gun I've found that looks exactly like a key?"

"Like a key? But it holds bullets? How big is it?"

"Oh, very small. It only fires one bullet, and the aim is dreadful, but it's quite cunning, really."

"I'd like to see it," Day said.

"I'm glad to hear you say so, because I've sent you one."

"You haven't."

"I found two of them and I thought to myself, 'Who would appreciate a thing like this more than my dear friend Walter Day?'"

"You shouldn't have. When did you send it? I haven't seen it arrive."

"I should think it would have got there yesterday. But really, watch for it any old day now."

"I shall. Thank you so much."

"When this is over, you must stop by the house. You'd be astonished by some of my recent finds. In fact, I have something I very much want to talk to you about. A proposition, you might say."

"I'm intrigued."

"By God, how I've missed your company. You have a knack for making a person feel like he's the most interesting fellow you've met. Do come for dinner. I'll have Jane make something special. And bring your lovely wife. How is Claire?"

"Oh, she's huge. The baby can't come fast enough for her at this point."

March laughed. "Don't worry. It'll come all *too* fast, and it will grow even faster. You'll wonder where the time went."

"I already do." Day glanced at the clock and grimaced. "Mr Hammersmith isn't coming back out of the office, is he?"

"You're anxious to get to the prison?"

"Of course. It'll be daylight soon, and we've got to get on the trail of those men before they hurt anyone."

"I'm not sure about all this. What will we possibly be able to accomplish at the prison itself? The escapees are long gone already, and I don't think it matters all that much how many men we're after, just so long as we catch them all."

"You may be right," Day said. "Ours is but to do and die, as the poet says."

"Yes, of course. Orders are orders. I tell you what, though: If I see one of those prisoners outside the walls, I'll shoot first and worry about capturing him later."

"You've got your weapon?"

"I'm always armed, my dear boy. And not only with single-shot jailer's guns. Made an enemy or two in my day, and it never hurts to be cautious. But I tell you what: You go ahead to the prison and I'll wait for your sergeant here."

"You're sure?"

"Absolutely. It'll give me a chance to get to know the lad. And you can get started unknotting Sir Edward's little mystery."

"Right, then. Good of you. I'm off. See you in a bit."

Day closed the railing behind him and hurried away down the hall. Adrian March paused to glance at the closed door of Sir Edward's office and clucked his tongue. "Bloody disgrace," he said.

8

Cinderhouse was delighted to have a friend.

But there was a small voice nagging at him from the back of his mind. *He's a stranger,* the voice said. *He's an escaped prisoner. Who knows what terrible things he's done? Not the sort of friend we want, is he?*

But I am also an escaped prisoner, Cinderhouse thought back at the voice. *I have done terrible things. I needed to do terrible things, was forced to do them, but even so, who am I to judge anyone else?*

The voice did not stop nagging, but it moved further back where he could ignore it amidst the other chatter in his head.

He and Griffin followed the underground stream deep into the tunnels beneath the city. Griffin was quiet and seemed tense, but Cinderhouse found himself occasionally humming a merry tune.

They passed through a long narrow channel that seemed to grow closer and closer as they went, the walls pushing in on them. Moist red clay oozed in the light of Cinderhouse's lantern all around them, and their feet grew heavier as they walked, packing clay around the soles of their shoes. And then they passed out of that tunnel and there were steps cut into the clay ahead of them. Cinderhouse stopped and peered down into the darkness, and Griffin bumped into him as he emerged from the tunnel. Cinderhouse almost lost his balance and fell, and barely stopped himself from striking Griffin.

Remember, he's your friend, the nagging voice mocked him.

"Where do we go from here?" Cinderhouse said out loud.

"Down, I suppose," Griffin said. "There's nowhere else to go."

It was true. There was no way forward. The only choices they had were the staircase and the tunnel behind them, and Cinderhouse didn't want to have to turn back. But he couldn't bear the thought of descending into the blackness below, with no idea what might wait for them down there. He was about to suggest that they try the tunnel again and keep a sharper eye for branches that might be dug into the walls, but Griffin spoke first.

"Here," Griffin said, "let me see the lantern for a moment, will you?"

"Why?"

"I think I see something up above. Maybe some other way we might go."

Cinderhouse handed the lantern over. Griffin took it by its wire handle and turned around. He set it on the floor of the tunnel behind them and turned back to the bald man.

"Why did you—" Cinderhouse began.

Griffin swung a blow at him that the bald man did not see because the lantern was behind Griffin, making him nothing but a vague silhouette in the darkness, a yellow rim around a hole in the black mouth of the tunnel.

Cinderhouse yelled, but he was already turning away, covering his head. He ducked down, a thing he had seen many children do when he had punished them, crouching and covering their heads and necks. He felt the breeze from a second blow pass over him and heard a yelp as Griffin overcompensated. The other man had expected to meet resistance at the end of his fist and had not braced himself properly. The force of his swing pulled his shoulder around and he went forward across the top of Cinderhouse's cowering body. His left knee hit the bald man's back and he bent forward, his own weight carrying him over Cinderhouse and down the clay steps in front of them.

There was a great deal of thudding and thumping and yelling, moving away from Cinderhouse and down, and then there was silence again. Cinderhouse opened his eyes and stood. He picked up the lantern and held it out over the top of the steps.

"Griffin?"

There was no answer.

He tried again. "Griffin? Are you all right? Were you hurt just now?"

Again, no answer.

Well, this is a fine thing, the voice in Cinderhouse's head said. *Now you're alone again.*

Will you make up your mind? Cinderhouse thought back at it. *First you don't want him around, now you do.*

The voice went quiet and Cinderhouse thought about his choices. They were the same as before, only now Griffin might be waiting to ambush him at the bottom of the steps. Cinderhouse took a step back into the red clay tunnel and stopped. The prospect of traveling back down the entire length of it, completely alone, did not appeal to him one bit. He turned back and looked into the tunnel ahead that led down and down, past the edge of the lantern's light. He put a foot on the top step and then he put his other foot on the next step and he moved down like that, never resolving to actually go all the way down the entire staircase. But then he was far down it already and there seemed to be no point in turning back, and he had the lantern, which was more than Griffin had. If Griffin was even awake down there. *Or alive.* And then there were no more steps ahead of him, just hard-packed mud with traces of the red clay from above.

Griffin lay on the floor of this much larger passage, five feet from the bottom of the steps. Cinderhouse could see from his perch on the bottommost step that Griffin was still breathing, but his leg looked strange. When Cinderhouse drew cautiously near the other man, he could see a bit of pink-smeared bone sticking out through the trouser leg of Griffin's prison uniform. Cinderhouse's stomach turned over and he almost vomited, but he had eaten nothing since the evening meal at Bridewell and was able to swallow his rising gorge.

Then Griffin opened his eyes. They locked on Cinderhouse's eyes, and Griffin screamed.

Cinderhouse swung the lantern in a wide arc, saw the mouth of a tunnel beyond Griffin, and ran. He felt Griffin's fingers grasp for him as he passed, felt them snag the hem of his trousers and then fall away, and Cinderhouse was free. He ran and he ran, and it took some time before he finally heard that voice in the back of his mind giggling.

It sounded like the voice of a small child.

9

I nspector Walter Day scanned the crowd outside the prison entrance, looking for other policemen, and specifically for other members of the Murder Squad. His wagon had broken a wheel and he had run the final half mile to Bridewell, cursing his luck all the way. He spotted Inspectors Tiffany and Blacker near the edge of the gathering and made his way over to them.

"I didn't expect to see you here," he said.

Tiffany scowled at him. Jimmy Tiffany wasn't the most sociable of animals in the best of times, and this clearly didn't qualify as the best of times. "We're to start out there"—he pointed to some distant point—"and make our way back to here." He pointed at his own feet.

"We thought it might be useful to take a look at here before we went to there," Blacker said. "Are you doing the same?"

"Sort of," Day said. He didn't know whether the others were supposed to know about his assignment.

"How's the wife, old beast?" Blacker said. Tiffany scowled even more.

"The baby's coming any day now," Day said. "Or, well, in two weeks, but these things aren't precisely timed."

"I'm meant to be on my honeymoon at this very moment," Blacker said. "Inconvenient timing all round, if you ask me. Bad people ought to stay in prison where they belong and leave the rest of us to get on with our lives."

Day nodded. He felt selfish. And foolish. Babies were born every minute of every day. Why was he having so much trouble reconciling himself to the fact that one of those babies would be his own? Everyone else had worries of some sort. Such was life. He closed his eyes and opened them again, resolved to put his problems aside. Cinderhouse must be caught before he could threaten what little peace of mind Day had left.

"Where are the others?" Day said. "Has anyone seen Sergeant Hammersmith? Is he here yet?"

"They're all about somewhere," Blacker said. "Them what's not at the mile mark. Oh, speak of the devil."

Day turned and saw Constable John Jones pushing through the crowd toward them. Hammersmith was following close behind him. The sergeant had taken the time to rebutton his jacket and had done something with his hair so that he looked moderately presentable. Day let Jones pass and grabbed Hammersmith's elbow, stopping him.

"Is Inspector March with you?"

"Haven't seen him," Hammersmith said. "I thought he was with you."

"Well, I suppose he'll catch up to us," Day said. "You're all right?"

"I think I need to pay closer attention to my appearance," Hammersmith said. "It's the impression Sir Edward has left me with."

Day grinned and clapped his sergeant on the shoulder. Hammersmith nodded, resigned. Changing the subject, he indicated the milling crowd.

"It seems Jones has left us behind. He's got a key to the place," Hammersmith said. "It's locked up tighter than a drum."

"How does Jones have a key? How many keys are there to this gate?"

"He just grabbed me and said to follow," Hammersmith said. "I don't really know what he's got and what he doesn't have."

Day felt a hand on his elbow and turned. Jones was standing directly behind him, hemmed in by the onlookers milling about. "I was looking for you," he said. "You two are to come with me." Without waiting for any acknowledgment, he trotted away.

Day tipped his hat to Blacker and Tiffany and followed after Jones, with Hammersmith at his heels. They reached the high gates at the front of the stone fence that ringed the prison. Jones saluted the warders there and they nodded, slipped the bolt on the other side, and drew the gates open. They creaked on their hinges and moved reluctantly. Jones didn't wait for them to open wide, but slipped through as soon as there was a crack wide enough for his body. Day hesitated, but Jones beckoned him through with Hammersmith. They wound their way up the gravel path to the prison's main entrance and Jones produced his key, inserted it into the lock, and opened the door.

Inside was chaos. Warders of every size and shape, all dressed in dark blue uniforms that made them look like policemen, hurried to and fro, their sidearms out, busy on their various missions. Nobody gave them a second glance, dressed as they were in their police uniforms and Day in his suit. Jones led the way through a succession of doors, using his key at each of them. Day marveled at the fact that a single key granted them access to so many areas. He wondered how secure the prison was and whether he might be able to get through those doors with his lock picks.

At last they reached Bridewell's south wing. A man stationed at the door gave them a nod and unlocked the door behind him.

"This is the head warder," Jones said.

The warder held out his hand, and Day shook it. "Warden Munt," the man said.

"Inspector Day. Rough night you've had."

"The roughest. The boys are pulling it all together, though. Good crew we've got here."

"Glad to hear it. There are some discrepancies in the information I've got. I'm hoping you and your men can clear up a thing or two for me."

The warden motioned for the policemen to follow him. He turned and walked through the door, talking over his shoulder as he walked. "Discrepancies?"

"Yes," Day said. "Regarding the number of men who actually escaped."

"There's no question of that."

"I'm told there's a clerk who is questioning that number."

The warden made a scoffing sound that echoed down the ruined corridor, but he didn't turn around and Day couldn't see the man's face as he replied. "You're talking about Folger. He's made a mistake, that's all."

"Well, I'd like to talk to him anyway, if it's all the same to you."

The warden and Constable Jones both spoke at the same time.

"I'll fetch Mr Folger, sir," Jones said. And: "There's no need for that," the warden said. Then, hearing what Jones had said, he sniffed and turned around to face Day. "Oh, very well. Talk to him if you wish, but he'll only confuse the issues."

"I'll go with you, Jones," Hammersmith said. He gave Day a nod and followed Jones back through the door and away toward the prison's hub. Day smiled at the warden and picked his way carefully down the tight stone hall of the south wing. Six cells stood in a row in the rubble, their back walls shorn off, their doors hanging open. Across from them, six identical cells also stood open.

"Nine bodies?"

"Nine," said the warden.

"The train ruined the cells, but it couldn't have opened the doors on the other side of the hall," Day said.

"No."

"Then what did?"

"No idea."

Day bent and examined one of the steel bolts. He pulled the flat leather case from his waistcoat and opened it, took out a succession of tiny keys. He tried each of them in the lock, shook his head, replaced them in the leather case. He produced a tension wrench, like a small pair of tongs, and manipulated them in the keyhole, poking about with another crooked little tool.

"Good locks," he said.

"The best," the warden said. "Gibbons locks on every cell and every door we've got here."

"Someone had a key to these."

"Impossible. I have the only key."

"Do you?"

Day stood and watched as the warden produced a huge key ring and flipped through it, key by key, until he found one he liked. He poked it into the keyhole of the first cell and turned it, snicking the bolt forward and back. He looked up at Day with a triumphant smile. "This one opens every door here."

"Hmm," Day said. "Is there a duplicate of that key?"

"No. Only this one and the one ordinarily held by the warder on duty at the main gate. Your constable's got it right now."

"So there is one other."

"Well, I suppose, but—"

"Please, don't say no when you mean yes."

The skin around the warden's eyes tightened. "Of course," he said. "My mistake."

Day sighed. "I apologize. Damned awkward situation."

"Indeed."

Day moved past the first cell and stepped into the second. Grit crunched under his shoes. He stood over the body of a man and stared for a long moment at the mangled remains, the black darts emblazoned on the white canvas blouse. He stepped back out and walked over the rubble to the end of the corridor. Another body lay there, the prison shirt loose over its torso.

"Do we know the names of the dead?" he said.

"Yes. This is one of mine. A warder. Name of Mallory. Not among the best I've got. Best I've had, I mean."

"How so?"

"A shirker. Never one for following procedure."

"He's wearing the uniform of a convict."

"Not really wearing it."

"Well, it's there, even if he's not got it on properly. Was he guarding this wing tonight?"

"I believe he was."

"I see," Day said. "He's suffered a head injury there. An accident, I wonder, or was he struck by one of the escapees? He certainly wasn't involved in the escape plan, unless something went very wrong."

"How so?"

"There's dust under the body. And rocks from the wall. The

uniform couldn't have been changed out before the crash or the body would be under the debris, not the other way round. So his jacket was switched directly after the derailment occurred."

The warden bent and reached out toward the dead man.

"Don't touch him," Day said. "Leave him until Dr Kingsley gets here. I want to know what killed him."

"The crash killed him. That much is obvious. I think we ought to—"

A deep voice interrupted him. "What is obvious to you may well prove to be false."

The warden jumped and nearly fell, but Day caught his elbow and turned to the new arrival with a grim smile. "Good to see you, Doctor," he said. Then his face fell. "I'm sorry. I thought you were . . ."

A man in his late sixties, enormously fat with a great shock of silvery hair, approached them carefully, stepping around the body and kneeling with some effort in the dust. He looked up at Day and nodded. "Bickford-Buckley. On night duty at University College Hospital. Dr Kingsley sends his regrets. He's up to some important paperwork and couldn't tear himself away from his office. But you'll want to know whether this one was killed after the train hit, am I right?"

"Is it possible to figure that out?"

Bickford-Buckley nodded. "It may indeed be possible." He stood, his overburdened knees creaking, strode toward the back wall, and pushed. Loose rock tumbled back and out into the prison yard. He pushed again and a large chunk of the wall fell aside. "Although I must say I don't like the conditions."

Day left the doctor to his work and moved farther down the corridor. He poked his finger at each of the cells in turn as he walked. The warden followed silently. Finally, Day turned to him.

"There are nine bodies, including the warder. Twelve cells. These other dead men are all wearing the prison uniform, but are they guards or prisoners?"

"All prisoners, sir."

"You're quite sure?"

"Quite."

"So one prisoner has apparently changed jackets with a guard. He either killed that guard or simply saw an opportunity after the train hit. Four prisoners have escaped, but there could very well be a fifth man. This man in the stolen guard's clothing has disappeared."

"We don't know about a fifth man," the warden said. "That's pure conjecture. Too much chaos to be sure of anything yet."

"What about the other cells?" Day didn't look at the warden, but gazed at one of the empty cells as he talked. "Are there any empty cells in the other wings?"

"A few, I suppose."

"But you have no idea how many?"

"No, sir. That's not right. We keep excellent records."

Day said nothing. He raised one eyebrow and waited.

"Well," the warden said, "today is rather an unusual case, isn't it?"

"I certainly hope so." Day knew he was being hard on the man, but couldn't seem to help himself. He looked away at the piles of stone and twisted iron bars around them and considered his next question carefully. He didn't want to completely alienate the warden before he'd got all the information the official might be able to provide. The warden had lost several dangerous prisoners, but through no fault of his own. A runaway locomotive wasn't something he could have expected or planned for. If the escapees were found and returned quickly enough, Munt might be able to salvage his reputation and keep his position at the prison.

Day's train of thought was interrupted by the sight of Sergeant Hammersmith, who rounded the corner at the end of the hall, leading a small thin man by the elbow.

"Sergeant," Day said. "Good to see you."

"This is the clerk," Hammersmith said. "Mr Folger."

Day shook Folger's hand and introduced himself. The little man clutched a sheaf of file folders. "The prisoners," he said. "The ones who've gone missing."

"Four of them?"

"Perhaps."

"But there's an irregularity, correct?"

"There is."

"What sort?"

"Well." Folger was warming up now, his expression grim, but his body animated. "I can account for four men. The four we know about. Or at least tell you who they are, what to look for." He was clearly anxious to help and, Day was sure, anxious to avoid as much personal embarrassment as possible.

"But there's something unusual about one of them?"

"No," Folger said. "I mean, yes. But not one of the four. It's just that I think there was a fifth man."

"So you've indicated to my commissioner."

"See here now," the warden said. "I've already explained it to you, Folger. You've made a mistake. There's no reason to go about—"

"Please," Day said. "Perhaps it's a mistake, perhaps not, but I'd like to hear what he has to say, if you don't mind."

"Well, sir, there's one empty cell in the next wing that confuses me."

"How so?"

"There's evidence of habitation."

"Perhaps it wasn't properly cleaned after the last prisoner there left it," the head warder said. "As I said, we do have shirkers among the men."

"Quite so," Day said. "But if there was someone in that cell last night, that prisoner is also missing. In addition to these in here, that would make five men gone, not four."

"It might appear so," Munt said. "But my thinking is that the cell was probably always empty."

"You and Mr Folger seem to disagree on the facts. I'd like to hear more from him."

The warden threw up his arms and walked several steps away down the corridor toward where the doctor was huddled over the dead warder. But Day noted that he had remained just close enough to be able to hear anything Folger told them.

"Go on, sir," Day said.

"Right," Folger said. He glanced at his employer. "Yes. Well. A fifth man. I think there was one, in that cell. But I don't know who he was. That's the irregularity, you see?"

"You've lost the missing man's file?"

"No. I never *had* his file."

Day shook his head, confused, not sure what question to ask next. Behind him, he could hear the low murmur of words as the warden talked to Dr Bickford-Buckley. Short snatches of their conversation drifted to him. ". . . it's a shame . . . overzealous, is all . . ." Day narrowed his eyes as if that might help him eavesdrop, but Folger mistook his expression for irritation and held up his free hand.

"The fifth man wasn't a prisoner here," he said. "Or, rather, we don't know if he was a . . . We don't know who he was, that's all."

"Are you saying that someone broke in to the prison right before the others broke out of it? And then left again with the escapees?"

"Well, I know that doesn't make any sense at all, but I can't think of another explanation."

"Why are you so sure there was anyone in that empty cell?"

"I have records indicating that meals were taken there. Regular meals over the course of the past two days."

"Is it possible one of the warders was stealing food?"

"Well, I suppose it's possible. But I don't know why he would. The warders are fed much better meals than the prisoners are. It's not as if they're starving, you know."

Day took a moment to consider. An extra meal or two delivered to an empty cell was a curious thing, but it was hardly proof that a mystery man had invaded the prison.

"We know for a certainty that there are four men who escaped," he said. "That is correct?"

"Yes."

"Can you tell me anything about them?"

"Oh, a great deal." Folger seemed relieved to have something definitive and constructive to offer. He cleared his throat and opened the topmost folder in the little stack he was carrying. "Let's see, over here, we had a man named Hoffmann." He pointed at one of the empty cells. "Quite deviant. Seems he fell in love with his cousin and murdered her young gentleman friend to get him out of the way."

"Is that all?" Hammersmith said. "That's obviously deviant enough, of course, but we've seen men—"

"Oh, but he didn't stop at that. He blinded the poor girl and tried to pose as the fiancé he had murdered, somehow thinking she wouldn't know the difference."

"Ah," Hammersmith said. "Yes, that is strange."

"I would imagine he'd go back to try to reconcile with the girl now," Folger said. "He was completely obsessed with her. Talked of nothing else."

Day and Hammersmith gave each other a look. Hammersmith drew his pad of paper and pen from his jacket pocket and made a note. The clerk had given them a solid lead in finding one of the missing men.

"And here," Folger went on, pointing to a cell on the other

side of the corridor. "Well, that's a dead man in there, so we can close his file. But then next to him"—he pointed at the next cell in the row—"next to him we had Napper. Nasty little fellow. Followed a man from the Strand at the end of a workday, entered his home right behind him, and immediately killed him. Then he spent days with the man's wife, alone in the house, before finally being caught."

"What did he do to her?" Day said.

"Why, he ate her," Folger said. He moved on to the next empty cell and so failed to see the expression on Day's face. "And on the other side again, these two cells side by side, we had a bit of a John Doe."

"You don't have a name for him?"

"No. Never did. But he's been in and out of institutions like this nearly his entire life. Family all killed when he was a child, and the boy was found living with their bodies, completely unaware that they were dead. Isn't that odd?"

"Um, yes," Day said.

"After that he started sneaking into people's attics and hiding until they were asleep. He'd creep out at night, kill them. The whole family, I mean, kill them all and live in the house. He was found serving food to a family of rotting corpses the last time and eventually brought here."

"But you don't know his name?"

"He's never spoken. Completely mute."

"You must have called him something."

"Well, some of the warders and the other inmates called him by a buggy sort of name. Some insect. Let me see here." Folger looked through his file, then looked up at Day and smiled. "Oh, yes. Well, it makes perfect sense. They called him the Harvest Man after the species of spider. You know, it lives in attics. Quite an appropriate moniker, I suppose."

"Yes," Day said. "And what about this cell?" He indicated the last empty cell in the row.

"That one was . . . let me see. Ah, his name is Cinderhouse." Folger looked up from his stack of files at Day. "Oh, it seems you're familiar with his history."

"We've met."

"You arrested him."

"After he went to my home and threatened my wife."

"And after he abducted a child," Hammersmith said.

"And after he killed several other children and two good policemen," Day said.

"Well, it looks like you'll have to arrest him all over again," Folger said. "I remember interviewing him. I didn't think he seemed particularly dangerous."

"He was dangerous enough," Hammersmith said. "He just wasn't very smart."

10

Jack heard footsteps coming in the dark, wet shoes slapping the ground, someone moving quickly. It wasn't the doctor; the doctor hadn't visited him in days. And it wasn't the policeman. This was someone new, a gait he didn't recognize. Whoever it was, he was alone. Jack kept his muscles loose, his breath hot and steady under the canvas hood, and he listened. The footsteps slowed and then stopped as the stranger neared the opening of Jack's cell.

"Isn't this exciting?" Jack raised his voice so that the stranger would hear him. "I haven't had a new visitor in quite some time."

"What . . ." The stranger stopped, then started again, nervous. "What is this? Who are you?"

Oh, the stranger didn't know! He had stumbled upon Jack by ac-

cident. Under the hood, Jack smiled. His cracked lips broke and he tasted copper.

"Come closer, little fly," he said.

"I need to . . . There's no time."

"Someone is following you," Jack said.

"I don't know. I mean, yes, they're looking for me."

"And where will you hide?"

"Here. Down here."

"But this is my home. You may only hide here if I allow it."

"Why are you chained like that?"

"Come closer."

He heard the stranger shuffle in place, undecided.

"It's all right," Jack said. "I can't hurt you, can I? You can see that. So where's the harm?" Every word scorched his dry throat. He savored the pain. "Come and take this off my head so that we might see each other and converse like the gentlemen we surely are."

The stranger didn't move.

"What's your name, little fly?"

"Cinder . . . My name is Cinderhouse, but I fail to see how that matters." The stranger, Cinderhouse, feeling brave now after his initial confusion, feeling like Jack couldn't hurt him, chained and hooded in the dark as he was. Jack smiled again. Such a perfect little fly, a tender morsel already caught in Jack's web, but still unaware of the danger.

"Oh, it matters to me, Mr Cinderhouse. Do you mind if I call you Peter?"

"But that's not my name."

"It's not meant to be a name. It's a title."

"I don't understand."

"Tell me, do you understand this: Exitus probatur?"

"What?"

"Never mind. They're not close. The men following you. They're far away, aren't they?"

"I don't know where they are. I think I killed one."

"We have time before they follow you here. You're quite safe with me, Peter. I can protect you."

"Don't call me that."

"But why not? I should think you'd be honored."

Cinderhouse shuffled closer, the soles of his shoes dragging grit from the floor.

"Take the hood from my head and face me," Jack said.

There was a long moment of silence, and then Jack could feel the presence of the other man, hovering close, and suddenly the canvas was lifted and dull orange light sliced through Jack's eyes and stabbed into his brain. He hadn't even known that his eyes were open; there was no difference in the darkness either way and he had long ago lost track. Now his eyelids slammed shut and he gradually lifted them again, a fraction of an inch, letting them grow used to the idea of something besides their accustomed blackness. He let his eyes deal with the light, droplets of color filtering through his lashes, and concentrated on listening to Cinderhouse. The other man had stepped back from him, was loitering at the mouth of the cell, no doubt planning to run.

Frightened little fly.

"If you leave, you will never fulfill your destiny." Jack's voice was *little more than a whisper, filling the space, echoing from stone to stone. "If you leave now, you will always be lost and afraid, running here and there like a rabbit until you are caught."*

"Who did that to you?"

"I did."

"I meant the chains. Who chained you here?"

"I told you. I did."

"You didn't chain yourself."

"Of course I did."

"How?"

Such a stupid little fly.

"You've heard of a man, lived centuries ago, who worked miracles? A man who walked on the surface of the sea, laid his healing hands on the sick, and turned water into blood?"

"It was wine. You're talking about . . . He turned water into wine."

"Did he? Perhaps we read different accounts."

"What does that have to do with . . . ?"

"Oh, it has everything to do. The man I speak of, when he had done what he needed to do to establish his power, he allowed lesser beings to take him, to tear his flesh and spill his blood on the thirsty ground."

"He died."

"Do you think so? I don't. No, he had gone too far to die, taken too much power into himself. He allowed them to think he was gone and then he showed them that power. But only when he was ready and only after he had prepared his disciples."

The light didn't hurt so badly anymore and Jack's eyes were fully open, drinking in the sight of the cell, really a cave, the tall gaunt man in prison dress standing at the edge of the darkness beyond. Cinderhouse was holding a lantern and the light from it reflected on his bald scalp, pink and vulnerable. Jack took a deep breath of cool, fresh-smelling air. He glanced down and saw that his own blood and sweat and shit and piss had turned the ground at his feet black, had soaked into the earth so deeply that it would never wash away, even if these tunnels flooded. He closed his eyes and smiled again.

"How many have you killed?" he said. "Aside from the man who followed you. Anyone might have done that. How many did you put your hands on simply because you could?"

"How did you know?"

"More than one, am I right?"

With his eyes still closed, he heard a rustle of fabric as the bald man moved, and he guessed that Cinderhouse had nodded.

"You are an infernal machine," Jack said. "I knew that you were. But you were simply reacting, not following any sort of plan, am I right?" Jack said. Another nod from the bald man. "Wouldn't you like to finally understand the importance of what you do?"

"Importance?"

"There is a plan, you know."

"I don't understand."

"I know. But you will."

Jack licked the blood from his lips. It was time. He had performed his miracles, had allowed himself to be tortured, and had taken root in the soil. London grew up through him now, and he had spread out into the city, into the world, completely. He had achieved immortality. He was deathless.

He was death.

He was London.

"There is still work to do," he said. "Come, Peter, come closer and let me whisper in your ear. You are no longer alone. You are mine now, and I call you my rock."

Cinderhouse's left foot moved as if he weren't in control, as if he had become a puppet. He took a step toward Jack, and then his shoulders set and he raised his lantern and he moved fully into the little cell.

"Tell me what to do," the bald man said.

Silly little fly.

11

I've been sent to watch over you, ma'am," the constable said.

He was at least an inch taller than Claire's husband and broader through the shoulders, she thought, but he was not nearly so handsome, nor did he possess that glint of intelligence she saw in Walter's eyes. He had knocked on the door a few minutes after Walter had left, and Fiona had answered without looking through the judas hole first, which Claire intended to lecture her about when they were alone.

Claire looked at the rather large young man who stood in her parlor with his hat in his hand and an earnest expression on his face and she suddenly felt very tired and very irritated and wanted nothing more than to have a salty snack of some sort and then go back to bed and sleep for at least a month and a half.

"Do you have a name?"

"Of course I do, ma'am."

"Well, what is it?"

"Oh, it's Rupert, ma'am. Constable Rupert Winthrop. At your service, ma'am."

"I didn't ask for any. Service, that is. And please stop calling me ma'am. My name is Mrs Day."

"Yes, ma . . . Yes, Mrs Day. But you didn't have to ask, ma'am. Mrs Day, I mean. You didn't have to ask for anything, Mrs Day. Sir Edward sent me to protect you."

"Protect me from what? Primrose Hill is a very safe area."

"There's been a prison break."

"I know that. My husband is a detective inspector with the Murder Squad. He has just been called out to find those prisoners and catch them all over again."

"Yes, Mrs Day. I know Inspector Day, ma'am. It's just that one of those prisoners might mean to do you harm. Bodily harm, I mean. And with your being pregnant and all . . . I mean, you're going to have a baby."

"Am I?" Claire realized she was being very cross with this dim young man, but she couldn't seem to help herself. "I hadn't realized. Thank you very much for the news, Constable Winthrop."

"You're welcome, ma'am."

"I'll put on some tea," Fiona said. She was doing a poor job of hiding a smile, which only made Claire feel more cross. Fiona didn't wait for her to answer, but bustled away down the hall and through the door to the kitchen. Claire frowned at the air where Fiona had just been.

"Why would any of the prisoners mean to do me harm?"

"He's come to your house before, Mrs Day. He's that fellow what killed two policemen last year and your husband arrested him."

"What, the tailor?"

"Yes, Mrs Day. His name's Ciderhead, or something of the sort."

"His name was Cinderhouse."

"Yes, that's it." The boy beamed as though Claire had accomplished something remarkable in remembering the murderer's name.

"And he's coming here?" Claire pulled the top of her robe tighter around her throat.

"No, ma'am. I don't think so. Sir Edward just wanted to be sure you were looked after. That's all. Nothing to be afraid of."

"Well, what am I supposed to do with you now? Prop you in the corner?"

"That sounds uncomfortable, Mrs Day. But if you want me to . . ."

"No. I apologize. I'm quite tired and not at all myself."

"Well, it is early. The sun'll be up soon enough. If it's all the same, I'll sit in the hall. From there, I ought to be able to see in both directions, straight through to the dining room. And the front door, too, of course."

"I don't have a comfortable chair there."

"It's all right. I'll stand."

"Not at all. Help me move this." There was a heavy armchair in front of the fireplace and she tried to pick it up, but a sudden sharp pain in her belly made her gasp and double over. Rupert was immediately standing next to her and he hefted the chair in one hand, swinging it in a wide arc away from her.

"You shouldn't lift heavy things, Mrs Day."

She smiled. "No, I probably shouldn't."

The cramp subsided and she followed behind as Rupert carried the chair through the parlor door. He set it down in the hall, sat down on it, and nodded at her. "Now you just pretend I'm not here. I don't want to be a bother."

"Nonsense. You'll have tea, won't you?"

"Well . . ."

"Of course you will. I'll be right back."

She left him there and went down the hall, through the dining room, to the kitchen. Fiona was already putting on a pot, so Claire sat down at the little table and sighed. Cinderhouse was free and roaming about London and her husband was out there, once more in grave danger. She put a hand on her swollen belly and looked up at the ceiling. Tired as she was, she knew she wouldn't sleep until Walter came safely home.

12

Did we learn anything useful?" Day said. They walked back out through the big door in the center of Bridewell's hub, stepping into the narrow courtyard that represented the whole of the outside world to the unwilling residents of the prison. They stopped and Day looked up at the stars.

"Depends what you'd call useful," Hammersmith said. He was looking down at his little tablet of brown paper, the pages dog-eared from being carried around in the pocket of his rumpled jacket, pulled out and shoved back in and pulled out again. "We still don't really know how many prisoners escaped."

"Who do you believe?" Day said. "The head warder or the clerk?"

"I leave that sort of question to you. You point, I fetch."

"But surely you have an opinion."

"We don't have to believe that one of them's lying in order to believe that he's wrong."

"Of course not. But I got the distinct feeling that the head warder actually was lying. Something in the way he moved his eyes about, never quite resting them on any one thing when he spoke."

"You noticed that?"

"I did," Day said.

"So you see why I leave the pointing to you, while I am content to do the fetching."

"In your imagination, we are both hunting dogs then?"

"Is there anything more apt?"

"Perhaps not. Anyway, I think there are five missing men."

"So do I," Hammersmith said.

Day tore his eyes away from the stars above and looked at his sergeant. "Well, why didn't you say so?"

"I wanted to know what you would say."

"And what if I'd said there were four missing men?"

"I would have silently disagreed."

"Silently? Why silently?"

"Because I would have assumed that my opinion was the wrong one."

"Don't do that," Day said. "I want to know what you think."

Hammersmith nodded, and Day let the matter drop. He was still tense and he didn't want to take his worries out on the sergeant.

He led the way across the courtyard to the gate, where the same warder looked them over and worked the lock and swung the heavy bars outward so that they could leave. Day wondered whether a prisoner might be able to simply walk out of the place if he laid his hands on a cheap suit of clothes or a constable's uniform. But he said nothing, only nodded at the warder as they passed. The warder tipped his cap and swung the gate closed after them, locking himself in with the remaining prisoners, his world as small as theirs for the majority of his waking day.

The strip of poorly maintained grass outside the gate was less crowded than it had been when Day and Hammersmith had entered Bridewell. But Blacker and Tiffany still waited there. When he saw them, Blacker tapped Tiffany on the shoulder and hurried over to them.

"You're still here," Day said.

"Decided our time was better spent checking in with you, rather than tramping around this place without a clue," Blacker said. "Please tell me you've found us a clue."

"I think we have," Day said. He looked at Hammersmith, who flipped through the most recently filled pages in his little pad of paper.

"Best clue we've got," he said, "is this fellow Hoffmann."

"One of the missing men?"

"Yes. Seems he's in love with a girl," Day said. "It's possible he'd seek her out again, now he's free to go after her."

"You don't think he'd find himself a new girl somewhere?"

"Love knows no bounds."

"Or logic," Hammersmith said.

"Precisely."

"Do we know who the girl is? A name?"

"Her name is Priscilla Murphy."

Tiffany had his own pad of paper out and was writing as fast as Hammersmith could talk, the tiny stub of a pencil lost in his curled fist. He looked up and raised his eyebrows. "Address?"

"Not an exact address. There was an arrest record, but the details are a bit sketchy."

"Christ," Tiffany said. "There must be a dozen Priscilla Murphys in London. Your clue isn't much of one, is it?"

Hammersmith shrugged. "Take it or leave it."

"We'll take it," Blacker said.

"Good. She's somewhere on Victoria Road, near New Hampstead. The arresting officer was working that beat and responded to the girl's screams. So we know the general vicinity."

"See there, Mr Tiffany?" Blacker said. "That narrows the search down by a good deal. And it's not far from here, either. It's a cinch he'd seek out his old girlfriend."

"She's his cousin," Day said.

"Well, I might've gone after my cousin, too," Blacker said, "if she didn't know me too well to be interested. She's a proper bit of frock." He winked and Day chuckled.

"Listen," Day said, "we've no evidence of this, so I'm not telling you a fact here . . ."

"What is it?"

Day glanced over at Hammersmith and took a breath. "We're reasonably certain that we're looking for five men, not four."

"Another one escaped?"

"No, they all escaped together, but the prison's missing the records of one of them. We don't know what happened or who he is."

"Probably the same sort of record-keeping that doesn't bother with proper addresses," Tiffany said.

"Perhaps. But I think we need to keep our minds open to the possibility that there's another man out there. We can't stop when we've found four men."

"But we don't have a name? Of the fifth man?"

"Nothing at all. As I say, he may not even exist. But watch for suspicious characters. Mr Hammersmith and I will try to find out more."

"We'll be off, then," Tiffany said. He closed the cardboard cover of his tablet and stowed it carefully in his pocket again, along with his miniature pencil. Day noticed that Tiffany's pad of paper still looked brand-new, despite being well used. A stark contrast to Hammersmith's notebook.

"Right," Blacker said. "Wish us luck, gents. Sun'll be up soon."

"Too soon," Day said. "Godspeed."

Tiffany didn't bother to say his good-byes. He was already stalking away down the street and Blacker had to hurry to catch up to him.

"I wouldn't want to be paired with either of them," Hammersmith said.

"Blacker's not so bad," Day said. "I worked my first case with him. He tends to lighten the drudgery with his quips."

"So we've given them our only good clue," Hammersmith said.

"We'll get more," Day said.

"Of course we will," Hammersmith said.

"Then let's get back to it, shall we?"

13

The cell was well furnished. His captors had left behind the key to his shackles. They had left the barrel of water from which he drank every day and a paper bag with three dry crusts of bread. Jack looked at these things and held them in his mind, knowing that he only needed to endure the present pain in order to enjoy the riches before him. Most of all, his eyes focused on the black satchel, the medical bag, which the doctor kept there in the cell. Jack thought about the doctor, tried to recollect any clues he might have heard to the man's identity, as he concentrated on everything but the pain in his wrists and ankles. The fool Cinderhouse had used the left-behind key and was working at the shackles now, the shackles that Jack's skin had healed around and grown over. Jack thought about the black bag and the doctor who left it each day, and he imagined that the doctor had a *life up there with a wife who worried over him and might ask about an extra bag. The bag was safer here, safer left in the place where the doctor used it, where the doctor cut Jack the way that Jack had cut all of his ladies: Nichols and Chapman and Stride, Eddowes and Kelly and Tabram, oh my. So many ladies. Jack, you lucky boy.*

The doctor had left his bag so that his own lady would not question its purpose. Which meant that all Jack had to do was survive the shackles and the bag would be his.

The things he might do with all those lovely silver tools that lay within!

Cinderhouse mistook Jack's cry for a cry of pain and he stopped. He backed away from the shackle around Jack's left ankle as if he'd been burned.

"No," Jack said. His voice was barely a whisper. "Don't stop."

Cinderhouse said something that Jack couldn't hear above the red roar in his ears and went back to work. The iron had dug deep, had buried itself under a warm layer of flesh, and the bald man was now on his hands and knees tearing it away from Jack's bones.

Jack glanced down at the red river of blood that trickled between his toes into the dirt, into that soft, malleable clay beneath London, and he smiled and he screamed again and he returned his gaze to that beautiful black bag and its dreadful instruments of instruction.

14

Day spotted Adrian March outside the prison walls, squatting on the curb and staring at a spot in the road. Day held out a hand to stop Hammersmith, and they waited until March stood back up before approaching him.

"What did you find over there?" Hammersmith said.

"Nothing," March said. "Well, something." He waved his hand abstractly at the road and the empty field and the train tracks nearby as he walked toward them. "Just something left behind by children."

"I can't imagine children out here."

"Did you discover anything inside Bridewell?"

"Sir Edward was right," Day said. "At least, I think he was. By the way, where were you?"

"Me? I waited for a bit at Scotland Yard, then followed you out here."

"Why didn't you come with the sergeant?"

"I never saw him leave Sir Edward's office," March said.

"Well, it's good to have you here now," Day said.

"Take a look at this, Inspector," Hammersmith said. He had knelt on the road and was pointing to the spot where March had been looking.

"It's nothing, I tell you," March said.

"I don't know about that," Hammersmith said. "I think you might have stumbled across something after all."

Day squatted next to Hammersmith. He was privately amused that Hammersmith gave no thought to grinding the knees of his trousers into the dirt, even after being reprimanded that very morning for his appearance.

He squinted and brought his lantern in closer to the road and saw a smudge of blue chalk, distorted by uneven cobblestones. The chalk appeared to have been clumsily rubbed out, but there was still a faint impression where it had ground down into the stones.

"It's an *h*," Day said.

"From here, it looks like a four," Hammersmith said.

"No, you're right," Day said. "It's a four, all right. And an arrow."

"You think it means something after all?" March said.

"Well," Day said, "probably not. I don't mean to contradict you, sir."

"Not at all," March said. "Your eyes are no doubt better than mine in the dark. To me it looked like a child's scribble and nothing more."

"It may well be," Day said.

"But it may be something else," Hammersmith said. "The arrow's pointing that way, across the field."

"Shall we follow it?"

"It may be a waste of time."

"On the other hand . . ."

Hammersmith stood and held out his hand to Day, pulled him to his feet, and they set off moving slowly away from the prison, their lanterns held high. March hesitated a moment, then drew his revolver and followed them into the high grass.

15

The ground beneath was uneven, and Jack was still unsteady on his feet. Cinderhouse needed to help him occasionally when it came time for them to pick their way over broken stones or across overfull streambeds. They left a trail of Jack's blood behind them, and he imagined each drop that fell from his wrists blossoming from the dark soil into tall black flowers, screaming and swaying like sirens. Jack was dismayed by how much muscle tone he had lost. He assumed his coordination and strength would return, but it would clearly take some time. Cinderhouse had given him his jacket, with the black darts dotted across the front and down the sleeves, but Jack was still naked from the waist down. His legs were skinny and scratched. Cinderhouse carried both the lantern and the black medical bag from the cell.

They found a shallow place and crossed an underground pond, small darting white creatures swarming around their ankles and between their toes. They walked through dense catacombs, human bones stacked high and deep, skulls piled high over their heads, and into a large open chamber that Jack imagined was the inside of some enormous whale carcass, grey wooden ribs arcing above them.

There they found the man's unconscious body. Cinderhouse ignored it, walked right past it and started up a staircase that he said would lead them to a higher tunnel, but Jack stopped, his hand against the wall to help hold him up. He stood over the body and watched the man breathe, his chest rising and falling arrhythmically. There was a gash in the man's head and his leg was badly broken. Dark sticky blood had pooled beneath him, but the wounded leg had begun to clot.

"Who do we have here?" Jack said.

Jack barely whispered, but the chamber caught his question and bounced it around the walls until it boomed down at Cinderhouse. The bald man turned and stood next to Jack, looking at the other man's still and silent form, the legs and arms splayed across the cobblestones like those of a snipped marionette.

"He's nobody," Cinderhouse said. "An irritant."

"Oh, but I like irritants," Jack said. "For instance, I've become quite fond of you."

Cinderhouse scowled, but accepted the insult. "He followed me down here. He was in Bridewell."

Jack lowered himself slowly to his knees with a grunt and bent over the unconscious man. He brushed his hair out of his eyes and sniffed the man's face, squeezed his mouth open and smelled his breath, sucked in the air from his lungs. Jack smiled and looked up at Cinderhouse.

"What was his name? Did you know it?"

"He called himself Griffin."

"You say he was in the prison with you?"

"Yes. He was."

"For how long was he there?"

"Not long. I know I saw him there the day before we escaped."

"But not before that? How odd."

"I don't know," Cinderhouse said. He squinted and scrunched his features so that he looked like a child trying to remember instructions. "I don't think I saw him before that."

"Almost as if he arrived just in time to escape, would you say?"

"I don't know what you mean."

"That's all right," Jack said. "Of course you don't, my lovely little fly. Don't trouble yourself."

Cinderhouse smiled weakly, unsure of whether he had disappointed Jack. Jack stared down at Griffin and reached out, gently probed the wound on his leg. Griffin stirred and groaned in his sleep. Jack put his lips to the unconscious man's ear and murmured. "Exitus probatur," *he said.*

"Ergo acta probantur." *Griffin's voice was thick and gravelly, but Jack heard him clearly.*

He looked up at Cinderhouse and grinned. "Do you know what we have here, Peter?"

Cinderhouse shook his head, thoroughly confused.

"We have another acolyte. Isn't that wonderful?"

"Is it?"

"Oh, yes," Jack said. "Very wonderful, indeed. Why is he bleeding? Did you do this to him?"

Cinderhouse took a step back. "He attacked me." His voice was filled with fear.

"But you got the upper hand, did you?" Jack didn't wait for the bald man to answer. "Help me here," he said. "Don't worry, little fly. Here, get him under the arms, lift him up."

"Let's leave him here," Cinderhouse said. "He's of no use to us."

"You will do as I tell you." Jack's voice came from somewhere deep in his chest, rumbled up and out and surrounded the bald man with his anger and his authority. His head swiveled around to Cinderhouse, and his eyes flashed with rage. His lips drew back in a snarl. With an inaudible grunt, Jack pulled himself to his feet so that he towered over Cinderhouse. "You will never question me again. You will do exactly as I say at all times."

Cinderhouse's eyes grew wide and his mouth fell open. A runner of drool escaped his lower lip and spooled off his chin. He stood still and useless, confused for a moment, then nodded.

"I hate to have to raise my voice to you, Peter," Jack said. "You know that, right?"

Cinderhouse nodded again.

"Good," Jack said. "Don't give me a reason to be displeased with you and we will get along together like the best of friends. Always the very best of friends."

Cinderhouse handed the lantern and bag to Jack, then bent and hoisted Griffin's upper body.

"That's my boy," Jack said. He was tired. Standing so quickly and raising his voice had exhausted him. His knees were sore and wet from the damp ground. His wrists and ankles were torn open, the *bloody imprint of his shackles pressed deep in his flesh. The weight of the lantern pulled at him and he thought he might follow it and sink into the dirt. He didn't think he had any inner reserves of strength left, but he did not want Cinderhouse to see how frail he really was. For all his stupidity and his weakness of will, Cinderhouse was still a predator and would be sure to take advantage of any shift in their balance of power. Jack gestured toward the tunnel they had come through.*

"Carry him."

"He's heavy. I don't think I—"

"Then drag him."

"But that's the way we came."

"Are you arguing with me again, fly?"

"No, not at all." Cinderhouse cowered.

"Then go. I will follow."

Cinderhouse put his head down and maneuvered Griffin's body around, twisting the insensible convict's legs unnaturally, then shuffled backward across the chamber and into the tunnel. Jack had meant for Cinderhouse to be facing forward; he wanted to use the wall to hold himself up and he didn't want the bald man to see him doing it.

He closed his eyes and drew himself up to his full height and followed along behind Cinderhouse and Griffin and did not reach out for the wall and did not think about food or water or any of the temptations that would weaken him more than he was already weak. He didn't see the catacombs as they walked through them a second time, didn't feel the blind white creatures beneath his feet as they forded the pond again, didn't hear Cinderhouse gasping and grunting in the dark as he staggered with Griffin's body over tumbles of rock and dirt and bone.

And then they were on familiar ground. Jack had not seen his cell until this very morning, but he had lived in it for a very long time and knew the quality of the air, the sound of it, the scent of it. Jack's body odor had seeped into the stone around them and the dirt under them had absorbed his fluids, had drunk them up until he was a part of that place and it of him. He felt as though he could almost reach out and control the walls of the tunnel, bend them to his will as he would any limb of his body.

He motioned for Cinderhouse to take Griffin's body into the cell, Jack's own cell, and he finally leaned back against the wall as he watched Cinderhouse fasten the old iron shackles about Griffin's legs and wrists. Griffin's shattered leg hung uselessly. Jack smiled to think that Griffin's skin was being stained by Jack's blood. When Cinderhouse was done, Jack pushed himself off the wall and put a hand on the bald man's shoulder.

"You've done well, my Peter. Now wait for me out there." He gestured to the black tunnel outside the cell.

Cinderhouse went quietly out and was swallowed by the dark. Jack listened until he was sure that Cinderhouse was out of earshot. Then he leaned close to Griffin's hanging head. When he spoke, his voice was the slightest of whispers.

"Can you hear me in there?" He licked Griffin's earlobe, bit gently on the flesh. "Surely some part of you can hear me. I know you. I didn't know what you looked like until now, but I know the smell of you, your foul breath. You have been delivered unto me as I knew you would be. You are the first. I will bring the others here. But for now,

I will let you rot, hanging from these chains as I did for so long. I will let you stew in your own sour sweat, let you fear every approaching sound lest it be me. And I will return. I will do wonderful things to you. I will transform you as I have transformed so many others and, with your last breath, you will thank me as they thanked me. Wait for me now."

Jack stepped away, feeling stronger, feeling mighty in his righteousness. He held up the lantern and let its light shine on the black walls that no longer held any power to cage him. He walked away from the cell and found Cinderhouse in the darkness and led him away through the passages, across the rivers and the graveyards and the ancient silent city streets.

Up and back to London.

16

Fiona knocked lightly on Claire's bedroom door and waited until she heard Claire answer before she turned the knob and entered. The room was dark, only a single candle on the windowsill to dispel the shadows. Or perhaps the tiny flame was there to serve as a beacon for Walter, to bring him back safely. Claire was curled under an old off-white coverlet that was pulled up under her chin. Her blond hair glowed vivid orange in the candlelight, and the pillowy folds of the coverlet were grooved with deep purple bruises.

"Constable Winthrop is settled in now," Fiona said. "He ate all the biscuits we had in the place. And he drank three cups of tea with milk. It'll be a wonder if he can stand up from the chair."

"He ate them all? All the biscuits?"

"I think so."

"I was saving those."

"I'm sorry."

"No, it's fine," Claire said. She laughed. "I wasn't really saving the biscuits. I suppose I'm just put out that we have a policeman underfoot and it's the wrong one."

"Yes," Fiona said. "Why couldn't they have sent Mr Hammersmith? We know him already. We would have felt completely safe with him right away."

"I was talking about my husband. He's a policeman, too."

"Of course he is!" Fiona covered her mouth and turned to leave. "I'm so sorry."

"Don't go," Claire said.

"I have things. I should do them."

"Would you bring me a glass of water before you leave?"

"Of course."

Fiona kept her eyes down and let her long hair fall across her face. She was a slender, pale girl with a calm demeanor and an inexpressive face. The youngest Kingsley girl had grown up without a mother. She had spent much of her childhood helping her father at his work in order to be close to him. She had walked around countless crime scenes with him, observing the bodies of murder victims, sketching the placement of their limbs, and making note of their wounds, a junior coroner's assistant. Until the day Dr Kingsley decided that the morgue might not, after all, be the best environment for his daughter. He had sent her away, asked her to assist Claire until a permanent housekeeper could be found. But it was not the sort of work Fiona enjoyed.

She went to the washstand, where a ceramic cup sat next to a pitcher of water that had gone room temperature over the course of the night. Fiona noticed that the pail of dirty water from the morning's stand-up wash was still sitting on the floor under the table. She wondered if she was supposed to empty it. Her duties in the Day household were still unclear, and it sometimes frustrated her that she didn't know exactly what Claire wanted from her aside from simple companionship. She filled the cup and carried it to the bed, put it in Claire's waiting hand.

"We ought to interview housekeepers again," Fiona said. "And cooks. Cooks especially."

"Oh, I know," Claire said. "It's just, I have no energy for it. We already know how hopeless it all is." She took a long drink of water. Some of it dribbled down her chin and soaked into the coverlet.

They had had miserable luck in trying to find someone appropriate to help around the house. For some reason, the only women to apply for any position were horrible. On two separate occasions, they had hired a woman despite their misgivings, and both women had failed to return after their first days' work. It really did seem like they were doomed to make do without help.

"So," Claire said, "tell me about Sergeant Hammersmith. You seem terribly attached to the idea of him."

Fiona felt herself blush. Her gaze fell on the coverlet, and she noticed a long squiggly seam of red thread. She bent and focused on it. In the shivering light of the candle, the red threads looked like letters and words, like a long sentence that progressed down the side of the coverlet from top to bottom and around its corner.

"What's this?"

Claire set the water cup on the bedside table and pulled the coverlet down, bunched the side of it in her hands, and pulled it closer to her face. She smiled.

"Those," she said, "are the names of everybody—of every woman, at least—in my family, going back for, oh, simply generations. More than a hundred years. Perhaps even more than two hundred years."

"Their names? You mean your grandmother's name?"

"And her grandmother. Look, here's my mother's name stitched in there."

Claire pulled her feet up and Fiona sat on the edge of the bed.

"And, look, beside it there . . ." Fiona said.

"My name," Claire said. "My mother added my name to this when I was born. It's a sort of record of the family, passed down from daughter to daughter."

Fiona could see the pride in Claire's face as she read the names of her ancestors, all marching side by side down the sturdy white fabric. How many generations of housekeepers had carefully washed the heirloom? And how long since it *had* been cleaned? A thought occurred to Fiona, and she smiled at Claire, her eyes wide.

"If your baby is a girl . . ."

"It can't happen."

"Mr Day wants a boy?"

"No, no, I mean I'm rubbish at sewing. I could never ruin this old thing by stitching it up with some illegible clump of a name. Future generations would look at it and say, 'What went wrong over here?' And my great-great-great-granddaughter would say, 'Oh, well, that's where Claire Day, the infamously bad seamstress, destroyed everything.' And besides, you're avoiding the question about our dear Mr Hammersmith. I suppose he is rather handsome, isn't he? Or he would be if you could somehow get him in a clean shirt every once in a while."

"But you could hire someone to sew in the name," Fiona said. "If it's a girl, I mean. You mustn't let the tradition die out."

"Do you know that my mother has asked for it back? The coverlet, I mean. She's decided I shouldn't be the one to have it after all, and she's going to give it to my cousin."

"Oh, no."

"But I won't give it back. She gave it to me and it's mine."

"But why? Why would she take it back?"

"We differ in our opinions about Walter."

"She doesn't care for Mr Day?"

"It's really my father, I suppose. She's simply echoing his opinions like one of those nasty birds that speak."

"A mynah bird, you mean."

"One of those, with its croaking voice. Very like my mother, actually."

"Oh, dear. But Mr Day is wonderful, isn't he?"

"Yes. And therein lies the difference of our opinions on the matter. They had another boy all picked out for me, and I went and married a valet's son."

"I adore Mr Day, of course, but why did you choose him, if there was someone else?"

"Because he's the kindest person I've ever known. Had I married the boy my father picked for me, I would have become tough and bitter and a little bit dead inside. But with Walter I can be the person I would like to be. He thinks I am already that person, that ideal person of my imagination. That is why I love him. He is gentle and good and thoughtful and he loves me for who he thinks I am. I would so like to be that person. And when he looks at me, I am."

"How old were you? When you married?"

"Not much older than you, I suppose. But a handful of years makes all the difference at your age. You must be patient."

"Have you noticed Mr Hammersmith's hands? His fingers?"

"They're long."

"They're delicate. I imagine him at a piano sometimes in a beautiful shiny black suit, and he's playing something wonderful and moving, his fingers dancing to and fro over the keys."

"I can't imagine Mr Hammersmith playing a piano or wearing anything but a soiled police uniform."

"You must use your imagination," Fiona said.

"And you must be more careful about your imaginings. Men are not strong enough to endure our ideas. They are what and who they are, and they will always be that. Our imaginations betray us."

"Do you feel betrayed?"

"Not in the least. But Mr Day is exactly what I thought he was and would be."

"Well, anyway, you shouldn't give this back. Not ever." Fiona held the coverlet up to the light.

"I won't."

"Good," Fiona said. "I'll help you hide it if they ever come visiting. Your family, I mean."

"Let's make a pact."

"We should have a code. I love codes."

"I don't know any," Claire said.

"We'll think of one."

Claire winced and Fiona leaned toward her.

"What is it?"

"Nothing," Claire said. "A cramp, is all."

"That's normal enough. My father says there should be some cramping this far along, but we need to fetch him round if they start coming regularly."

"How regularly?"

"Ten minutes, I think. Every ten minutes or so."

"Well, it's not that. It's only every so often. I'm sure I'm fine."

"I could send for him now. Just to be safe."

"No, I really am fine. Just tired. The sun will be up soon, won't it?"

"Yes," Fiona said. "You should try to sleep."

"I think I'll just rest a bit. Do you mind?"

"Not at all. I'll be just down the hall. And Constable Winthrop is right downstairs."

"Thank you."

Fiona stood, and Claire stretched out under the coverlet and closed her eyes. Fiona leaned across her and blew out the candle. She picked up the water cup and carried it back to the washstand. She eyed the pail of dirty water suspiciously, then bent and grabbed it by its wire handle and took it to the door.

"Fiona?"

She stopped and looked back. "Yes?"

"Thank you. I mean, really. Thank you."

Fiona smiled and said nothing. There was no way to respond that would adequately express how she felt. Language was often frustrating when it came to simple human emotions.

"And Fiona?"

"Yes?"

"Nevil Hammersmith has the longest eyelashes I have ever seen on a man. Have you told him how you think about him?"

Fiona nearly dropped the water pail. She hunched her shoulders and the water sloshed about, but none of it spilled.

"Good night, Claire," she said.

"Good night."

Fiona stepped into the hallway, pulled the door shut behind her, and let out a huge sigh. Then she went looking for a place to dump the dirty water.

17

After a long walk underground, Jack and Cinderhouse came up to the surface inside a small obelisk at the corner of the St John of God cemetery. The door that was set back in the obelisk was ancient oak banded with iron, and the hinges squeaked and stuck. They were only able to open it halfway, and they squeezed through the crack into the grey predawn. There was not a person in sight in any direction they looked. The sky was overcast and there was a cool spring breeze blowing through the grass and along the tops of the tombstones.

Jack swayed in the wind. He closed his eyes and inhaled deeply, bringing in the fresh moist air and blowing out the dust and blood that had filled his nostrils for so long. He felt the wind brush against his bare testicles and he opened his eyes. He gave Cinderhouse a quick glance, just to make sure he was still there, then walked away through the stones, letting the grass poke up between his toes and the first few drops of rain spatter against his face. His legs gave way and he fell and tumbled until he fetched up against the side of a stone. He looked up at the name engraved in the front of the stone, but he didn't recognize it. It was not the name of anyone he had touched, and so he felt a mild disappointment. He knew that the odds were against the body under him being one of his own, but the entire day had felt so much like it belonged to him that he had half expected it to be a familiar corpse. It was his birthday all over again and everything ought to be his.

From that prone position, he looked around at the sea of stones and wondered at the number of graveyards in London, so many of them filled with people he had not managed to transform before they met their ends in other ways, at other hands. He silently apologized to them all for being so slow in his work. He wondered what would happen as the city continued to grow and lap over its current boundaries. Would the bodies beneath him be plowed into the soil and homes built atop their bones? Or would they sink farther under and join the forgotten dead in the catacombs beneath?

When he had caught his breath, he pulled himself up and staggered over to where Cinderhouse still stood in the shadow of the obelisk. He took the bald man by the arm and leaned against him and allowed himself to be led across the graveyard to Cambridge Street. They were somewhere in Agar Town, he knew. Not the best area to be caught out after dark. Jack had come up far from his old stomping grounds and even farther from his home. He imagined his landlady would have given up on him by now. She wouldn't wait more than a few weeks to decide he wasn't coming back. Perhaps she thought he was dead. No matter. *Whatever she thought, she would have cleaned the place out and found someone new to pay the rent. His things would have been donated or put out in the street. There were no relatives to claim them. His old life was gone and there was no going back.*

But he was content to be alive and aboveground and free.

"Forward," he said, "into the future. On with a brand-new life."

The bald man gave him a puzzled look, but said nothing, which was a relief. Jack didn't like the man's voice. It was high and reedy and grated on his nerves.

Jack heard running water and he pulled Cinderhouse across the street, to where they could see down past the towpath to the black surface of Regent's Canal. The early-morning air was wet and clung to them like gossamer. Jack felt a cool mist on his face, but did not know whether it came up from the canal or down from the heavy grey sky.

In the predawn hour there was little traffic, but Jack knew that carriages would choke the street as soon as the first signs of approaching daylight began to show on the horizon. They needed to find a place to hide before the sun came up. And something to wear. There was no way they could pass unnoticed in the city without proper clothing.

He turned his back on the canal and Cinderhouse mirrored him, turning when he did, doing as he did, unless instructed otherwise. He appreciated how quick the bald man was to follow his orders.

A dog trotted by on the other side of the street, then stopped and looked at the two men. It wagged its tail hopefully and altered its course, heading slowly toward them, perhaps in search of food, but too wild to come directly to them. It circled, its ears laid back but its tail limply moving back and forth. Jack frowned and squinted down the length of the street to where a splinter of darkness had peeled away from the purple sky and was moving steadily toward them, growing as it came, fashioning itself into the shape of a large black omnibus, four horses out front, chuffing away toward the day's first destination. Behind the bus came a wave of water pouring from the sky in a solid sheet, advancing as if pulled along by the steady horses, as if they were a harbinger of the weather. Thor's chariot.

The dog, wild and stupid, thin and hungry, almost as thin as Jack, advanced toward the two men, unaware of the bus. Perhaps it was deaf, or perhaps the sound of the rain masked the rumbling of the wheels. Jack felt his heart begin to beat faster in anticipation. He felt Cinderhouse tense next to him.

The horses clopped past the two men. There was a solid thunk and a sharp yip of pain, and then the rain poured down and the bus disappeared into the grey, headed somewhere on the other side of the canal. Rain drove down and splashed up and settled down again in waves, running off the sides of the towpath and joining the black water below.

Jack stepped out into the street and looked for the dog. He found a spatter of blood, already being washed away, and a trail. He followed the red swath, which led him to a small pile of organs, a rope of intestines replacing the blood trail. Soon he found the dog itself, weak now and stopped by the curb on the other side of Cambridge Street, unable to step up out of the lane. It had pulled itself into a tiny bundle, shivering in the rain, ripped apart by the callous horses, by the wheels of the black bus. It looked up at Jack, and he knelt beside it on the bloody stones. He put out his hand and touched the dog's snout. The tip of its tongue extended far enough to lick his fingers.

"We should put it out of its misery," Cinderhouse said. "Show some mercy."

Jack looked up, surprised to hear the bald man speak. He had not heard Cinderhouse follow him, had barely heard his voice over the sound of the rain.

"'The quality of mercy is not strained,'" Jack said. "'It droppeth as the gentle rain from heaven.'"

"But it is raining."

"Is it? I hadn't noticed." God, but the fly was a stupid creature. His company was quickly becoming tedious. "I mean to say that you cannot ask me to show mercy. It must be freely given or it means nothing."

"I'll do it then. The poor thing."

Jack motioned for Cinderhouse to move back and he looked down at the dog again. It was panting and whining, staring up at Jack, its insides painted across the curb, blood welling from its ear. Jack smiled at it and ran the tips of his fingers over its wet muzzle again.

"Death is not a thing to be feared, little fly." Jack spoke to Cinderhouse, but he looked at the dog. "We are larvae, all of us, awaiting transformation. We must be patient and we must understand that all change is painful."

"Just bash its head with something."

Jack looked up at Cinderhouse again. They were sharing a precious moment with the dog, a once-in-a-lifetime experience, and Cinderhouse was unable to appreciate what was happening. The bald man was pacing about uselessly, looking for a rock to use. Jack decided to ignore him. He turned his attention to the dog just in time to see that pleading expression leave its eyes. Its paws twitched one last time and it went still. He watched as it ceased being a dog and became some-

thing else entirely. He stopped breathing and his lips parted in awe. He felt he might pass out. This was the ultimate communication with the universe, and it had been denied him for so long.

Someone ought to pay for that.

He touched the dog again, but it no longer held any interest for him. It was already going cold. The rain beat against its blank eyeballs.

Cinderhouse shoved something at him, breaking his field of vision. A wooden rod, perhaps thrown off by a passing carriage.

"Use this," Cinderhouse said.

Jack stood and stepped toward the rail. "You use it," he said.

He kept his back to the bald man and listened, but could hear nothing over the sound of the rain. It was entirely possible that Cinderhouse would hit Jack with the rod and gain his freedom. Jack wouldn't blame him at all. He would use the rod if he were in the bald man's shoes. Or any shoes.

"It's already dead."

Jack turned and smiled. He reached out his hand and took the rod from Cinderhouse.

"You missed it," Jack said.

"Poor thing."

"Maybe. But we're all going to die, aren't we? We can't all expect pity."

"It didn't have to die like that."

"But it did have to die like that. It had no choice."

"Not after the bus hit it."

"The bus was simply a part of the process. The mechanism of transformation. We are surrounded every day by such machines. We are such machines."

Cinderhouse stepped up to the rail as a carriage rolled by. Its wheels sluiced water up over the curb, over their toes. Jack watched the rain bounce off Cinderhouse's smooth scalp as traffic began to pick up on the bridge. It was still dark, but the rain had already begun to ease into a gentle sprinkle. No carriages stopped for them, nobody wondered about the two men and the dead dog. Everyone had a place to go. Jack knew that if he gave the bald man enough time, he would speak again. Until then, he was content to stand and listen to the soft patter of rain on the canal.

"It was mostly children for me," Cinderhouse said. "The ones I killed. I mean, as you say, transformed. The ones I transformed."

"Ah, that is not something I can appreciate. Not children."

"But surely you . . ."

"Never a child. Children are already in the midst of transformation. They're not yet ripe, are they?"

"Ripe?"

"Promise me you'll leave the children be."

"I . . . I'll try."

"You would not want to break a promise you make to me."

"I won't."

"Was it only children?"

"No. I killed two policemen."

Jack stopped looking at the canal. He had been just about to push Cinderhouse over the wall. "Policemen? You surprise me, little fly."

"They were going to take a child away from me."

"And so you lashed out, did you?"

"Yes."

"But they caught you."

"Yes."

"Well, you can't very well kill one policeman without expecting to be caught, let alone two of them. They're a bit overprotective of their own, aren't they?"

"They beat me. Broke my nose."

"But they did not kill you outright in return for what you had done."

"No."

"That was unkind of them."

"Was it?"

"Do you know their names?"

"One of them was named Day. Detective Inspector Walter Day."

"One of the ones you killed?"

"No. The one who caught me. One of them."

"I meant the dead ones. The ones you killed. Surely you kept their names. Out of respect."

"One was named Pringle. He was a customer of mine. Constable Pringle. I don't remember his full name. I don't know the other one's name at all."

"You do them a disservice. They shared their experience with you, allowed you to be a part of it. The least you can do is remember them."

"I don't. I'm sorry."

"More's the pity."

Jack turned and walked along the footpath toward the city and Cinderhouse followed. Jack didn't turn around when the bald man spoke again.

"His wife's name was Claire."

"Who?"

"The policeman who caught me. The one who sent me to Bridewell."

"His wife's name was Claire?"

"I visited her one time. At their house in Primrose Hill. It's not very far from here, actually."

"Ah, you remember that, do you? Their house? The woman?"

"Quite clearly. She was lovely."

"My dear little fly, you sound as if you have unfinished business to attend to."

"Do you think so?"

"I do," Jack said. He licked his lips and tasted rain. "I really do."

"What should I do?"

"Don't worry, Peter. I'll help you figure it out."

He looked up at the dark sky as he walked and he let the rain hit his eyeballs the way it had drummed against the dog's eyes. Finally he had to blink. He splashed along through the puddles underfoot, and he led his dear stupid little fly toward the city.

18

They crossed the field carefully. The rain had gone as quickly as it had come, and clouds scudded away across the sky, the only movement in sight. Day and Hammersmith shuttered their lanterns and, when their eyes had grown used to the starlight and moonlight, they crept through the grass, watching for movement against the blue horizon. Day drew his Colt Navy, but kept it held down at his side. There was a handful of loose tombstones scattered about, tumbled down by rain and snow and years, but there were no men hiding behind those stones. The three policemen were alone.

When they reached the road, they stopped and listened. Day held up his hand and motioned toward their right, where the road sloped up over a culvert. Hammersmith nodded and crossed the cobblestones silently. Under the cover of the trees on the other side, he went slowly uphill, watching the windows and doors of the houses that bordered the field. Day turned and walked along the road to his left, and March followed him.

Day began to feel foolish. There was no reason to suppose the chalk marks meant something, no reason to suspect any of the prisoners had escaped across the field. While the three of them wasted their time out here, the prisoners might be ten or a dozen miles away in the other direction. He hoped Blacker and Tiffany and the others were on the right track, even if he wasn't.

"Ssst."

Day looked around. March was across the road, walking at the edge of the tall grass and looking in the other direction. Behind him, he could see Hammersmith's head and shoulders, his policeman's uniform purple in the yellow moonlight. He wasn't looking in Day's direction, either.

"Ssst," came the voice again. "Up here."

Day looked up into the trees. Nothing. Then a quick movement in the shadows behind the leaves. Day moved his head and saw an old lady leaning out of a window on the top floor of a house, partially obscured by a jutting rooftop from the story below her.

"Hello, mother," he said. "It's late."

"It's early," she said. "And keep your voice down. That other one might still be around."

"Other one?"

"Come out from behind them trees, so I can see you proper."

Day stepped out, away from the row of houses, out of the

shadows, looking both ways to be sure he wasn't presenting a target. The woman was not much more than a blur in the darkness of the room behind her, but even though he couldn't see anything Day felt it was improper to peer into a lady's bedroom. He averted his eyes.

"You're a policeman?"

"Inspector Day, ma'am."

"My pleasure."

"You said there was another one," Day said. "Another man? Was he another policeman besides me?" With so many of the police combing every neighborhood near the prison, it was quite likely the woman had seen a lot more activity on the street than she was used to.

"Not the man I mean. Dressed different. Not a policeman, just different."

Day felt his breath come quicker and his heart beat faster. Had the convicts come this way after all? "How was he dressed, ma'am? Was he wearing a white uniform? Big black darts up and down the sleeves?"

"One of them was wearing something very like that, yes. How did you know?"

"You say one of them was? Do you mean there was more than one of them?"

"Of course I mean there was two men. Please keep up if you want to talk to me."

"Yes, ma'am. My apologies." Day turned at a sudden sound behind him. March had crossed the road and was standing at his elbow.

"What's she saying?"

"She's seen two men tonight," Day said.

"Who were they?" March said. He apparently had no compunction about looking into women's bedrooms, because he was scowling up into the shadows as if he'd already caught the woman in a lie.

"I'm sure I don't know who they were," the old lady said. "I don't associate with strange men after midnight. Nor coppers, neither."

March muttered something under his breath that Day didn't catch and took a step forward. Day caught him by the arm. "If you don't mind, sir," he said in a low voice, "I think I might be the one to talk to her."

"Go ahead, then," March said. "But I wouldn't expect much out of that one, if I were you."

"Of course, sir." Day raised his voice so that the woman could hear him. "Mother, we're terribly sorry to disturb you at this hour, of course, but we would greatly appreciate your help."

"You would, would you?" The old lady's voice still sounded chilly, but she hadn't closed her window yet. Day took that as an encouraging sign.

"I don't mean to worry you," he said, "but we're on the trail of dangerous fugitives. And you are the most important witness we've got."

"I am?" Day could practically hear her drawing herself up to her full height, enjoying the sudden authority she'd been given. "Well, I'm not surprised. They didn't act at all civilized."

"What did they do?"

"Why are you looking at that tree when I'm speaking to you?"

"My apologies, mother. I don't mean to offend you."

"You're a good boy, but I'm far too old to be offended easy."

She had already proved herself to be easily offended, but Day glanced cautiously up at her. She was leaning farther out the window now, and he was surprised to see that she was fully dressed, her hair up and her face powdered. It occurred to him that she had been expecting him, or someone like him.

"Mother, what did the other men do?"

"This is ridiculous," March said. "We're going to wake the entire street. She doesn't know anything."

"I do so know anything," the old lady said. "They come from up the field there and got into a row right under my window. I wasn't sleeping. Haven't slept good in years. It's my back. Hurts most awful at night when I'm laying down. I ought to get another mattress, but those ain't cheap, you know?"

"A good mattress can be quite pricey indeed."

She nodded, clearly happy he was in agreement. "So I was awake anyhow and I looked down on them, but not too close. I didn't want them to see me looking and come round on me."

"If they were the men we're looking for, they were dangerous fellows."

"I thought they were. The one dressed half like a policeman did something to the other one and they went away up the street there and then the other one fell down."

"One was dressed as a policeman?" Day was confused. "Like me, you mean?"

"No, only half. And more like him." The old lady pointed and

Day looked around the tree trunk where Hammersmith was just jogging up even with March.

"One of the men was dressed like him?" Day pulled Hammersmith forward and the sergeant smiled and took off his hat, then looked away at the same tree Day had been staring at.

"Not just like him, no. But very like him, I suppose. His top didn't match his trousers, though."

"So he had a jacket," Day said. "A blue jacket, like this." He tugged at Hammersmith's sleeve.

"Precisely what I'm saying, yes."

"And they went off in that direction?" Day pointed down the lane. There was a small green building there, a few yards away, butted right up against the curb.

"Yes. Then the man who was half a copper went off again and I never seen him no more tonight."

Day felt a raindrop hit his cheek and roll down. A moment later another drop hit his hand. More rain wasn't what he needed.

"And the other man?" he said.

"Well, he's still here, isn't he?"

"Still where, mother?"

"Why, there." And the old lady pointed directly at the tiny green tea shop.

19

⁂

They lingered in the shelter of a copse of trees until a man passed by. He was tall and thin and carried a heavy attaché case. His hair was dark, going grey at the temples. His shoes were shiny black. The rain had abated, but his umbrella was still open. He was a busy man, hurrying along with no interest in the bald man and the half-naked bogeyman that trailed after him down the road.

They followed him along Old St Pancras Road to Aldenham and then up Ossulston to Phoenix Street, which Jack felt was entirely too appropriate at the dawn of his rebirth. The man turned in at the gate of a small tidy whitewashed terrace house, unlocked two bolts on the red front door, and stepped inside. Jack took the black medical bag from Cinderhouse, and the bald man trotted across the street. He pushed through the gate as it was swinging shut and put out his hand *just before the businessman closed the door. Jack came along after him and they forced their way inside before the man could do more than furrow his brow and open his mouth to complain.*

Jack shut the door and turned the topmost bolt. He already felt sure the man was alone in the house. Anyone inside was unlikely to have fastened both locks. He sniffed the air and his supposition was confirmed. The atmosphere inside was stuffy and empty. There was nobody moving around in here to stir the dust and bring the rooms to life. He sighed deeply and smiled at the man, grateful to have a place to call his own, even if their arrangement was only temporary.

"Who are you? How dare . . ." the man said. He was still holding his umbrella, and now he pointed it at them like a weapon. "I demand that you leave. Leave immediately."

"To answer your initial question," Jack said, "I am who I am. And this is my colleague, the shadowy Mr Evans of Fleet Street." Jack indicated Cinderhouse, who gave him a confused look, but said nothing.

"Well, Mr Evans and Mr . . ." The man looked for the first time at Jack's naked legs, at his cock hanging down past the end of the prison shirt. His gaze traveled up and took in the darts on the white canvas uniform, and Jack saw comprehension suddenly spark in his eyes. "I don't want trouble," the man said.

"Nobody wants trouble," Jack said. "Who would want that? Trouble is not something we seek, dear sir. Trouble is the thing that seeks us."

The man turned to run, headed for the hallway and, Jack assumed, a back door through the kitchen or scullery. But Cinderhouse was prepared and blocked the way. Jack felt electric excitement shudder through his spine and flicker down his arms and legs. He set his bag on the floor against the wall, grabbed the man from behind, and pro-

pelled him to the floor. He bit into him, but the man's suit was thick and padded in the shoulders and Jack's teeth were weak. Still, Jack laughed.

He was free.

The man crawled across the foyer with Jack clinging to his back. Jack grabbed a handful of distinguished greying hair and pulled the man's head back, smashed it forward into the floor. Once, twice, three times, and the man stopped crawling, crumpled across his forearms, his fingers twisted into claws. A clear ooze mixed with blood trickled from the man's left ear, and Jack tasted it. He listened to the man, relished the sound of the hot salty life coursing through his throat. He ground himself against the man's still body.

Finally he rolled off the man and rose to his feet. Cinderhouse stood there, uselessly, staring at the wall as if he were a machine that had been switched off.

"Take him into the parlor," Jack said. "Put him in a chair and find something to tie him with."

"Why not finish him and be done?"

"Always in such a hurry, Peter. You have much to learn about art. Now do as I say."

"I think it's a mistake to leave him alive for any length of time."

"Tell me you aren't arguing, little fly?"

"Please stop calling me that."

"Ah, they grow up so fast, don't they?" Jack said.

Cinderhouse frowned, wondering who Jack was talking to.

"You must never contradict me," Jack said.

"It's only that I don't like it when you call me an insect."

"Then I will stop."

"Thank you."

After that, Cinderhouse went quietly about his chores as Jack watched. He lit candles all through the house, then dragged the man through the inside door and down the hall to the parlor, propped him up, and levered him into a plush armchair piled with embroidered burgundy pillows. Jack surmised that the man was married and that the wife was currently away. Why else the burgundy pillows? They were not the sort of thing a man would choose for himself. Jack wondered if the man had children, too, and how old they might be. And what the insides of their bodies might look like. Jack shrugged. There were things even he wasn't meant to know.

While Cinderhouse went looking for twine or wire, something to tie the man with, Jack cast his eye about the house, his gaze finally coming to rest on the attaché case. It was unlikely the case held clues to the man's home life. It was probably full of business papers, which would be completely boring. Jack kicked the case under a settee. The man wouldn't need it again. He wouldn't be returning to work. Jack had already liberated him from the humdrum life of the worker bee.

There was a silver letter opener on the mantel over the fireplace and Jack picked it up. It was well polished and gleamed in the candlelight. Jack tucked it into the sleeve of his shirt, holding it against his arm with his fingertips, relishing the cold metallic feel of it. He decided to add the letter opener to his collection of instruments in the black leather bag. But it occurred to him that he needed pockets. He needed a decent pair of trousers and a waistcoat and a long jacket, all of them with loads of pockets.

The rest of the house was drab and ordinary, but with those occa-

sional women's touches he had noted. Floral-patterned draperies and gilt chandeliers. Nothing expensive, and nothing too terribly tasteful, either.

Cinderhouse returned from the back of the house with a spool of rough mailing twine. He set to work wrapping it around the unconscious body of the man in the chair.

"We should name him," Jack said. "What shall we call him?"

"I'm sure he already has a name."

"Had. He had a name, dear fly, when he was a simple worker. But we are going to do things to him and he will never return to that ordinary life he once led. Nor should he desire to. This is a new day for him. For us all. And he shall have a new name to go with the new day."

"I asked you not to call me that."

"What's that?"

"I asked you not to refer to me as an insect anymore."

"I didn't realize I had."

"Well, don't do it again, please." The bald man cocked his head to one side and seemed to think for a long moment before speaking again. "I'm fond of the name Fenn," he said.

"Fenn?"

"For him." Cinderhouse pointed at the bound man. "Isn't Fenn a pretty name?"

"No. I don't like it."

"Well, I do."

"I like the name Elizabeth," Jack said.

"But he's a man," Cinderhouse said. "You can't call a man Elizabeth."

"I can and I have. His name is now Elizabeth."

Cinderhouse shook his head, but he didn't argue further. He returned to the work of tying Elizabeth to his chair. Jack was unhappy with the bald man's attitude. There was entirely too much arguing going on.

"What did you say," Jack said, "that you used to do before you were in prison?"

"I was a tailor," Cinderhouse said.

"Fascinating," Jack said. "And how close in size do you think I am to Elizabeth?"

Cinderhouse sized them both up expertly with his eyes. "You are taller than he is, and I would guess that you were once a very large man, but you're quite thin now. Still, I think I could let out his hems and cuffs and get his suits to match you well enough."

"But I'm not interested in 'well enough.' I want to look every bit as dashing as I did before those evil men got hold of me."

"I can make you look good. That's a thing I do well."

"That's the spirit," Jack said. "And it appears you've got our boy good and fastened down. Be a good fellow and come here a moment."

Cinderhouse narrowed his eyes, but put down the nearly empty wooden spool that had held the twine. He cautiously approached Jack, walking very slowly. Jack became impatient.

"You are becoming entirely too insolent," Jack said. "I'm afraid I shall have to punish you now. Please remember, I do this out of love."

Cinderhouse started to back away as Jack reached for him, but it was too late. Jack mustered all of his strength and chopped his knuckles at the base of Cinderhouse's skull, where it connected to his spine. When the bald man stumbled and fell to his knees, Jack pulled the letter opener from his sleeve and held it to Cinderhouse's throat. He leaned down and brought him close and whispered in the bald man's ear.

"This is going to hurt me more than it hurts you," he said. "Or perhaps not as much. Let's decide when it's done."

Cinderhouse began to scream, wordlessly, but Jack didn't hear him. He heard nothing but the blood pounding in his own ears.

20

They approached the little green building cautiously. Day walked straight toward it along the pathway, while March and Hammersmith split up and circled around it. March flowed through the gloom under the trees, nearly invisible. Hammersmith came at it from the road, out in plain sight, but varying his gait and direction by small increments to make it harder for anyone inside to take aim at him.

If there was anyone inside. And if they were armed.

It was still only sprinkling. The rain hadn't come back in force yet, and Day hoped it would remain at bay. At least until they caught the missing men. He carried his Colt Navy loose in his hand, ready, but not anxious.

By the time Day reached the front door of the tea shop, he

could no longer see March or Hammersmith, but he knew they were nearby, within six feet of him on either side of the building. The sun was beginning to peek over the horizon and it filtered through the leaves of the trees, glanced along the rooftops of the houses. The tiny shop twinkled emerald green as raindrops pattered against the leaves overhead, moving the tree branches up and down around it, alternately dappling it with light and shadow. Day arrived at the front door and switched the revolver to his other hand. He reached out toward the doorknob, but then pulled his hand back and frowned.

"It's locked," he said.

He took a step back and looked around him. The street was still deserted, but it wouldn't be for much longer. Soon, people would be coming out of those homes, men headed away to the train or the cabstand or simply walking to work, children running to school or playing in their gardens. The road would be crowded with people.

March materialized next to him from somewhere around the corner of the building.

"Surely you can unlock it, Walter," he said.

"I can. But look." He pointed at the heavy steel padlock, its swinging arm looped through a bolt on the outside of the door. "This has been locked from the outside, not the inside. It's not possible for someone to be in there." He raised his voice. "Sergeant, I think it's clear."

"Take a look at this," came Hammersmith's voice from around the corner of the shop.

Day stowed his weapon and walked around to the road.

March followed him. Hammersmith was squatting, looking at something against the curb. Day leaned down and used one hand to steady himself against the wall of the building.

"Another one," he said.

A jagged line smeared by rain, but still clearly visible in the wan light, was drawn in blue chalk on the curb. Above it was an arrow, pointing toward the wall above it.

"The rain'll eventually wash this away," Hammersmith said.

"We need a sketch of it. Too bad we don't have Fiona Kingsley with us. She's a good artist."

"A terrific artist," Hammersmith said. "But we hardly need her talents for this." He pulled out his dog-eared pad of paper, turned to a blank page, and sketched a duplicate of the tiny chalk diagram with his pencil. "That'll do, won't it?"

"Looks just like it to me."

"But it's nothing," March said. "What does it mean?"

"Well, it must be a relation to the other one we saw," Hammersmith said. "Don't you think?"

"I think so," Day said.

"But what is it?" March said. "It looks like it might be a long arrow, but a piece of it's missing. Rubbed out or washed away by rain."

"Or maybe whoever chalked it there, maybe his hand slipped and made that gap," Day said. "What did the other one look like?"

Hammersmith flipped a page in his notebook. "I think it was a number four, but I'll . . . Yes, a number four with an arrow below it."

"And this might be a number one," Day said. "With an arrow up top of it. Maybe it's not a gap in the line. Maybe it's two separate lines."

"What do you think it means?"

"Besides nothing at all," March said.

"I think it means that four people escaped Bridewell," Day said. "Somebody's helping us find them."

"Or somebody has his own agenda we don't understand," Hammersmith said.

"Or children play with chalk in the roads round here and you two are so desperate for a clue that you're seeing meaning where there isn't any." March sighed and ran a hand through his hair. "I don't mean to be a naysayer, I really don't, but a manhunt doesn't come down to chalk lines in the road. Believe me, I've been involved in my fair share of manhunts."

"Yes," Hammersmith said. "You did a brilliant job bringing in that Ripper fellow."

"Nevil!" Day said. "I say, man."

"I apologize."

"No, no," March said. "From your perspective, you're perfectly correct."

"I shouldn't have said that," Hammersmith said. "It's just, you've been insufferable tonight. I don't understand. We're doing our best here, and yet it's never quite right for you, is it?"

"I suppose I have been difficult," March said. "Success, finding these men tonight, it's important to me. More important than you know. I did not retire from the Yard under the best of circumstances and I would like to correct the impression I made in the Ripper case, if I can. I would like to win back some modicum of respect. I haven't wanted to follow false clues because I fear those prisoners are getting farther and farther away from us with every passing moment."

"We're all tired," Day said. "And we've all got a lot on our minds. Tempers fray. But we'll find those missing men. We will."

March smiled. "I believe you, Walter."

Hammersmith held out his hand. March hesitated, then clasped it in both of his own hands and smiled.

"Again," Hammersmith said, "I apologize, sir."

"All is forgiven. Shows you care about what you're doing, that's all."

"So," Day said, "what say we take a quick look in this shop and then move on to the next clue?" He didn't mention that he had no idea where they might find another clue.

The other two followed him round the side of the little green building to the door. Day leaned down and took another look at the padlock. He reached into the pocket of his waistcoat, produced the flat leather case, opened it, and took out two tools. One was a small pointed hook. The other tool was a tension wrench that resembled a thick pair of tweezers. He inserted the angled ends of the wrench into the keyhole and maneuvered it until he felt pressure against them, then slipped the tiny hook between them and turned it. It took him two tries, but the clasp sprang open and the heavy end of the lock fell loose and dangled against the doorjamb. Day smiled at his mentor and was pleased to see March smiling back.

Day motioned for Hammersmith to remove the lock from its bolt. He and March readied their firearms and took up positions on either side of the door. Day nodded to Hammersmith, and the sergeant pushed the door open with the toe of his boot and stepped back, all in one fluid motion. Day entered the room at a crouch and stood against the wall, just inside the door. He heard March and Hammersmith enter behind him, but he didn't look around at them. He waited for his eyes to adjust to the gloom.

If anything, the shop's interior seemed even smaller than it looked from without. Grey sunlight pushed into the room through the open door and around the loose-fitted shutters that covered half the opposite wall. Dust motes sparked silver and disappeared. There was a lantern on a peg over the long counter below the window. Under the counter were several deep drawers. At a right angle to it were shelves stacked with saucers, cups, trays, spoons, and tiny china milk jugs. All of it plain, unadorned, easily replaced if broken. A mesh bag full of lemons hung from a nail on the side of the topmost shelf. There was a hot plate on the counter and two teakettles set neatly beside it, but no oven. Day supposed the vendor must bring in cakes and sandwiches from somewhere else every morning, rather than trying to create them in this cramped space.

Lying on the floor at his feet was a man, moving slightly, but bound at the hands and feet with rough swaths of canvas that bunched and mounded over him and across the worn planks beneath him. A thin strip of canvas had been tied around his mouth and behind his head so that it bit into his jaw on both sides. The man's eyes were wide and staring, the whites of them almost glowing. He was trying to speak, but his tongue was caught up in the gag and all he could muster was a weak grunting sound.

Day put his Colt Navy away and bent down next to the man. There was a nasty gash on his head, but it wasn't bleeding and had already crusted over in his hair. He looked up at Day, who shifted slightly from side to side. The man's eyes followed his movements and seemed to be tracking correctly. He had pulled at his bonds hard enough that the canvas had knotted itself into something resembling a wooden ball. It was instantly clear that there was no point in trying to untie him.

"I need a knife," Day said. "Have you got one?"

March shook his head and stepped past Day to the counter, where he began poking about in the drawers. "There's this," he said, and held up a wedge-shaped cake knife. "It's serrated along the edge."

"That might work."

March knelt down and began sawing at the canvas on the man's ankles while Day worked the gag slowly up and down until he could pull it away from the man's mouth.

The man gasped and gulped in air, worked his jaw back and forth. Then: "About goddamn time," he said.

Day eased the gag back into his mouth.

"What's your name?" he said.

He maneuvered the gag again so that the man could move his tongue around the saturated cloth.

"Get this shite off me!"

Day put the gag in place again. He straightened up and stood next to Hammersmith.

"Well, I don't think he's the proprietor of this place," Hammersmith said.

"Could be," Day said. "The escapee might have changed clothing with him."

"Almost got this," March said. He was still sawing away at the man's feet.

"How are you holding up?" Hammersmith said.

"Me?" Day said. "I'm fine."

"You've seemed a bit anxious of late."

"Oh, you know, just the usual sort of thing."

"Baby coming and all that?"

"Yes, exactly. I shouldn't worry, I suppose. Been plenty of babies born before mine and they turned out all right, some of them without fathers of any sort."

"Well, I hate to disagree, but really too many babies grow up and become this sort of person." Hammersmith pointed at the man on the ground.

"Ah, that's got it," March said. He stood up and laid the cake knife on the counter, then reached down and hoisted the man to his feet. He held the man's elbow, steadying him, and leaned him against the counter. Then March held up a finger and grabbed the cake knife back off the countertop. "Wouldn't do to leave that within your reach, would it?"

"Let's try this again," Day said. "I'm going to take off your gag and you're going to tell us your name. Leave the profanities out of it."

The man nodded and Day pulled the gag down over his chin. The canvas was sodden with drool, and he wiped his fingers on the man's filthy prison shirt.

"George," the man said. "My name's George."

"George what?"

"George Hampstead. This is my shop. Someone broke in, some mad bloke with a murderous gleam in his eye, and he tied me up. Switched his clothes for mine and left me here for dead, he did."

"He heard us suggest that just now," Hammersmith said.

"Did not," the man calling himself George Hampstead said.

"You were right here when we said it."

"I wasn't listening."

Day grimaced. "Mr Hammersmith, do you remember those sketches we were shown of the escaped prisoners?"

"I do, sir."

"Does this man resemble any of them?"

"He does, sir."

"Which one? Do you remember?"

"The one called Napper, sir."

"I never was!" the man in the prison uniform said. "You can't go off a thing like that! It's not no kinda proof."

Day nodded. "We'll get this whole thing straightened out. Don't you worry."

He turned and opened the door. The others had to shuffle about to make room for the door to swing inward. Day stepped outside and took a deep breath of fresh air. He hadn't realized how stuffy it was inside the tea shop until he was out of it. Dawn had brought with it a bustle of people, up and down the street, most of them headed toward the far corner and away. Day presumed that was the direction of the commuter train to central London. He whistled and motioned to a little boy, who was sitting idly on a step in front of one of the homes. The lad ran over to him and Day produced a ha'penny from the pocket of his waistcoat.

"Would you like to earn a coin?"

"Like to earn a bigger one than that, if you've got it," the boy said.

"How about a second coin just like it?" Day fished in his pocket again.

"What've I got to do?"

"Get to Scotland Yard and ask them to send round a wagon. Tell them one of the men's been caught."

"One of which men?"

"Never you mind. Just find Sergeant Kett and he'll know what you mean."

"Sergeant Kett," the boy said. "He's to send a wagon, you've caught a man."

"Exactly right."

The boy nodded once, sharply, and marched away, joining the throngs of men headed for that nearby train. Day turned around and almost bumped into an elderly man, who was stopped outside the tea shop and was staring at him with a puzzled expression.

"I say," the man said.

"Terribly sorry," Day said.

"What are you doing?"

"Police," Day said. "My name is Inspector Day. Nothing to worry about. Please go about your business, sir."

"But I can't go about my business."

"You can't?"

"You're blocking the way. That's my tea shop."

Day smiled. "Ah, very good, sir. Then you have the opportunity to clear up a small mystery for me."

"A mystery?"

"Do you have anyone working for you here? Small fellow named George Hampstead? A bit jumpy?"

"No." The man pulled himself up to his full height. "I've never had anyone working here except me. Never a need. What's going on here?"

"Well," Day said, "it's all a bit complicated. Do you have a few minutes to spare?"

21

The contractions were coming every few minutes, and Claire didn't know what to do. She curled up under the coverlet and hugged her knees and closed her eyes and tried to imagine the tiny life inside her. One day that life would be a person. One day that life would be a policeman or a housewife, a mother or a father, a living breathing human being. But right now, that life wanted to come out.

Claire reached under the edge of the mattress and brought out her diary. She unsnapped the catch and opened it and looked over the last entry she had made. Nothing much. Nothing that made her proud. Just a jot about feeling lonely and having trouble getting the buttons right on Walter's shirts. There ought to be something more there. What if she died in childbirth? It was more than possible. Dr Kingsley told her not to think of such things, told her she was safe and healthy and that he would do his all for her. But he didn't know. He'd never felt a contraction, he'd never given birth.

She turned a page and took her pencil and bit her lower lip. Another contraction hit and she grimaced, almost made a sound, but didn't. At least there was that. She felt like pushing back against that pressure, but she was afraid of what might happen if she did.

Instead, she thought of her baby and what she could tell it. Her eyes closed, she felt the room moving, and she remembered skipping rope when she was a girl and hadn't worried about dying. She thought about what it was like to be a child, and she hoped that she would be able to make her baby feel the way that she had when she was young. She opened her eyes and she wrote in her diary:

> *My skipping rope,*
> *It passes over and it passes down.*
> *My skipping rope,*

She couldn't think of anything that rhymed with *down*. She felt dizzy and unconnected, so she concentrated harder on the words. She crossed out the second line and wrote *It passes under and it passes up*. This posed the same problem. *Cup?* What did that have to do with skipping rope? *Pup?* Maybe the child was skipping rope with a dog? That seemed unlikely.

She tossed her diary aside and lay watching the ceiling swim around above her. There were more than enough nursery rhymes for children. She didn't need to write her own.

Another contraction hit. She clenched her teeth and moved her hand to her stomach. And then she felt something warm and wet moving under her bottom and up to the small of her back, and she pulled aside the blanket and there was liquid soaking into her fresh linens, a whole day's work undone by her rebel body. Tears sprang to her eyes and she wiped them away.

Another contraction, this one the worst yet. Terrible pain, and why was it necessary to feel such pain when childbirth was such a common thing? She tensed up into a ball in the wet spot, but it wasn't a spot, it was an ocean, and she clenched her hands into fists and thought about her horse, the little horse her father had given to her on the occasion of her thirteenth birthday, and she wondered if that horse was still galloping about somewhere on her parents' land wondering why she didn't visit it anymore. Why didn't she take it apples and ride it anymore?

The pain passed, although she could still feel it, a faint drumbeat like her pulse somewhere far away. She sat up and looked down and there was blood in the bed, blood mixed with something clear and viscous, flecking the coverlet and soaking into her nightgown.

"Fiona!"

She licked her lips and concentrated on not panicking, except that everything felt wrong. Her body was somebody else's body and it didn't fit her properly, hadn't been hers to begin with. She gasped and closed her eyes; again there was a twinge low in her belly, a soft strum of muscle and grit, and she screamed as loud as she could.

"Fiona!"

22

※

Jack stood patiently in the center of the parlor while Cinder-house moved around him. The tailor had Jack try on the jacket first. Elizabeth sat quietly in his chair in the corner of the room, watching them alter one of his suits. The jacket's shoulders were broader than Jack's own shoulders, but not by much, and the slight difference helped with the sleeves. Jack's arms had always been much longer than average and his enforced starvation hadn't altered their length. Cinderhouse silently noted a few things, then had Jack try on the trousers. They were a bit long, but the tailor pinned up the hem of the left leg, made sure it broke properly against the top of Jack's foot. He measured Jack's waist, using a piece of the same twine they'd tied Elizabeth with, and had Jack take the suit off again.

Cinderhouse retired to the dining room table and began to sew, *while Jack rooted through the drawers in Elizabeth's bedroom until he found a pair of underpants that fit him well enough if he bunched them up at the waist. He found a smoking jacket in the closet in the hall and put that on, too, and paced about the house, barefoot. He hovered over the bald man for a while, watching him work, but the tailor kept pricking himself, his hands shaking with fear, and so Jack wandered away. He didn't want blood on his new suit. At least, not just yet.*

He found half a stale loaf of bread in the kitchen cupboard, along with a cheese that wasn't much more than rind. He ate them too quickly and was only halfway through the bread when he had to step out the back door and vomit it all back up. After that, he ate slowly, swallowed a little bit of water with each mouthful.

When he felt satisfied that he would hold the bread down, he went back to the parlor and stood in the shadows under the stairs and watched Elizabeth struggle with his bonds, unaware that he was being observed. Jack's gaze settled on the mantel. Cinderhouse's tongue was nailed to the forward edge. It had stopped dripping and was beginning to shrivel a bit around the edges. It had always fascinated Jack how long a person's tongue was once it was out of the mouth, free to stretch itself out a bit.

Now he missed Cinderhouse's chattering. Only a little. The bald man still expressed himself with grunts and gestures, but of course that was the most rudimentary and imprecise of languages. Jack frowned and wondered if he ought to have punished Cinderhouse in some other way. Left him with his words so they could have a proper conversation.

Then he realized that what was really needed was a second tongue on the mantel. Two tongues might converse with each other. What secrets would they tell? He left the shadows and went in search of his medical bag. It was still on the floor against the wall where he'd left it when they'd first entered the house. He opened it and rummaged through until he found a fine scalpel, still dotted here and there along its short sharp blade with Jack's own blood. He went back to the parlor, and Elizabeth stopped struggling when he saw him. Jack smiled at him in what he hoped was a reassuring way and removed the gag from the homeowner's mouth. Elizabeth started to say something, but Jack shushed him and went right to work.

When he had finished, he left the gag loose around Elizabeth's neck so he wouldn't choke to death on his own blood. Jack pounded a nail through Elizabeth's tongue into the edge of the mantel. It made a fine companion piece to Cinderhouse's tongue, although there were subtle differences between the two pieces of meat, not the least of which was that the bald man's tongue was much more ragged at the far edge where it had been torn out. Absolutely fascinating to see the many variations the human body worked upon itself. God's wonders were truly infinite.

Jack stepped back and wiped his fingers on the front of the smoking jacket. He hefted the hammer once or twice, tested its weight, and slashed at the air with it, letting it swing his arm around, wondering at the simple power of it. He saw Elizabeth out of the corner of his eye, still drooling blood down the front of his shirt, his eyes wide with pain and terror. Jack sighed and put the hammer down on the mantel top. He hadn't intended to frighten the poor fellow. Hammers were not his style. Didn't everyone know that by now? He patted Elizabeth on the shoulder and left the room.

He checked on Cinderhouse, who was still toiling away over the *suit at the dining room table, then took the stairs up to the bedroom once more. He closed the door and turned the lock and lay down on the bed. The ceiling was tin, painted white, with swirling decorative grooves that looped across its whole expanse. He followed the grooves with his eyes, making pictures in the patterns up there, until he fell asleep.*

23

They were waiting for the wagon from Scotland Yard, and Hammersmith was visibly chafing at the sense of wasted time. Day offered him his flask of brandy, but Hammersmith waved it away. Day took a long pull at the flask, recorked it, and stowed it in his jacket, on the other side from the Colt Navy so that their weight balanced and didn't pull the jacket off-center.

"I hope the others have caught somebody, too," Hammersmith said.

"How are you, Nevil?"

"What?"

"You asked after me earlier," Day said. "What about you?"

"I'm fine."

"I see."

Day stared at the green tea shop where Adrian March stood guard over the prisoner. The air was better out here on the street, even if the sky remained suspiciously grey.

"I've got to find a new flatmate," Hammersmith said.

"It's been six months. More than that, hasn't it?"

Hammersmith nodded, looked away at the sky, both of them waiting for it to open up and soak them. "His family came. Took his things. What things they wanted."

Constable Colin Pringle had been off duty when he was murdered, helping his friend Hammersmith on a case he wasn't even supposed to be working. Hammersmith hadn't mentioned Pringle even once since then. Day was surprised to hear him speak of him now, but he stayed silent, afraid any sound he made might chase the sergeant back into whatever hole he'd been living in for seven months.

"Left me with his suits."

Day looked down at the footpath and waited.

"Can you imagine me in a suit?"

Day smiled at him. "Maybe when you make inspector."

"Never happen. I'd give them to you, but they wouldn't fit. You're bigger than he was."

"So are you."

"I suppose so. Where would I put them if some new chap moved in? He wouldn't want a dead man's clothing taking up all the space in his room."

"You could donate them to the poor."

"Would Colin like that, do you think? Would he be pleased to see his suits worn by shit-shovelers and knocker-uppers?"

"It might amuse him. But I didn't know him as well as you did."

There was a long companionable silence. Day looked up at the sky and Hammersmith looked down at the tops of his shoes.

"You shouldn't worry, you know," Hammersmith said.

"About what?"

"I was thinking about my father."

"You've lost a lot in the past year."

"I was thinking about him the way that I remember him, not the way that he was at the end of things. By then his body had failed and his mind had gone. He wasn't the same man. But when I was younger . . ."

"I'm sure he was a good father."

"Well, I don't know. I don't know what's a good father and what's a perfectly average father, since I never had more than one to compare, you know? But what I remember best of all are the small things, not the big events, not the things you think you'll remember, like a trip to the Crystal Palace."

"But the small things?"

"Yes. When he would put his hand on my shoulder as we walked along. Or when he showed me how to tie my boots. He was patient with me."

"Nevil, your boots are untied."

"That's what reminded me just now. I never quite got the knack of it."

"Do you want another lesson?"

"Ha." Hammersmith looked up and grinned at him. "But that's what I mean. You'll show your son. Or your daughter. You'll show them how to tie their shoes. Or you'll just take a walk with them and be quiet and let them talk. You'll listen the way that you always do. And they'll remember that one small moment, maybe, when they're older. And that's all they'll need from you. Only that you were there."

"If that's really all it took, Nevil . . ."

"I think that it is."

"Thank you, Sergeant."

"I didn't mean to offer you unasked-for advice. And it's hardly my place . . ."

"Not at all," Day said. "I'm glad that you did."

"Good."

Both men quietly watched the far corner of the street until the wagon came around it and rolled smoothly toward them. At last, the escapee would be taken off their hands and they could get back to the business of catching prisoners.

"And it's good to know," Day said, "that their uncle Nevil will be such a font of good advice."

He clapped Hammersmith on the back and stepped out into the street and hailed the wagon driver.

24

inderhouse poked his fingers through the gap in the curtain and peered outside. Clouds were moving fast across the sky, and shining slivers of bright blue and pink slashed through the grey. He was aware of Elizabeth, whimpering in the chair beside him, but he ignored the damaged homeowner. Cinderhouse had been punished, but he was still Peter, still the rock. Elizabeth was nothing, not even a fly. Jack would dispose of him eventually, when he grew bored.

A carriage rolled by outside and a bird fluttered up past the window, on its way to some roost above. Cinderhouse smiled, then grimaced at the pain in his mouth. His punishment had been too severe, he thought. But then, who was he to judge? He set his face carefully, found an expression that didn't hurt his tender lips too much. Jack had pushed hard against the bald man's jaw for leverage as he'd yanked.

The bird flew back down past the window—or perhaps it was a different bird; what did he know about birds?—and grabbed at something in the dirt. Across the street, a door opened and a little girl stepped out into a sudden patch of sunlight. It glinted on her shiny blond ringlets. She wore a pink dress covered with bows and dots, and it ended just above her ankles. Cinderhouse found himself staring at her delicate ankles. He was panting.

He wanted that girl.

But Jack had told him he could not have any more children.

A ridiculous notion. Surely Jack hadn't meant it. It was like telling the bird not to claw at worms in the dirt.

The girl leaned against the fence across the street and Cinderhouse pulled the curtains partially shut. He didn't want her to see him. Not yet. He wasn't properly dressed. Elizabeth jounced in his chair, trying to get the bald man's attention. Cinderhouse turned and picked up the shovel from the fireplace. He pounded the injured man—the *other* injured man—on top of his skull until Elizabeth slumped silent in the chair. That was better.

Cinderhouse checked to be sure the girl was still there. Then he turned and hurried to gather his new suit, the second suit from Elizabeth's wardrobe that he had altered. He would make himself look nice for the girl.

Jack couldn't possibly be angry about that. Not if he simply visited the little girl. Surely he wouldn't punish Cinderhouse for obeying his nature. That wouldn't be fair at all.

Just the thought of that pretty little girl was giving Cinderhouse strength. Just the thought of her! He almost smiled again.

He absolutely couldn't wait to meet her.

25

Fiona Kingsley dropped her umbrella in the foyer and rushed through the door into University College Hospital. Her feet left damp tracks across the smooth polished wood as she scampered along the dark hallway. She barely glanced at the skeleton in the corner, held together with wires and screwed into a wooden base. She had named it Bruce when she was three years old, and it was now like an old family pet, tolerated but barely seen. Her father's laboratory was in the hospital's basement, but his office was on the ground floor and so she tried it first. She knocked twice on the closed door and pushed it open, entering headfirst. Great piles of paper obscured her father's desk, and a single green-shaded lamp standing on a stool against the side of the table failed to illuminate the dark and dingy workspace. Fiona clicked her tongue and turned to leave, but there was a rustling sound from somewhere in the gloomy back half of the room, and Dr Kingsley's head popped up over a mound of yellowed vellum. His spectacles were up on top of his head, virtually lost amid drifts of wild grey hair. His necktie was skewed and stubbornly knotted as if the doctor had tried to pull it off without first loosening it.

"Shut the door," he said. "I'm busy." Then he peered harder in her direction and said, "Fiona? Is that you?" He touched his face and patted his hands gently about in the sea of paper.

"They're on your head, Father," Fiona said.

Dr Kingsley reached up and found the spectacles, extricated them from his hair, and adjusted them carefully on the bridge of his nose. He smiled at Fiona and walked around the desk, grabbed her in a big hug. Fiona noticed that she was nearly as tall as he was and wondered when that had happened.

"What brings you, my dear?"

"It's Claire," Fiona said. "She's having the baby."

"What, right this minute?"

"Very nearly so. She's having pains."

"Contractions, you mean? How close together?"

"Every five minutes at least."

"If I know Walter," Kingsley said, "he must be out of his mind with worry right now."

"He's gone."

"Where is he?"

"He was called out. Something's happened and he was sent for."

"How long ago?"

"Not long."

"Oh, of course. The thing at the prison."

"It was just after he left that Claire began to feel the cramping. Well, not long after, at any rate."

"Has her water broken?"

"I think so. But Father, there's blood."

"She's bleeding?"

"Yes, is that very bad?"

"Not necessarily. How much blood did you see?"

"A little bit. I'm not sure. There were other fluids, too."

"Well, a certain amount of bleeding is to be expected." Kingsley snatched his hat from the rack by the door and moved a stack of papers off the floor onto his desk. "Ah, here it is. You know, you should have sent someone to get me, stayed with her."

"I'm quicker than anyone I might have sent. And a policeman is there helping."

"That's good." He pulled up on the handle of the black medical bag that he always carried when he was outside the hospital. It didn't move. "But I'm sure she'd rather have you there with her right now."

"We'd both rather get you there sooner than later."

He stopped pulling on the bag and squinted at her. Fiona felt sure he could see through her, that he knew how frightened she was, that she had left Claire alone because she didn't know what else to do and she needed her father. He turned back to the bag and glared at it.

"Oh," he said. "There's the problem." He leaned on the corner of the desk and lifted it an inch and slid one of the handles out from beneath the desk's leg. He scooted the bag across the floor with the toe of his shoe and set the desk back down. He stepped over to the bag and picked it up, took his daughter by the elbow, and steered her toward the door.

"Well, what are we waiting for?" he said. "We have a baby to deliver."

26

Eunice Pye moved to a terrace house on Phoenix Street the same year she was married. Her husband, Giles, died in that terrace house the same year the London Underground was opened to the public. Right or wrong, she had always associated Giles's death with the advent of swift transportation and there was nothing within walking distance that interested her much, so she rarely left her home except for Saturday mornings when she visited the corner market.

She was returning from the market at eight o'clock when she saw a strange man leave the house with the red door. That particular house had been cause for much speculation by Eunice because Mrs Michael, who lived there, had left two weeks previously and had not returned. Giles would have told her to mind her own business, but Eunice couldn't help speculating. She had decided that there must have been a terrible row and that it was entirely possible Mrs Michael would not be returning. Mr Michael, whose hair had begun to grey (or perhaps he had stopped touching it up when his wife left), had lived there alone for those two weeks, but had not changed his routine. He left each morning for work and returned each evening with a bag of fish and chips from Benny's on the corner. (Eunice assumed it was fish and chips because she could not imagine sampling any of Benny's other greasy offerings.)

Eunice had not seen this new strange man enter the house, so she reasoned that he must have arrived while she was at the market or in the wee hours while she slept. But now here he was, a tall man in a nice grey suit that fitted him nearly perfectly (although she thought it seemed a bit scrunched in the shoulders). He closed the red door carefully, as if to make sure it would not latch behind him, and he came through the gate, letting it swing shut again.

He stopped then and stood on the curb, watching the little Anderson girl, who was playing in her tiny front garden. Eunice took a moment to smile at her, but the little girl had always been an absolute beast and she stuck her tongue out at Eunice.

Eunice was carrying two baskets of groceries and her gate was latched. She was trying to determine whether to set a basket down on the path in order to free up a hand to unlatch the gate when the stranger hurried over and opened the gate for her.

"Thank you, young man," Eunice said. She carried her baskets through the gate and turned back to the man. "Would you mind closing it again?"

The man said nothing. He closed and latched the gate and tipped his hat to her. He turned back to the house with the red door and paused only a moment for another look at the little Anderson girl. He glanced again at Eunice and then went in by his own gate and into the house.

She watched until the red door had shut behind him, then she shuddered. She had never liked bald men. Giles had maintained a full and healthy head of hair for the entirety of their married life. There was something about this particular bald man that interested her, though. Something she couldn't quite place. Perhaps it was his mouth, which looked swollen and sore. His lips didn't seem to close completely.

She set her baskets down on the narrow strip of grass that separated her garden from the front walk and found her key in her handbag. She unlocked the front door, picked up the baskets, and carried them through to the kitchen. The instant she reached the counter, she remembered why the bald man seemed so familiar.

She let go of her baskets, one of which landed safely on the counter. The other landed half on, half off the counter, and gravity propelled it the rest of the way to the floor. Eunice heard the crash and spatter of a jam jar, but did not turn around. She got to the front door as quickly as she could, shut it, and bolted it fast. She went to the parlor window and looked up and down the street, but the bald man had not come back outside. There was nothing in the lane but the usual foot traffic and the occasional carriage rolling past. Still, she kept watch for half an hour, waiting to see if the bald man would leave again.

When he did not, she reluctantly left her station and cleaned up the broken jar of jam (which had thankfully been contained in the basket and had not caused a mess on the floor). She emptied the basket into the garbage, considered washing the basket, then threw it in after. She put her groceries away and folded her remaining basket and stowed it under the kitchen table. Then she gathered her notecards, envelopes, and her best pen and sat down at the window seat where she commanded an excellent view of the entire street. She barely looked at the notecard as she wrote, and so her handwriting was not up to her usual standards, but she felt it necessary to keep a watchful eye on the little Anderson girl, even if the child *was* a beast.

When she saw the postman turn onto her street, she stuffed the card into an envelope and addressed it to the Metropolitan Police. She pulled her door open before the postman could get the mail through the slot and handed him her envelope.

Then she went back to watching the street.

She wondered what was going on in the house with the red door. And she wondered how soon the police would come to catch the bald man.

27

The boy driving the police wagon was perhaps twelve or thirteen years old. From his driver's seat he was able to look down on Day and Hammersmith, and it was for this reason that he refused to alight. Instead, he sat, stoic and silent, with the morning sun behind him. Sergeant Kett had obviously put young runners to work driving carriages for the day. Day wondered if the boy was trying to grow whiskers or had perhaps left a bit of wheat cereal on his lip. His thoughts wandered to his unborn child and he wondered if it would be a son and if it would be as dutiful as this boy was.

Hammersmith gave the horse's nose a pat and followed Day to the tea shop door, which was closed and refused to budge. Day tugged on the handle and then rapped on the green door.

"It sticks," said the shop's proprietor, who sat frustrated on the curb, watching for cabs in the street. Every time a two-wheeler or four-wheeler rolled by, he would mutter under his breath, "Another one lost."

Eventually, the door swung open and Adrian March beckoned them inside. Day shook his head.

"The wagon's arrived," he said. "Let's bring him out."

"One moment," March said.

The door closed, then opened again a minute later, and March pushed Napper out onto the footpath. The prisoner stumbled, but caught himself before falling and stood up straight. He was shorter than he had seemed inside the miniature shop. His hands were still bound in bunched and knotted canvas, but there were fresh wounds on his face and scalp, fresh blood on his prison-issue uniform. He spat at Day, but the inspector moved backward and watched the glistening spit break and spatter at his feet. Napper grinned at him. His teeth were small and pearl grey.

"Sorry," he said. "Meant that for him over there."

"What happened?" Day said. "Why's he got blood all over him?"

"He fell," March said. "Hit his head against the counter before I could catch him."

The shop's proprietor pushed past them all and disappeared into the gloom of the green building. Off-balance, Napper fell against Day. Day grabbed him by the collar and pulled him upright, but his attention was arrested by the gleam in the little prisoner's eyes.

"Heard something," Napper said.

"What do you mean?" Day said.

"The other one, Griffin," Napper said. "He told me a thing you might like to know."

"What's that?"

"I'll tell you," Napper said. "Or maybe I won't."

"He's lying," March said. "He didn't say anything like this when we were in there." He gestured at the tea shop.

"You didn't ask me nice," Napper said. "You was evil toward me. Not talkin' no more to you."

"If you have something to say," Day said, "say it."

"Only you. Only to you."

"Why me?"

"Nice eyes you got. Friendly eyes. Salty tasty eyes."

Day remembered that Napper was the one who had eaten a woman over the course of several days. He swallowed hard and turned away. "Let's get him in the wagon."

"He said he were gonna put me in a cell," Napper said. He was talking fast, realized he'd lost his audience, but probably had no idea what he'd said that was so wrong. "Said he was gonna take me underground, down there, and put me in a cell."

Day turned back around. "Who did? Who said that?"

"You weren't there."

"Who?"

Napper looked slyly around at the three of them. "Griffin. It were Griffin. Said he had it all ready and waitin' for me, for when the others come and took me there."

"Underground?"

"It's what he said. Swear it on my honor."

"Your honor? That means nothing."

"Catch 'im. He'll tell you same's I done."

The big shutters on the street side of the tea shop swung open and the proprietor stuck his head outside. "What happened in here? What did you do to my place?"

"It was this fellow and his friend," Day said. "Terribly sorry, sir."

"The whole day's gone. It'll take the whole day to clean this up."

"We'll try to send someone to help you with that," Day said. But he knew there was nobody to spare. They didn't even have proper drivers for the wagons.

Day opened the back of the wagon and eyed the dark interior. It had been built to transport prisoners and was sturdy enough, with heavy oak buttresses and inch-thick paneling. So heavy that Day wondered about the strength of the horse that had to pull it. The benches along the walls inside the van were utilitarian, not fashioned for any measure of comfort, and there was no window for illumination, no place to set a lamp or candle, nothing to break off and use as a weapon. He stepped back and glanced at the puffed-up boy holding the reins.

"We can't send Napper away with this child," Day said.

"I'm no child," the boy said.

"I'll be good," Napper said. "Real good."

Day ignored them both. "This lad would probably be safe enough during the ride, but there may not be anyone at the Yard to receive him. He might be stuck sitting there, useless, until someone comes to help move Napper into a cell. Or he might try to move the prisoner himself and be hurt in the attempt."

"I can move 'im," the boy said. "I'm plenty able."

"Well, that settles it," Hammersmith said. "He can move him." But he chuckled as he said it.

"He looks strong," Napper said. "Plenty of meat on them bones."

Hammersmith stopped laughing.

"One of us has to ride along," Day said.

"Mr Hammersmith," March said, "you're the best choice for it."

"I think you ought to go," Hammersmith said.

"I'm no longer quite so young as you are, my boy," March said. "And Inspector Day can't go because he's in charge of this investigation. It would be a waste of his time."

Hammersmith looked at Day and an entire conversation occurred without either of them saying a word. Hammersmith pursed his lips, raised his left eyebrow. Day shrugged at him. He didn't want Hammersmith to go, but March's logic was sound. Hammersmith sniffed and kicked at a stone in the street.

"Fine," he said at last. "I'll be back with you in an hour. Where will I find you?"

"Inspector March and I are going underground."

"Do you know how many miles of tunnels are down there? It would take us days to get through it all," March said. "And just on the word of this bloody convict?"

"I told you what's true," Napper said.

"Wasn't talking to you."

"I can't very well expect to find you underground," Hammersmith said.

A large crowd of passersby had gathered at a respectful distance, watching the police and the filthy little man trussed in bloody canvas. Napper clearly enjoyed the attention and was performing some sort of jig. The tea shop proprietor was still hanging halfway out his window, listening to their conversation, perhaps hoping one of them would come back inside and help him tidy the place up. Day waved at him.

"Where's the nearest entry to the tunnels under us?"

"I'm supposed to know that?"

"I can tell you," a heavyset man said. He was wearing a hat two sizes too small for him and carrying a broken umbrella. "There's a church right across there." He pointed vaguely at some spot in the distance. "Under it's a catacombs."

"How do you know that?"

"I work there. Play the organ at mass."

"What's the name of the church?"

"St John of God, sir."

Day turned back to Hammersmith. "Meet us at St John of God. We'll nose about and then come back to the door in an hour. If there's any sign that someone is down there, we'll all go down together."

"Don't deal with anything on your own," Hammersmith said. He held up a warning finger. "Wait for me if there's anything suspicious. Promise."

"I'll wait for you, Nevil."

Hammersmith nodded once and pushed Napper into the

back of the van. The prisoner was still hopping about, amusing the crowd, and he tripped, sprawled facedown on the floor of the wagon. Hammersmith lifted Napper's legs and shoved forward, propelling him all the way in on his belly.

"Here," Day said. He held out his lantern. "You'll need this."

"Further insurance that you'll stay aboveground," Hammersmith said.

"I'll stay away from the dark until you find me again."

Hammersmith took the lantern. He jumped up into the wagon and closed the doors behind him. The boy shouted "haw" and cracked the reins and the wagon lurched away from the curb. It rolled down the street, the horse straining against the immense weight of its load, turned the corner, and was gone.

Day turned to the fat man with the little hat. "Will you show us the way to St John of God?"

The man nodded, his face bright and eager. He waved the broken umbrella over his head and led the way down the street as if he were at the head of a parade. Day smiled at the tea shop proprietor, motioned to Adrian March, and followed the fat organ player as the crowd began to break up behind them.

28

There were fugitives loose in the city, but Constable Rupert Winthrop was not out there chasing them down. He was stuck in the foyer of a private home on Regent's Park Road, sitting on an uncomfortable chair and sipping tea. His stomach was growling and he wanted a pastry, but there was no one else in the house except a very pregnant lady, and Rupert didn't want to bother her.

He had tried watching the door like a hawk, just staring at it. It made him feel diligent and in charge of the situation, but that feeling had passed quickly. There was no situation. Everybody else was out there running down villains, and Rupert had apparently done something wrong because he was doing nothing. He couldn't figure out why Sergeant Kett should be unhappy with him. He'd spent the last hour thinking over every exchange he'd ever had with the sergeant, but there was nothing. It must have been something personal, something he'd had no idea would offend. The only thing to do was try to get back in Kett's good graces as soon as he possibly could.

He was puzzling over just how to accomplish that when he heard a woman scream upstairs. He dropped his cup of tea, which broke on the floor. Tea spattered everywhere, and Rupert wasted several seconds by dropping to his knees and trying to gather the shards of china into his palm. A second scream made him drop the shards, some of which split into even tinier sharp bits, and jump back to his feet. He rushed to the steps and stared up into the darkness. He looked back at the door again, the door he was supposed to be guarding, then took a cautious step up. He heard whimpering somewhere above and abandoned caution, taking the stairs three at a time. He didn't wait at the top of the stairs for his eyes to adjust, and so he ran into a wall and caromed off of it, then oriented himself and walked down the hallway, stopping outside the lady's bedroom. He rapped on the door, already embarrassed and unsure.

"Ma'am?"

A moment's silence. Then: "I'm fine."

Rupert tugged at his earlobe and sniffed. What if someone else was in the bedroom? What if someone had climbed up from the outside and through the window and had a knife to Claire Day's throat and was whispering in her ear, telling her to say that she was all right?

"Ma'am," he said, "can I open the door?"

"I'd rather you didn't."

"But are you really all right?"

"Yes." Her voice was small and far away, muffled by the thick door. She sounded like a little girl. "I mean, no. I don't know. Where's Fiona? I want Fiona."

Rupert stepped closer to the door and put his lips almost against it. He wanted to push himself through the grain of the wood and be able to see whether Mrs Day needed his help.

"She went to get the doctor for you," he said.

"She left me?"

"Only for a bit. I'm here, ma'am. Really, anything I can do . . ."

"Just leave me alone."

"Are you sure? I could—"

"I said leave me alone!"

Rupert pulled his head back away from the door as if he'd been struck. "I'm sorry, ma'am." He spoke quietly and wasn't sure she could hear him, but then she answered.

"I'm sorry, too, Constable."

"Yes, ma'am."

"Rupert?"

"Yes, ma'am?"

"I don't wish to offend you, but would you please leave me alone?"

"Of course."

"And please send Fiona to me as soon as she returns?"

"Yes, ma'am."

"She is going to return?"

"Yes, ma'am."

"Thank you, Rupert. And I'm terribly sorry. You seem like a nice person."

"Yes, ma'am. I try. Please don't hesitate . . . I mean, if you need anything . . ."

"Thank you, Rupert."

He nodded, though of course she couldn't see him. He retreated to the stairs and down and went to his chair in the foyer, but he didn't sit. He looked back up at the top of the stairs where they disappeared into shadow and then he looked at the dangerous puddle of tea and china that he had made on the floor. He clucked his tongue and went in search of a broom and dustpan.

There was something useful to do at last.

29

By the time they reached the church, the fat man with the tiny hat had grown nervous. They stopped at the edge of the church grounds and the man pointed across to a rear door.

"Perhaps," he said, "perhaps it would be a good idea if nobody knew I was involved."

"You're not involved," March said.

"Exactly right," the fat man said. "What say we keep it just between us?"

"There is no us," March said. "Here's the church and we have no further need of you."

"Just as well," the man said. "Just as well. But if you could see your way clear to not mention my name. To not mention, I mean to say, my name in connection with any of this."

"But we don't know your name," Day said. "How could we possibly mention it to anyone?"

"Yes, thank you. Thank you for understanding. It's just that I'm awfully fond of the organ here and I would hate to be asked to cease playing it."

"Understood. Have a wonderful day."

"It's a very nice organ. Old, but refurbished. Its very age lends it a rich tone I wouldn't be able to get from a newer instrument. Very nice, indeed."

"Glad for you," Day said.

"So." The man smiled at them nervously and held out his dimpled hand for them to shake. "Happy to have been of help. As long as we agree that I was of no help whatsoever."

"Complete agreement," March said.

"Very good of you. I say, I wonder if you might tell me?"

"Yes? Tell you what?"

"Exactly."

"I'm sorry?"

"Tell me what," the fat man said. "What's it all about, then."

March rolled his eyes and walked away from them across the wet grass toward the church. He waved a dismissive hand. Day smiled at the fat man.

"We're tracking a prisoner," he said.

"You caught him." The fat man seemed proud of himself for pointing out the obvious. As if Day were a small child trying to pound a square block into a round hole and the fat man had shown him the ball he ought to be using. "Sent him away not more than fifteen minutes ago in the wagon."

"Yes, that was one of them. But there are others. We have to catch them all."

The fat man's face fell, and Day saw him struggle with the new concept.

"So," Day said, "I'll just pop off now and catch this other prisoner. Thank you again. And mum's the word."

"It is? Why?"

"No reason," Day said. "We're all done now. You may go home. Good day."

He turned and walked briskly away before the fat man could say anything else. He heard the man clear his throat as if to get his attention, but he didn't look back. He wondered how the little hat stayed on the man's head.

The grass under his feet was wet from the recent rain and steamed slightly as a few stray sunbeams broke through the cloud cover and struck the churchyard. Glistening spiderwebs, like pearl strands, were slung low between blades of grass, and Day stepped carefully over them so as not to disturb their eight-legged tenants' morning work.

He wondered whether Claire had woken up yet, whether she had even gone back to bed after he left. He wondered whether sleeplessness would affect the unborn baby. Thoughts of the baby made him frown, squinting into the sun. He marched on, forgot about spiderwebs underfoot, and found his flask in his pocket. He uncorked it and took a long burning drink. Corked it back up and put it in his pocket, wiped his lips on the sleeve of his jacket.

March was at the back door of the church when Day caught up to him. He raised his eyebrows at Day and jiggled the handle. It moved freely. March held a finger to his lips, telling Day to be quiet in case the prisoner they sought was just on the other side of the door. He turned the handle again as Day brought out his revolver, then pushed hard against the door and stepped back out of the way. Day crouched and moved forward through the door into the darkness of a little windowless room.

In the light from the open door, Day could see that the room was used for storage. It was stacked floor to ceiling with the sort of superfluous items a church might collect over the course of several decades: old broomsticks, candelabras, incense burners, three long dusty pews with broken legs, chairs, buckets, bolts of fabric, an enormous chipped slab of marble, some sort of font that leaned to one side, a chandelier, carefully labeled boxes of clothing and vestments. But no people, no missing prisoners. There was another door on the far wall. It was closed, and Day stepped carefully around a hole in the floor and tested the doorknob. It didn't move. Locked from the other side. Which might mean that the prisoner had come through here and locked the door after him, but Day was willing to bet the door was always locked. It wouldn't do to let a child wander into the storeroom. Too many opportunities for an accident.

He went back to the hole in the floor he'd skirted a moment before. March was already there, on his hands and knees, peering down into the darkness. There was a flat slab of wooden flooring upended against a stack of boxes next to the hole, scattered dust and dirt and splinters around the opening where the floor had been pulled up and cast aside.

"He's down there, then," Day said. He was suddenly seized by an urge to do something, to make some difference. Things were happening all around him, things he couldn't control, and he wondered if he would feel better in action. Without time to worry, perhaps he would stop worrying altogether and feel better about everything in his life. What would Hammersmith do? Of course the sergeant would leap into the darkness, whatever the cost. Day had promised Hammersmith that he would stay aboveground, but Day wasn't a child. He certainly wasn't Hammersmith's child. He was on the cusp of becoming a father, after all, someone who made decisions and acted on them.

"I suppose he could be down there," March said. "It's possible."

"It's definite."

"By now?" March looked up. His features were pulled down into an ugly quizzical expression by the tension from his neck. "No, by now he's gone through there, whatever tunnels are down there, and come up somewhere else. Somewhere far away. We'd never find him."

"Maybe. Or maybe he's hiding down in the dark somewhere, waiting for us to stop looking for him so he can escape into Ireland next week."

"How would he do that? What would he eat for a week?"

"I don't know his plan, Adrian. But I'm saying I think we should go down there and look for him."

"I'm not going to let you get killed or lost in the sewer with a baby on the way."

"Baby's got nothing to do with anything."

"Anyway," March said, "we should look elsewhere for this man."

"Look where? There is nowhere else. We don't really know *who* we're looking for, we don't know *what* he looks like. We know almost nothing about him."

"We know he's wearing a prison warder's uniform. Or a part of one."

"I mean this is the only clue we've got," Day said. "We follow the clue. You taught me that."

March sat back, leaning on his arms, and smiled. "I did. Very well, then."

"Even if he's not there, we may find some trace of him, some indication of where he went, what direction he's traveling in. It's a starting point."

March put his hands up in front of him, palms out. "We'll go. You've made your point. But keep that revolver at the ready. And let's find another lantern."

They looked behind the pews and the marble and the bolts of moth-eaten fabric, and they dug through several of the boxes, but they didn't find a lantern. They did find a can of oil, but it was useless without something to put the oil in. Finally, they settled for pulling several of the candles out of the old chandelier. Day put four of them in his pocket, and March put several in his own pockets. They lit one candle apiece and poked them through the trapdoor as far as their arms would reach, looking around for signs of danger. They saw a crude staircase leading down and there were scuff marks in the dust, indicating that somebody had gone this way recently. But they already knew that much.

Day trained his Colt Navy on the center of the hole and March sat at the edge of it, swung his legs around, and descended slowly down the stairs. When he was out of the way, Day followed him into the shadows below. He felt barely a twinge at the thought that he was breaking his promise to Nevil.

30

Claire gritted her teeth and closed her eyes and held on tight to the thin sheet that covered her belly. Each contraction lasted a little bit longer than the one before it. They were stronger now and they were coming closer together. Claire wasn't sure what she was supposed to do, whether there was something she could do or not do to make the cramps less painful or to make them more productive somehow. She wanted the whole thing to be done with, her baby healthy and in her arms at last.

When it was over, she lay panting, waiting for the next contraction. She didn't know when it would come or how long it would last. She tried to remember the things Dr Kingsley had told her to expect, but it was hard to concentrate on that when she knew he'd be coming to help soon. He would tell her what to do. If he arrived in time.

She knew that Constable Winthrop was somewhere downstairs, but that didn't reassure her. He was nice, but seemed a bit hopeless about practical matters. Much like her husband sometimes was. She thought of Walter and hoped he was safe. She hoped he would come home very soon and hold her hand and simply be there with her. There was nothing he could do to help her, but he could be there. That would somehow be enough.

She rolled onto her side and sat up at the edge of the bed. She felt like some wild animal in a trap, a fox with the dogs at her heels. The lamplight hurt her eyes and so she closed the shutter. She stood and tottered the four steps to the window and opened the shade. Just enough light filtered through to illuminate the room, but it was diffuse enough that it didn't make her headache any worse. She got back into bed and breathed a sigh of relief. Then the next contraction hit.

Eventually, she opened her eyes again and lay there, drained. She wondered how she could be so limp and tired and yet so tense. It didn't seem possible.

Outside, a cloud moved in front of the sun and Claire watched the shadows on her wall flow. They contracted and then expanded, moved smoothly along the top of the baseboards and danced around the corners of the room. She wondered about the baby inside her, about what shapes and colors it would see with its new eyes.

She reached for her diary and the pencil on the table beside her and, using her belly for support, scratched out the fruitless lines about skipping rope. She began to write a new poem for her future child.

The door is closed, the candle snuffed.
Hear Mummy's footsteps in the hall.

Claire stuck the point of the pencil in her mouth and sucked on it while she thought. It was good to have something to puzzle over besides the workings of her own body.

Something moves, but nothing's there.
It's just a shadow on the wall.

She decided she didn't like the first two lines and crossed them out, thought a bit, and added more. She worked out the verse in her head and smiled as she rearranged the words on the paper, building couplets as she went.

Distracted, she only paused long enough to ride out each new contraction, and she didn't fret about the passage of time. She didn't notice the room grow darker and the shadows on her wall begin to converge.

31

The wagon had not yet reached HM Prison Bridewell when the cannibal had a seizure. Napper's eyes rolled back in his head and the handcuffs kept his hands restrained, but his right shoulder rotated forward and his right leg twisted up and across his left leg and he curled down and toppled off the bench onto the floor of the police wagon.

Watching this from the other side of the wagon, Hammersmith immediately drew his truncheon from his belt, but didn't otherwise move. He had no way of knowing whether Napper was tricking him, trying to get him to come closer, or if something was actually wrong. Hammersmith could hear Napper's teeth grinding above the sound of wheels on the cobblestones outside. It occurred to the sergeant that Napper might swallow his own tongue, and so he dropped down and knelt beside the cannibal, his truncheon at the ready. Napper made no move on him, but seemed to be breathing, and so Hammersmith eased back on his haunches, his spine resting against the front of the bench behind him, and waited. At last Napper's limbs relaxed and his eyes closed. A great streamer of thick drool escaped from his mouth and ran across the toe of Hammersmith's boot. Napper's breath steadied and slowed and he appeared to sleep.

Hammersmith put his truncheon away and made a half-hearted attempt to lever Napper back up onto the bench, but the prisoner was limp and unhelpful. Finally, Hammersmith gave up and kept a watchful eye as Napper slept.

Several minutes later, Napper's eyes opened to half-mast and he spoke. The words were slurred, and Hammersmith leaned marginally closer.

"What?"

"Not just us," Napper said. But Hammersmith thought he said *not justice*.

"Never mind justice for you," he said. "What about your victims, huh?"

"No," Napper said. "More than us now." This time Hammersmith heard him correctly.

"What does that mean?"

"You might catch us, but you'll never catch him."

"Catch who? Either make some sense or shut up, you."

"Somebody set the Devil free and it's too late to put him back," Napper said. Then he closed his eyes and began to snore.

Hammersmith frowned and settled back against the bench.

Outside, a cloud drifted in front of the sun and the interior of the wagon went darker and colder. The lantern's light seemed to dim. A shiver scurried up the sergeant's spine, and he felt the hair at the base of his neck stand up. He shook off the feeling, but he tightened his grip on his truncheon and fastened his eyes on the slumbering cannibal.

32

The crude staircase ended at a tunnel that led off in either direction, farther into the city and farther away from it. March argued that the prisoners would have run as far away from London as possible, but Day disagreed.

"These men were all scheduled to die in prison," Day said.

"Precisely why they would want to get far away from it," March said. "They would be heading north, toward open country."

"That's what you or I might do. We're rational people. But these escapees are the worst specimens London has to offer. They're animals, predators. I think they'll go looking for prey."

"Surely not right away. Surely they'd hide first. They'd want to be certain they wouldn't be caught."

"No," Day said. "They've been forced to deny their true natures for months and years. They'll be hungry. They'll want to experience a kill. They'd go where they can find the densest concentration of people. Of victims."

"There are people to the north of us."

"We don't know who's down here, if anyone is. But if Cinderhouse made it this far, if he's down in these tunnels, he'll want a child. I know this man, I captured him once before, and I know that he'll go looking for a child. He would go south."

March argued his point for a few more minutes, but finally gave in and followed Day into the tunnel going south.

As they walked, smaller tunnels branched off to either side of them, black mouths in the rough stone walls, only barely visible in the glow of candlelight. At first they would stop and advance a few feet into each of these offshoots, examining the ground for any sign that a person might recently have passed over it. But eventually they stopped bothering with the smaller tunnels and stuck to the big main passage where they could see occasional scuff marks in the dirt. Someone had used this tunnel. The same someone who had opened up the church floor.

Eventually the tunnel widened out and they found themselves in a huge chamber. The ceiling arced high above them, invisible in the darkness, and they could hear water streaming past them, off to their left. A stream traveling south and a bit west, burbling over ancient brick and cobblestone. Day ran his hand over the wall beside him and thrust his candle into an alcove. There was a pile of bones on the ground, heaped four feet tall and at least as deep. Above the bones, yellow skulls were stacked on some kind of shelf, row after row of them, grinning out at him, their black eye sockets glittering with imaginary wit. Day poked at one of the skulls with the barrel of his revolver and it rolled forward to reveal another skull behind it.

March came up behind him. "Catacombs," he said. "Probably attached to the church graveyard at some distant point in the past."

"All these people," Day said. "Forgotten."

"As we all will be. Every human being who has ever lived or ever will live. We'll all be forgotten when the people who loved us and remembered us die in their turn."

"There's a sad thought."

"Not at all," March said.

"By your way of thinking, nothing matters. Not a bit of it. Whether we catch these men today or not, whether they kill more innocent people or not. Hell, it doesn't matter whether anybody falls in love or has a child, dies young or dies old. We're all destined for this." He gestured at the wall of skulls, the blank hollow features dancing in the light of the shivering candle flame. The candle had nearly burned down to his fingers now. Day reached into his pocket and found another candle, lit it from the old stub. He held the stub up and blew out its flame. "I can't believe in that," Day said. "That's not a thought I want to wake to every morning."

March shook his head. "But that's not at all what I mean. It all matters. Everyone and everything matters because every moment that we have matters. We must make the most of our lives while we can."

"That would seem to run contrary to your philosophy."

"You don't know my philosophy, Walter." March's voice was barely audible. "Don't presume to know what I'm about."

Day looked at the skulls, big and small, young and old. He moved past March, out into the tunnel, and walked on. Ten feet down the passageway there was another alcove. Bones were stacked in the tunnel, mounded high and wide. Skulls had rolled down this enormous pile and were scattered randomly in the dirt. Day stuck his candle into the alcove opposite the bone pile and peered in after it. This niche in the tunnel wall was identical to the one next to it, but it was empty. Clearly the bones had been taken from it and thrown outside to make room. Day entered the alcove and looked around it. There was an iron ring hammered into the floor and chains fastened to the back wall. Shackles rested on the shelf under the chain, the shelf that had been built to hold skulls. He set his revolver on the shelf and picked up one of the shackles with his free hand. It was a simple grey iron band, not a speck of rust on it. The chains were also new, strong and shiny. Day frowned and turned to March, still holding the shackle. The older man reached past him and grabbed the revolver off the shelf. He backed up and pointed it at Day.

"What is this?" Day said.

"I'm sorry, Walter," March said. "You really don't seem to understand my philosophy, and I'm afraid we've come to a bit of a turning point here."

33

Kingsley waited on the top step of the porch and let Fiona go ahead of him. She rapped lightly at the front door, then opened it and led the way inside. An awkward young man with ginger hair was posed in the foyer, half-risen from his chair, his hand on the end of a truncheon stuck in his belt. His mouth was open and his forehead was creased, and he appeared to be frozen with indecision. Then he saw Fiona and smiled and let out a great sigh of relief.

"Oh, it's you," he said. "I was afraid . . . Well, I wasn't afraid, mind you, but I was worried, concerned you might be . . . you know, a fugitive."

Kingsley smiled and transferred his bag to his left hand. He took a step forward, past his daughter, and patted the young constable on the arm. "If we had been fugitives," Kingsley said, "I'm sure you would have dealt with us."

The boy nodded, his expression serious. Fiona closed the door and ran to the foot of the stairs.

"How is she?"

"It doesn't sound good," the boy said. "By the way, sir, my name's Winthrop. Constable Rupert Winthrop."

"Dr Bernard Kingsley."

"Kingsley? Are you . . . ?" He gestured vaguely at Fiona and back as if drawing a line in the air between them.

"Yes, we are. Tell me, you said just now it doesn't sound good?"

"Sir, she's done a good bit of screaming and shouting since Fiona left."

"Yes, well, she's having a baby. But she's a healthy young woman and her pregnancy has been relatively normal, so there's little enough to fear."

"Yes, sir."

"I'd better go check on her. I'll leave you to it, Constable."

"Sir? Is there anything . . . ? I mean, I wonder if there's something I could do to make things easier for her. I know you said . . . Still, it seems like it might be going rough."

Kingsley smiled at the boy. Rupert's hair had escaped from under his hat and was plastered across his forehead with sweat, like the wet tail feather of some nervous tropical bird. Kingsley felt a momentary urge to reach up and pull off the constable's hat and set the bird free. He could see that thirty seconds spent talking to Rupert Winthrop now would help calm the household. The last thing Claire needed was a frantic boy running about the place.

"How are you at fetching water?" Kingsley said.

"I can do that."

"Very good. I'm going to need clean water and lots of it, in both cold and warm varieties, so you'll need to heat some up for me at the fireplace. I'll also need every basin you can find in the house."

Constable Rupert Winthrop stood at attention and saluted, then turned and trotted off down the hall toward the kitchen.

"He seems like a nice boy," Kingsley said.

"He's a bit hopeless, isn't he?" Fiona said.

"Give him time. He just needs a bit of seasoning. Now, it's high time we looked in on our patient." And he followed his daughter up the stairs toward the bedroom where he could already hear Claire Day moaning.

34

The sun was higher in the sky when Jack awoke, but he was sure he hadn't slept for more than an hour. Sleep annoyed him. It smacked of weakness and mortality and inefficiency. But it was one of the many prices he had to pay in order to walk among his people as one of them.

He took a standing bath at the washbasin in Elizabeth's bedroom, soaking a cloth in fresh water and wringing it out in the pail on the floor, using Elizabeth's harsh soap, lye and ashes, scented with lavender. After, he pissed into the pail, watching the ripples spread across the surface of the dirty bathwater. There was a small tin of tooth powder that appeared to be brand-new and a toothbrush with a wooden handle behind the handbasin. He brushed his teeth hard, scrubbing *them until his gums bled. Then he drank the rest of the water in the pitcher beside the basin and wiped his mouth on his bare arm.*

Naked, he unlocked and opened the bedroom door and stepped over Cinderhouse's body in the hallway. He crouched over the tailor, who was sound asleep, his eyelids fluttering, a smear of old blood on his chin. His mouth had not yet healed, and Jack resisted an urge to pry the tailor's mouth open so he could see the stump of muscle that was left there. Cinderhouse was dressed very well in one of Elizabeth's altered suits, and he was clutching a kitchen knife in his right hand, his knuckles white, his fingers rigid.

Jack smiled and clucked his whole and healthy tongue. Cinderhouse had been waiting for him, thought he would be able to kill his master and go free. He might even have succeeded had he not fallen asleep at his post. Silly little fly.

Jack gently opened Cinderhouse's hand and took the knife from him. He stood and walked to the stairs and went down. He kept the knife with him, holding it loosely at his side. He liked the feel of it. He had always managed to find a use for knives.

He passed the open door to the parlor without glancing in and went into the kitchen. There was a heel of bread and a butt of ham on the butcher block by the back door. Jack used the knife he had taken from Cinderhouse to slice off a piece of the ham and made himself a sandwich. He stood at the back door in a beam of sunlight while he ate and watched honeybees flicker around the sweet purple flowers in the garden. When he had finished, he licked his fingers.

In the parlor was another of Elizabeth's suits draped over the back of a chair, tailored and pressed and waiting for him. He set the knife down on the seat of the chair and took the trousers off their hanger. He held them up for Elizabeth to see. There was a subtle blue stripe in the black material and it shimmered in the light from the window. The homeowner, still tied tightly to a chair near the hearth, did not acknowledge Jack in any way. He stared into space, his eyes dead, his chest moving shallowly with each breath. Jack decided he would have to find a way to cheer Elizabeth up. He'd give it some thought when the other business of the day had been tended to.

He pulled the trousers on, thrilling at the feel of fabric against his skin, and left them unfastened, spreading his legs wide to keep the trousers from falling back down. He unbuttoned a dazzling white shirt, almost purple it was so pure and fresh, and he slipped his arms into the sleeves, shrugged the shirt up over his shoulders. He gathered the buttons in one hand and inserted them back into the holes, starting from the collar and working his way down his chest and abdomen, taking care not to drop any of them on the floor. Getting dressed was a thing so many took for granted, and yet he had not performed this simple daily operation in a very long time. He wanted to enjoy the process. He tucked the tail of the shirt into the top of the trousers and fastened the hooks on the fly. He wondered briefly why the front of a pair of trousers was called a fly, and he thought of his own stupid fly, his Peter, his rock, on the floor in the hallway upstairs, sleeping and missing the splendor of this ritual. He found the cufflinks, pretty chunks of silver with a blue porcelain inlay, and fixed his cuffs. He moved the knife and sat in the chair and pulled on a pair of sheer black hose that the tailor had left for him there. Elizabeth's shoes were perhaps a bit loose, and Jack got up and went back to the kitchen, found a folded bit of butcher paper in the garbage that still smelled of meat. He took it back to the parlor, tore it in half, and stuffed the crumpled bits of it in the ends of the shoes. Elizabeth looked up at him when he heard the sound of tearing paper, but immediately lost interest and returned his gaze to the nothingness he saw in the middle of the room. The shoes were a better fit with the paper in them, so Jack tied them with a double knot, stood and put on the waistcoat and the jacket, went back to the kitchen, and gazed at himself in the mirror on the back of the pantry door.

He looked magnificent.

He smoothed his long hair and walked down the hall. He had seen a coin purse on the chimneypiece and he found it again. He weighed it in the palm of his hand before slipping it into his pocket. He picked up the knife from the chair in the parlor and took it with him. He did not say good-bye to Elizabeth. If the homeowner chose to be rude and uncommunicative, Jack could match him. He put the knife in his medical bag on the floor and took a tall hat from the rack by the front door. He quietly snicked back the latch and opened the door, stood for a moment in the stream of sunlight that rushed in to greet him, then stepped outside and pulled the red door almost shut behind him. He took the four steps along the path in the little front garden, swinging his black leather bag by the handle, and went out by the gate. He passed a little girl playing across the lane. She stuck her tongue out at him and he wondered how it would look lined up next to the other tongues he had nailed to the mantel in Elizabeth's parlor. But he smiled at the ill-mannered little girl and tipped his hat to the old lady he saw peering out the window next door. He walked away down the lane and turned the corner, and was gone.

35

Day put his hands up. It was a universal gesture, an automatic reaction to the gun pointed at him. Adrian March moved backward a step. His foot brushed up against a skull, and it rolled across the ground toward Day, zigzagging as its cheekbones took its weight, first left, then right, then left again. It bumped against the toe of Day's shoe and he looked down. It was very small, a child's skull, two front teeth missing and an open hole at the top of the head. Some sort of crushing blow had shattered the bone, exposing the brain and ending a life much too early. Day looked back up at March and took a deep breath. The air was damp and musty.

"I don't understand, Adrian. What is this?"

March smiled, a wry expression with no amusement in it. He

glanced down at the revolver as if surprised to find it in his hand. "This isn't, uh . . . Yes, well." He took his finger out of the trigger guard and slipped the revolver into the pocket of his jacket. "I'm not going to shoot you, Walter. That was never . . . Just didn't want you to shoot me."

Day lowered his hands but stayed where he was, his back to the empty alcove in the tunnel wall, the shiny new shackles waiting patiently in the darkness behind him. "Why would I shoot you?"

"Because it's time I told you a thing or two, and I feel fairly sure you won't like hearing about some of it. At least, not at first. But I want you to listen to me and weigh what I have to say. Weigh it carefully and consider who it is you're talking to. You know me well."

"And you should know that you can talk to me without a gun."

"You might still try to arrest me," March said. "That will be harder to do if I have your Colt."

"Adrian? You know what's going on down here, don't you? These catacombs have been made over into a prison of some sort. A dungeon. You had something to do with that." He kept his voice flat. It wasn't a question.

Clearly Adrian March was involved in something terrible and dangerous.

"Not just me," March said. "There are many of us."

"All morning you've tried to stall the manhunt. You didn't want me to come down here."

"I did, but I wanted to prepare you for this first. I wish you'd listened to me."

"Are those shackles for me, then? Are you going to lock me up down here?"

Day had a brief vision of his unborn child as an adult, squatting in a poorhouse somewhere, with no knowledge of his missing father. It was a surprising vision, and it awakened an emotion in Day that he didn't recognize.

"If I were going to leave you down here, Walter, I wouldn't have put the revolver away. I'd like you to listen to what I have to say and see what I have to show you. And then we'll go up again, out of here, and you can arrest me if you want to. But I think you'll choose to join us. I've always wanted you to join us. I've only been waiting for the right time to approach you, and I thought perhaps the prison escape might help me introduce the subject."

"What subject? And why now?"

"Because you have a child on the way," March said. "You are now responsible for the life of an innocent. It's an experience that changes a man, changes the way a man thinks. If today had gone the way I'd planned, I would have told you about us over a good meal and a bottle of red wine. I even sent a gift to your home. I wanted you to have questions and to ask me about these things in an atmosphere of fellowship and trust. There are so many things I could have—"

"You said 'us.' Who do you mean? Wait. Never mind. First tell me what this is." Day waved his hand to indicate the shallow cave behind him, then the entire length of the tunnel, all of the city, and everything that had happened over the past few hours.

"Come over here," March said. He led the way down the tunnel and pointed to another alcove, marked only by a vague area of darker black. "Shine your candle in there."

Day did as he was told and thrust his arm into the gloom of the recess, illuminating it with his fresh candle. It was identical to the one next to it: an iron ring in the floor, chains and shackles against the back wall. Day turned and approached the tunnel wall across from the alcove. There was another haphazard pile of bones, stacked high to a point under the ceiling, spreading out across the floor so that it all resembled some morbid pyramid.

March had already moved farther down the length of the tunnel. He pointed at another inky blotch on the wall.

"And there," he said.

Day shone the candle's flame into this third alcove. Again, the ring, the chains, the shackles. And across from it all, the pile of old bones.

"How many of these are there? What are they for?"

"There are eight of them," March said. "Eight so far. There's room here for more, but the work has been slow. Five of them are clustered here, and there are three more in another section of the catacombs."

Day tipped his candle and let wax drip onto the shelf next to the shackles. He pushed the bottom of the candle into the wax and held it there for a moment until the wax had cooled enough to hold the candle upright. He turned back to March, his hands free, and began to calculate the distance between them. He was in the center of the makeshift cell and March was outside in the tunnel. There were perhaps six or seven feet between them.

How quickly would March be able to get the revolver out of his pocket? How fast were the old man's reflexes?

"Do you mind if I reach for my flask?" Day said. "It's here in this pocket."

"Of course. By all means."

Day took out the flask and poured an ounce of brandy into his mouth. He swallowed and held the flask out to March, but his former mentor shook his head and smiled.

"No, thank you," March said. "I believe I'll stay right here, out of your reach."

"Suit yourself." Day corked the flask and slipped it back into his pocket.

"We are called the Karstphanomen," March said. "And we have existed for many decades. This"—he held his hands out in the air, far apart from each other—"this is all ours. Miles and miles of tunnels and caverns and abandoned buildings, waterways and burial grounds and lost treasure troves. We own it all."

"You live underground? Like rats?"

"Of course not. I live in my home in Acton. You've been there. You've supped with my wife and me. No, Walter, this place is where we do our work."

"What kind of work is that?"

"The work of justice."

"Justice?"

"Walter, you've spent the morning hours chasing prisoners. Why?"

"Because they escaped from prison."

"But you have skills. Aren't they better used to do something besides running round the city poking under rocks for villains?"

"You would rather let them be free?"

"Not at all," March said. "But what good is a prison? If prisons worked, if that were a system that functioned properly, why then these men would already be reformed, would they not? You wouldn't have to worry about where they are. You wouldn't have to catch them again."

"A prison is—"

"A prison is a cage," March said. "That is all it is. A cage where we keep our most dangerous animals, those men we deem not fit to mingle with society. We keep them all in one place, where we can see them and feel safe. We do it for ourselves, for our peace of mind. But what of the men in that cage?"

"What of them?"

"Have we not done them a disservice?"

"How so?"

"If we're to keep them in a cage, shouldn't we teach them something? What do they learn there? It's not a frivolous question. What do they learn by being caged? I believe the answer is nothing. They learn nothing."

"One hopes some of them might reform their ways."

"One hopes? Some of them? How often do you suppose that happens?"

"I wouldn't know. Ask the head warder when we find Cinderhouse and return him to Bridewell."

"Why would your Cinderhouse, or any of them, bother to reform at all? Listen, there's no incentive to reform. We give them no reason. Criminals are such stupid people, Walter. They're children, really. They must be taught. They must be shown the error of their ways. They must experience true justice."

"A prison sentence is justice."

"No, Walter, a prison sentence is law. Law and justice are very different concepts. How many people did Cinderhouse kill? Since you mentioned him by name, let's use him as an example. How many were murdered by him?"

"I don't know. Two policemen. There were children, certainly, but we don't know how many over the years. We think he killed his wife and son. There were three small skeletons buried behind a carriage house."

"Children."

Day nodded. He had moved incrementally closer to March as they talked. He was now roughly four feet away from him, close enough to grab March's arm before the retired detective inspector could get the revolver out of his pocket. He tensed, ready to spring at March, but the older man sensed the slight change in Day's body language and stepped back, farther into the shadows of the tunnel. He snuffed his candle and became a disembodied voice in the darkness. Day relaxed visibly, but began to slowly inch toward March again.

"So," March said, "this person killed children. What did he do to them? Did he hurt them first? Before he killed them?"

"I don't know. I'd rather not . . ." Day sighed. "I think he probably did, yes."

"Is it justice, then, that he be caged?"

"I wouldn't know. I haven't spoken to him. Perhaps if we find him, I could ask him."

"Don't be crude. No, of course there's no justice in it. Those children are gone. Those policemen are gone. And their killer hasn't learned anything, has he? How much better would it be for him if he experienced everything that he did to those children? What if he were made to feel what they felt, to truly feel their fear and their pain? What do you think? Wouldn't that be more likely to change a man than simply putting him away, out of sight, behind bars?"

"Perhaps."

"No, not perhaps. I'm right, Walter. That's justice. Make the man experience his crimes firsthand. It's the only way."

"The law is the only way."

"The law is a failure."

"The law is the law, *Inspector* March. You should know that. You were the best."

"I was deluded."

"And now? You've joined some secret club and you believe the scales have suddenly fallen from your eyes?"

"The Karstphanomen, Walter, is not a club. It's a society. And it's a great thing we're undertaking here. We are the ones who set those prisoners free. We caused the train wreck. We had a man inside Bridewell, and he made sure the right prisoners escaped."

"If that's true . . . Adrian, if what you say is true, then you set murderers free in this city. In *my* city. My wife and unborn son may be in danger because of you."

"It went wrong. There were supposed to be men at the gate to gather the prisoners up as they came through. They never would have made it beyond the main gate. We had a wagon, but it broke a wheel. We arrived just minutes too late."

Realization washed over Day and he turned from the voice, looked at the shackles again. Candle wax had dripped down over the metal and pooled, dull pink, like blood and water.

"This place . . ."

"Yes," March said. "This place is where we bring murderers, molesters, perversions of humanity. This place is the classroom where they receive instruction."

"You're mad."

"No, Walter, I'm angry. Madness would be to stand by and do nothing."

"Adrian, I . . . No, I understand now. It was the Ripper case. He did this to you, didn't he? You never caught him, and the stress of it all, the pressure you must have been under to catch Jack the Ripper . . . I can't imagine. But this isn't the answer, man. Come with me. There are doctors who could—"

"There are doctors among us, Walter. Does that surprise you? The Karstphanomen has doctors, lawyers, Lords . . . Yes, even policemen. There's a member of the royal family among us. We are not madmen. We are enthusiastic proponents of justice."

"How many of you are there?"

"Very many. And, Walter, I've proposed you for membership."

"Never."

"You're too quick to speak. Wait until you see what we've done."

"I don't want to see. I don't want to know any of this. Adrian, if anything you're saying is even remotely true, I'm going to have to arrest you."

"You won't arrest me. When you see what we do, when you see it firsthand, you'll help me."

"Help you to do what? Torture people?"

"They deserve it."

"I thought you said you were teaching them something."

"We are."

"Are you teaching them? Or are you hurting them because you feel they deserve it?"

"Both, actually. Why can't it be both?"

"Can you hear yourself? You've become a zealot."

"Walter, you're wrong. I didn't fail. I caught Jack. I really did catch him."

"You caught Jack the Ripper?"

"Lusk and Aberline and I. We caught him. Saucy Jack is down here right now. Has been for more than a year."

"Oh my God."

"Would you like to see him?"

"I . . ."

"Come with me. Just let me show you what we've done, and then you can arrest me if you still want to. I'll go quietly."

"I don't want to see."

"Yes, you do."

Day took a step back. His heel hit the iron ring in the floor and it clanked against the stones. He turned and looked at the chains, at the hard-packed walls, at the dim glow of the candle.

He could barely breathe. Monstrous things had happened here among the bones of untold previous generations. These men thought he could be one of them, had discussed him down here in the mud and clay. While he lay beside his wife and unborn child above them, evil men had made plans for Walter Day.

He turned back to the dark tunnel where his mentor lurked.

"Very well," he said. His voice sounded far away to him, like someone else speaking. "Give me back my revolver. Then show me Jack the Ripper."

36

When the Devil tipped his hat to her, Eunice Pye clapped her hands to her chest and waited for her heart to stop beating. She knew exactly what he was as soon as she saw him, and she cursed herself for staying in the window long enough that he noticed her. But the Devil kept on walking and turned the corner out of sight and her heart kept beating and she didn't die. She sent up a silent prayer of thanks to Giles for watching over her. Then she rushed out of her home and across the lane without looking to see if there were carriages coming. She banged through the black iron gate and into the tiny courtyard in front of the Anderson home. She scooped up the girl who was playing there and hugged the child tight. The girl yelped and protested and squirmed, but Eunice didn't even notice. She rang the doorbell, and when the Andersons' house-keeper came to the door, Eunice handed the struggling child over to her.

"You keep watch over her today, Miss Bonnie," Eunice said. "There's evil about, and you ought to keep her safe inside."

She didn't wait for a response, but turned and marched back across the street. This time she remembered to watch for wagons in the lane. Of course the Andersons' housekeeper would think Eunice was a madwoman, but that was fine with her. Whether they were worried about the Devil in the lane or worried about the madwoman in the house across the way, they were likely to make their girl stay indoors for the day, and that was all that really mattered.

Eunice didn't go straight back to her own house, but veered to her right and went through the gate next door and crept through the garden to the front window of the Michaels' home.

In a single morning she had seen one of the escaped prisoners whose likeness decorated the front page of the morning tabloid and then she had seen the Devil himself, and they had both come out of this house. She didn't know whether the bald murderer of children had turned himself into the Devil or whether they were different people and the bald man was still inside somewhere, but she knew that she was not safe anywhere, not even in her own home where she could put up wards, as long as the Devil was about in the neighborhood. She felt she had to do something constructive, and she was not afraid of death as long as she knew where she was going when she died and that Giles was up there waiting for her. Good people did not hide and wait for evil to pass by. They acted.

The curtains were closed across the Michaels' window, but there was a gap of perhaps an inch and a half where they did not quite meet in the middle. She went up on her tiptoes and held on to the bricks of the outside window ledge with her fingertips and peered inside.

The house was very dark, but when her eyes got used to the gloom she was able to see well enough. The parlor looked normal at first glance, and she was unable to see beyond it except for a wedge of the hall that she assumed led to the kitchen in back. She was certain that the Michaels' home followed the same floor plan as her own, and so the stairway to the upper floors would be just out of sight across from the parlor, but she couldn't see it from where she was.

Her toes started to hurt. They weren't used to bearing all of her weight, even though she was not a large person by any stretch of the imagination. She scowled, disappointed, at the empty room beyond the window and decided there was nothing to see. She would have to go directly to the police and bring them round, rather than waiting for them to respond to her earlier correspondence. But just at the moment she began to lower herself back to the ground, something moved at the periphery of her vision and she sprang back up on her toes and focused on the corner of the room between the window and the fireplace. There near the hearth was a blind spot where she could not see, but there was a foot, or more precisely a shoe with a foot in it, and the shoe was moving. Just a little bit, but it was enough to command her attention. She pressed her cheek against the glass and followed the shoe with her eyes, up a leg, and there was a hand, but the hand was twisted at a very odd angle, and there was a bit of rope about the wrist, and that was as much as she could possibly see.

Her toes hurt and her eyes hurt and her back hurt, but she paid them no mind.

There was a person tied to a chair in the parlor of the Michaels' house.

Her eyes widened with the realization and she drew a deep breath, and then she noticed something else. Nailed above the fireplace were two objects. They were small and oblong and dark in color. Then one of the objects moved, shriveled a bit and curled up on itself just the slightest amount, and it looked to her like it might be talking to her.

And it was a tongue. There were two tongues nailed to the mantel.

Eunice let herself drop back down into the garden. She went to the gate and around to her own little garden and inside her house. She opened the door under the stairs and found her stoutest garden hoe and went back out of the house and next door again.

There was no time for policemen now.

The red door was not latched. The Devil had left it open for her, and she did not know whether that had been a mistake or he had set a trap, but she knew that she had to do something or she would hate herself forever.

Eunice Pye pushed open the door and, brandishing her garden hoe, she stepped over the threshold and into the Devil's house.

37

Adrian March knew the tunnels beneath this part of London as well as he knew the streets above them. He lit his candle again and led the way past sunken buildings, through an underground train station, to a large pond, which they crossed in a two-man skiff. Day followed along, but his mind wandered despite the marvels he saw around him. He knew that he wouldn't be able to backtrack through the tunnels without becoming hopelessly lost. He remembered that they were supposed to meet Hammersmith at the door of the church before they struck out underground, but Day didn't know where the church was anymore or how to get back there. It was entirely possible that March intended to abandon him down here, leave him to wander in the darkness until he died.

He turned his mind to the twin concerns of food and water, as if March's betrayal were a certainty: The water in the underground pond was fresh, and they saw wildlife living in the tunnels, deer and foxes and rats. There were fish in the pond, too, blind white things, and Day thought he might be able to fashion some kind of hook and line. He could catch a fish, he assumed, more easily than he could hunt a deer in the dark. Of course, he was unlikely to find a cask of brandy in any of the caverns they passed through. There would be no cases of wine that hadn't long ago turned to vinegar. He might live for a time, but he wouldn't be comfortable. And he wouldn't be present at the birth of his child.

Still, he followed March deeper and deeper down and he prayed that his mentor had not completely lost his mind, that there was still a trustworthy man somewhere in there.

Beyond the pond, March led the way into a side passage that grew narrower as they traveled. The ceiling angled down so that Day had to stoop to walk, and the walls were unfinished red clay rather than the hard-packed soil and stone he had seen in the larger tunnels. He followed March down a series of steps that might have been accidental shapes in the earth, not anything hewn by men. He thought again of his friend Hammersmith, who had grown up working the coal mines of Wales and who still feared enclosed spaces. Perhaps it was best after all that they had not gone back for the sergeant.

At the bottom of the soft clay steps, March leaned down and waved his candle over the ground at his feet.

"What do you make of this?"

Day came down off the bottom step and stood next to his mentor. There were dark spots in the dirt and they gleamed in the candle's light. Day squatted and touched one of the spots. It was thick and gummy. He brought his fingers to his nose and sniffed at the black liquid, then stuck out his tongue and tasted it.

"Blood," he said. "It's been here for some time, but it hasn't dried yet."

"Oh, no," March said. He stood up straight and reached out his arm so that the candle illuminated a tiny bit more of the dark passage ahead of them.

Day found his flask and took a drink of brandy, swished it around his mouth to get rid of the metallic taste of blood and clay.

"One of the prisoners, perhaps," he said when he had swallowed the brandy.

"Or an animal," March said. "I hope it's an animal. A wild dog or rats fighting each other. That's possible, isn't it? Rats fight each other."

"That's a lot of blood to have come out of a rat," Day said. "And there's a trail running off down there. No way of knowing if it's human blood, but we should be careful."

Day drew his Colt Navy and they proceeded down the tunnel.

"How far do we have to go?"

"Not much farther," March said.

"I'll take the lead."

"Not necessary."

"I've got the gun."

"It could be one of us," March said. "A Karstphanomen. He wouldn't know you."

Day didn't bother to reply. He held the gun out at his side and led the way down the passage, the clay underfoot muffling his footsteps. He worried that the candlelight might give them away to anyone waiting ahead of them, but there was no getting around that. They couldn't very well douse the only light sources they had.

The tunnel widened out as they went along, and they passed waterways and narrow branches. Day began to see more of the alcoves along the sides, shallow recesses that had been dug to contain bones. He guessed they were in another section of catacombs, perhaps beneath another church in another parish. He walked carefully, but the blood trail led directly down the center of the tunnel floor.

"Here," March said. He was close behind Day. "Just up here to your right."

Day slowed down and stopped when he saw another pile of bones in the passageway. The alcove opposite the bones seemed larger than the others, as if it had been hollowed out and expanded.

"Not this one," March said. "It's the last one down here."

Day stepped past the bones and found another pile of bones, another large alcove, and then a third pile and a third alcove. The tunnel abruptly ended two feet beyond the third alcove. It was the last one. Day crept up to it and shone the candle into it, his gun held up even with his chest, at the ready.

Inside, a man was chained to the wall. The man was wearing a dark blue uniform jacket, much like that worn by the police, and a dirty white pair of trousers decorated with black darts. His leg was badly broken, a splintered fragment of bone jutting from the fabric of his trousers. He raised his head and looked at Day, an expression of horror on his face.

"Behind you," he said.

Day heard a muffled cry and a thump, and he turned to see March's body falling. Day swung the gun around and brought the candle up at the same time. A man stood in the darkness beyond March's silent body. The man was only a dark shape cut out of the tunnel's air, his eyes black and glittering in the candlelight.

"Welcome," the man said, "to my home away from home."

Day pointed his gun and squeezed the trigger just as the man's arm came up and something lashed across Day's face. The gun's report was deafening in the enclosed space of the tunnel, and Day reeled backward. He felt blood running into his eyes and he thought he could hear someone laughing, but he couldn't be sure because the gun blast was echoing around and out and back at him. Then something struck him in the head and his knees turned to tissue paper and he fell into the darkness. He saw the candle fall next to his face and he saw a boot come down on it, extinguishing its flame. Then he saw nothing at all. The tunnel went quiet and closed in on him and crushed the breath out of him, and he lost consciousness.

38

⸻◦⟨⟩◦⸻

Dr Kingsley smiled at Claire Day and then at his daughter, who stood anxiously by the door, wringing her hands. He put the stethoscope back in his bag and took a look around the bedroom. There was a table next to the wall that was being used as a bath, with a basin, towels, a pitcher, and a pail. There was the usual complement of tooth powder and soap and talcum. He set his bag on the table and scooped those small items up and went across the room to the giant wardrobe. The wardrobe was useless for his purposes, and so he opened its doors and tossed the toiletries inside and closed it again. He moved the curtains and took a look out the window. They were on the corner and above the ground floor, and there were no nearby homes with windows that looked out on the

Days' upper floors. He pulled the sash and opened the curtains and cranked open the window to let in some fresh air. The room was stuffy and dark, and he imagined both Claire and Fiona might appreciate a light breeze.

"I would prefer to take you to a hospital," he said. He turned from the window and scowled at Claire. Her hair was sweaty and plastered to her neck. She sucked in her breath as a contraction hit, then relaxed a bit as it passed. "You're moving ahead earlier than I'd like."

"I didn't mean to," Claire said.

"No, of course not. Babies come when they're ready to come, and we have little say in the matter. You'll have the child right here and it will be fine."

"Will it, though? Is everything all right? It hurts and there's blood and I don't feel very good."

"No, you don't feel very good. You're having a baby. It's not meant to be a picnic."

"But is anything wrong?"

"There is only a small amount of blood, and you mustn't let it alarm you. It's perfectly normal and I should have told you to expect it. We doctors call it the 'bloody show,' and that's frankly an apt description of the entire process."

"Father," Fiona said, "she's scared."

Kingsley sighed. Childbirth was always a risky proposition. His record was good, better than that of any other doctor in London. He had helped in the delivery of nearly a hundred babies and had lost only seven of them. Only three of the women had died. He remembered them all and they haunted him still, but he knew the numbers were regarded as acceptable. Years ago, after the first young mother's death, he had learned to keep them all at arm's length. He did his work and he did it well, but he did not need to be a friend to these women. He was their doctor, and if they died . . . well, people died. He did his best and he hoped they would not die, but he could not control the process as well as he would prefer. There were too many things that could go wrong in an instant.

But Claire Day was already a friend, and there was no way he could maintain his usual formal distance.

"Fiona, would you please go find as many towels and blankets as you can find? And I saw two small occasional tables in the hallway downstairs. Please ask the young man to bring them up here. I need more surfaces."

Fiona turned to the door. He could see the frustration on her face.

"Wait," he said. "Take this, will you? It's ruined. Throw it out."

He gathered the sticky coverlet from the bed and bundled it up, handed it over to his daughter, and guided her out the door by her elbow. He shut it after her and turned to Claire. She had stood and was pacing restlessly around the room. Her nightgown was spotted with the evidence of her ordeal. Kingsley guided her back to the bed, then dragged a chair over from the corner. He sat next to Claire, where she wouldn't have to strain to see him, but where he could avert his eyes so as to allow her some modesty at this stage.

"Here are the facts," he said. "This is advancing weeks earlier than expected. That is not a good sign. But it is not the worst."

"Have I lost him?"

"The baby, you mean?"

"Yes."

"No. I don't know why you call it 'him.' There's no way to know what gender the child will be. But there is a heartbeat, and that means your baby is alive inside you."

Claire smiled weakly.

"Claire, your baby is alive and it wants to come out here and meet you. It is our job—mostly yours, but I'll help where I can—it's our job to allow the baby to do just that. To allow him or her to come out and be your child. And that's what we're going to do now, you and I together. You are not alone and, although it will not be an entirely easy process, it's a process that countless other women have endured. My mother did it, and your mother did it, and everybody's mother has done it. And you will do it, too."

"It hurts."

He nodded. "It does hurt, and it will hurt even more. And then it will all be over and you will forget how much it hurt and you won't even care about that anymore because you'll have a new baby."

"Have you ever seen anybody die doing this?"

He nodded again. He wanted to lie to her, but lying was not a thing he was in the habit of doing and he didn't know how to start.

"I have, Claire. But not many times. And for the most part those women were older than you are and they were poor and unhealthy. I do not anticipate that you will have the same problems they did. Have you been eating lots of butter and eggs, like I told you to?"

Claire gasped and her fists clenched as she felt another contraction. When it passed, she whispered into her closed fist, "I want Walter to come home. I want him here."

"He'll come as soon as he can come. He's trying to make things safe for your baby. Isn't that good? I'm sure he's thinking of you and the baby even now."

"I just wish he were here."

"Well." Kingsley let out a deep breath and stood, pushing down on his knees to help himself up. He went around to the back of the chair and dragged it to the foot of the bed. "Let's see how this is progressing. Maybe you can surprise him with the new arrival when he does get here. Wouldn't that be nice?"

He paused, his hands on the back of the chair.

"Claire, I am a very good doctor. Do you believe that?"

She nodded.

"Good. Because it's true. And you are going to be just fine because I am going to take care of you now. I promise."

He smiled, and she smiled back.

Then he sent up a silent prayer to a god he did not believe in that he would be able to keep his promise.

39

D ay woke to the sound of a man screaming. He opened his eyes, but it made no difference. The world was still black. There was something covering his face, a bag or a hood. It reeked of sweat. There was a slit in the bag near his chin, and he breathed through his mouth. He was shivering and tried to move his arms, but they wouldn't respond. *I'm paralyzed,* he thought. *I've been hit in the head and I can't move, and I'll never move again.* Then he heard the faint clink of metal ringing against stone behind him and realized that he was in chains. Now that he concentrated, he could feel shackles on his wrists and ankles. He couldn't feel the comfortable weight of his gun and his flask and he understood that his jacket had been taken from him. His hat was gone, too. He remembered dropping his gun, so it wouldn't have been in his jacket anyway. Perhaps it was still on the tunnel floor. Maybe it was within reach, if he could only move a little.

The man stopped screaming and panted as if out of breath. The sound of him was nearby, yet distant, on the other side of a wall. Day realized he was chained up in one of the three alcoves he had seen and someone else was chained in an alcove next to him.

"March!"

There was no answer. He tried again.

"Adrian! Inspector Adrian March! Can you hear me?"

Something moved. Day felt a change in the air in front of him, but there was no change in the darkness under the hood. Then there was a voice, a low rasp, and it was directly in his ear. Someone was standing with his lips against the rough fabric of the hood, pressing it against Day's ear. He smelled copper and fish.

"You'll get your turn," the voice said. It was deep and muffled. "Be patient."

"Who is it? Who's there?"

But there was no answer. Day couldn't tell whether the man had gone or was still standing right there next to him. He turned his head, but it moved slowly, as if his neck needed to be oiled, and a sharp pain lanced through his skull, radiated outward through his face. Warmth moved down his spine and spread out into his torso, down his limbs to his fingertips and his toes.

He blacked out again.

When he woke up, he sensed he was alone. He could feel his

pulse in his temples, beating at his brain. He heard low murmuring somewhere far away and he concentrated on the sound, dragged his attention away from his throbbing head. The voice he heard was somewhere to his left, the opposite side of him from the screaming man he had heard before. There was another wall. There were walls on either side of him and, he could tell by the movement of air around him, a wall behind him. But the space was empty in front of him. He was in one of the cells and it opened out into the tunnel. There were other men, possibly also shackled, on either side of him. He listened harder to the murmuring voice.

"Say anything," it said. "Anything at all."

"Go to hell, you monster." That was March's voice. Loud and defiant, but there was pain evident in the way he clipped his consonants.

"Oh, I will," the voice said. "But you'll be there with me. I *thought* I knew you. And now I do. By your voice. I heard your voice nearly every day of the past . . . What has it been? Did you keep me here for a year? I should look at a newspaper."

Day heard March coughing.

"Would you like some water? Here."

March's cough turned into sputtering and gasping.

"Leave him be!" Day said.

March continued to cough, but Day heard the sound of footsteps approaching. The stranger came through the tunnel, and Day could hear him breathing, standing not more than two feet away.

"I don't know your voice," the man said.

"Which one are you? Hoffmann? You're not Cinderhouse. I'd know his voice."

"Oh, we're both playing a game of place-the-voice," the man said. "Delightful."

"This is no game."

"Everything's a game. Tell me something . . ."

"What? What is it you want?"

"*Exitus probatur*. What do you say to that?"

"I don't know," Day said. "I don't understand. Tell me what you want."

"What I want? I haven't decided yet what I want. What's your name, bluebottle?"

"Tell me your name first."

"Your name, I said. Don't make me hurt you. Better yet, don't make me hurt your friend next door."

"My name is Day. Detective Inspector Day."

He heard the man gasp and then the sound of hands clapping, three loud echoing reports.

"Day? Not Walter Day, by chance?"

Day felt his stomach turn over and he suddenly couldn't breathe. The man knew his name. Did he know where he lived? Was Claire in danger?

"Oh, my," the man said. "Have I guessed correctly? Do you know, Walter Day, that we have a friend in common?"

Day shook his head, and the motion sent another spike of pain through the base of his skull. He sucked in a sharp breath. "Who? Who do you mean?"

"It's really nobody," the man said. "I thought he was some-body, but I was mistaken. But now I don't know what to do with you, Walter Day. I think I'll keep you for a time. Perhaps I'll feed you to my fly."

"Listen—"

"Yes?"

"By order of the Queen, I'm placing you under arrest. Sur-render now, while you can, and I'll see that you're treated well."

The man took a step back. Day heard his shoes scuffing on the stones. Then he began to laugh. Day felt himself slipping away. When the man stopped laughing, he sniffed and Day heard him blow his nose.

"Thank you for that," the man said. "I needed a good hearty chuckle. You know, I quite like you, Walter Day."

The man's voice had lost its mocking tone. He sounded sin-cere. And surprised.

"I really really do," he said. "You're so marvelously uncompli-cated."

"Let us go free," Day said.

A hand clamped against the fabric of the hood over his mouth and Day smelled something sharp and acrid, a chemical seeping into the hood.

"Shh," the voice said. "No more talking. I still have work to do, and I'm suddenly peckish. Why don't you take a nap?"

As if the man had given him a hypnotic command, Day felt the floor open up under him and he fell into a deep and dream-less sleep.

40

Eunice Pye stood just inside the doorway and squinted into the gloom of the Michaels' house. She listened very hard, harder than she had ever listened before, but heard nothing, no movement, no voice or rustle of paper or cloth anywhere in the house. And so she crept cautiously into the hall, past the coatrack and the little pile of mail on the floor. She left the front door open behind her and sunlight bounced off its painted red exterior, now angled into the hall, and shone deep orange against the wall next to her.

She moved her feet forward, one at a time, barely lifting them from the smooth uneven floorboards. She held her best garden hoe out in front of her with both hands. She knew there was little she could do with it to threaten anyone or protect herself, but it made her feel better and safer to hold it.

The stairway was in front of her, along the right-hand wall. She stopped and looked up. There was a red runner that swam up the middle of the stairs, and she wondered briefly at the extravagance of it. She had a small rug made of rags and cast-off remnants next to her bed that Giles had given her on some long-ago Christmas Eve. She could not even imagine how much such a long strip of carpet must have cost. She blinked and held still and remembered why she was there in that house, and then she took a deep breath and moved forward.

Nothing stirred in the shadows at the top of the stairs, and so she turned her attention to the parlor door, which was now near to her left elbow. That door was standing open, and she could see a giant table painted black just inside the room. She moved two steps sideways and she was standing in the doorway with the table to her right. There were chairs around the table, four of them, but the chairs were empty. There was a bookcase against the wall directly ahead of her, behind the table and next to the fireplace. It held a collection of knickknacks and small painted family portraits and perhaps a dozen books of the kind sold by door-to-door salesmen to the lady of the house. Among the portraits she spotted two or three framed photographs of stiffly posed people in their Sunday finest. She wondered if Mrs Michael would ever be coming back to that house. She wondered if Mrs Michael was dead, perhaps buried in the back garden. But no, that was silly. Eunice had seen Mrs Michael leave the house with three big trunks and ride away in a four-wheeler while Mr Michael was at work.

Eunice finally turned her head and looked at the two objects nailed to the mantelpiece over the hearth. She stared at them for a long time, hoping that they would turn into things one might normally see on a mantel, things that were not tongues. But they didn't change.

She tore her gaze away from the tongues and saw Mr Michael sitting in a straight-backed padded chair next to the fireplace. He was tied there with mailing twine, and he was watching her. He held perfectly still and his eyes were open, and for just a moment she wondered if he was dead, but then she saw that his chest was rising and falling rhythmically. His hair was tousled and his eyes were red and his mouth was puffy and crusted with blood, much the way the mouth of the bald prisoner had been when she had seen him in the street.

She took a quick glance around the rest of the room, then laid down her hoe and rushed to his side. He turned his head to watch her as she approached, but didn't make any other movement. She hunched over his wrists where they were bound to the chair and her gnarled fingers worried at the knots, which had been pulled tight and small like hard little seeds. She shook her head and whispered to Mr Michael.

"Rheumatism," she said. "Can't move my fingers so well as I might have done once upon a time. But don't you worry. You sit tight and I'll be right back."

She scurried away back to the hall and clucked her tongue at herself. She murmured under her breath. "Of course he's going to sit tight, you silly old woman. Man can't move if he wants to."

She glanced up the stairs again as she passed them and went along the hallway to the kitchen. She tried to move quickly, but she didn't want to be surprised by anything, so she stopped at the kitchen doorway and entered slowly, checking both corners by the door before she went all the way inside. Nobody was waiting for her there, but the back door was standing open. She went to it and looked around the empty garden before exploring the kitchen. It wouldn't do to have someone walk in while she was distracted.

There was a knife block on the counter and the biggest knife was missing. There was a butt of ham and some bread crumbs on the butcher block. A honeybee sat on the ham. She brushed it away with the back of her hand and it buzzed around her head.

"Go on, little bee," she said. "You don't eat ham and I know you're not gonna sting me."

It lost interest in her and *zee*'d across the kitchen and zigzagged out through the open door. She selected the smallest knife from the block and ran her thumb along its blade to see if it was sharp. She nodded to herself and crept back down the hallway to the parlor, checked it carefully for new people, and then hurried over to the chair where Mr Michael sat in enforced patience, waiting for her.

The knife was very sharp indeed and made short work of the mailing twine. She rubbed Mr Michael's wrists to get the blood moving in them again.

"Can you stand?"

Mr Michael nodded, but didn't speak. Eunice looked at his mouth and then looked at the horrible tongues hanging above the hearth, and she blinked back tears at the thought of what the poor man must have endured.

She patted him on his arm and helped pull him up. He clutched the back of the chair and leaned hard against it, and they waited for the feeling to come back to his legs. When he could walk, she led him out of the parlor and turned right and guided him down his own hall to the door, which was still standing open. She was so anxious to leave that house that she practically pulled him out into the sunlight. He stood blinking in the tiny front garden while she pulled the door closed behind them. She didn't hear it latch, but she turned and took Mr Michael by the arm and led him into her house and put on a kettle for tea. While she waited for the water to heat, she went and got a roll of gauze bandages, a little bottle of iodine, and the pint of rye that Giles had always kept in the back of the cupboard. Then she broke open her jar of pin money that she had saved from sewing work. She would need pennies to pay the neighborhood boys.

She was going to send out as many runners as she could afford. She was going to send them to Scotland Yard and she was going to send them to HM Prison Bridewell. She wanted every policeman and warder in London to come and look at the tongues hanging in the parlor next door. She would only feel safe when they had caught the Devil and sent him back where he belonged.

41

Jack was hungry.

He sat at a table, far back in the main room of the pub, ignoring what went on upstairs, and when the wench came to ask what he wanted, he tipped his hat forward, dropped two of Elizabeth's coins on the table, and asked for as much as that would buy.

He sat and waited and watched the people interact. He felt nothing but a distant fondness for their messy flesh. They were his life's work, and he hoped to someday understand them.

When his food came, the wench had to pull over another table to *make enough room for all the plates and bowls. She asked him if he wanted anything else, and he could see the smirk hiding behind her smile. He wanted to leap up and take a scalpel to the corners of her mouth, peel back her cheeks, and expose the ugliness within, but instead he smiled back at her and said, "No, thank you. This will do." And watched as she walked away with a sway in her hips. He had money and she was advertising her like of it.*

He took a bite of kidney pie. Delicious. It was too hot and it burned his tongue and made the roof of his mouth sore, but he ignored the pain and took a sniff of the blood sausage. That turned out to be cool and sliced wafer-thin. His mouth was still sore and so he ate it carefully, and it was perfectly spiced.

He took a deep draught of ale, wiped his hand on his sleeve—or, more precisely, Elizabeth's sleeve—and took a look around the room. Many of the people there were watching him, but they quickly looked away when his gaze fell on them. One woman didn't look away. Her hand was on another man's elbow and she was pressed close against him, but when he looked at her, she raised her eyebrows and he licked his lips. She was his for the taking.

He wondered about the meaty organs grinding and churning inside her. He knew how beautiful they must be, glistening and wet.

And he looked away at the glob of pork on the plate in front of him, encased in fat, cold and dead and salty. And he ate it.

There was more than he could hold. He had not eaten, really eaten, in a year, and his stomach had shrunk. A few bites of this and that, and there was no room left in him. He turned his gaze inward and wondered at his own organs, wondered how well they were digesting the food he had just eaten. Wondered whether he should chew more thoroughly or whether he had done the job.

He did not look at the women again, but stood and walked out of the pub and away.

He hoped someone would finish his food. He hated to waste anything, but he clearly no longer had the appetite he'd once possessed.

42

⬡

Day!"

He was dreaming about a time when he was nine or ten years old, fording a brook in Devon with his trousers rolled up past his ankles . . .

"Walter! Can you hear me?"

There was someone with him, another boy standing in the water, but the sun was behind him and the boy was a rainbow halo blur that was talking, shouting at him . . .

"Walter, did he hurt you?"

His words made no sense because they were flavored like orange custards. Day was not fond of orange custards. He turned from the other boy and walked upstream, watching as the water broke against his shins and soaked the ends of his trouser legs where they were rolled and heavy. It became harder to walk and the boy behind him was hollering about something and the lovely sunny childhood afternoon began to seem tedious. His arms were sore and his legs hurt with the effort of pushing back against the streaming water and he wanted to go home.

And so he woke up.

"Walter?"

"I'm here. I'm awake."

"Oh, thank God. I thought perhaps . . . Well, I wasn't sure you were still with us."

Adrian March's voice came from someplace nearby, behind the wall.

"I don't know where I am," Day said. "But I think we're still in the tunnels."

"We are. He's got us in these cells we made in the catacombs."

"Your gentlemen's club, you mean." So he was, as he had assumed, shackled in one of the alcoves underground. "Adrian, I think there's a bag over my head. Something made of cloth. I can't see anything."

"It's probably the hood we used on him. Has he hurt you?"

"I'm chained here. My wrists and ankles."

"I am, too. But give me a moment. I've got my cufflinks on, the set with the lockpick hidden inside."

Day bent his wrist against the shackle around it, curled his fingers, and strained until his fingers cramped.

"Funny," he said.

"What is?"

"I'm wearing those same cufflinks, remember?"

"Yes."

"But I can't reach them. I'm trying, but my sleeve's been pushed too far up my arm."

"Don't worry. I'll get us out of here, if given the time."

"Are we alone here?"

"I think so. Griffin stopped screaming more than an hour ago, if my sense of time hasn't deserted me."

"Who is Griffin? Is Griffin the one who did this to us?"

"No."

"Is he one of the prisoners?"

"No," March said. "Well, yes, actually, I suppose he is, but not in the way you mean."

"Are you able to get at the pick?"

"I've already got it. It's just a matter of bending my wrist properly so I can get at the lock on this shackle. Once I get an arm free, the rest will be simple. I'll be over to fetch you soon enough."

"Do please hurry."

"Believe me, I'm doing what I can. Now be silent so I can work at this. It's not easy picking a lock that is about one's own wrist."

"Godspeed, Adrian."

"If he comes back, if he comes before I finish, keep him busy. Make him talk."

"Saucy Jack, you mean."

"He called himself Jack, but I never knew whether it was his real name. He seems to have taken a liking to you."

"I can't explain it."

"It's no great mystery, my dear boy. The man has been caged for months. You're the first person to actually listen to him. You are, quite literally, a captive audience. You must continue to listen, to provoke, to distract him if you can. But do be careful."

"I'm not afraid of him," Day said.

"Why not?"

"All he can do is kill me."

"That's not all he can do."

"What else is there?"

"Don't be so unimaginative, Walter. You really should be afraid of him."

"How did you catch him?" he said. The sound of his own muffled voice echoing in the little cell was, at least, better than silence.

"After all those months of chasing Jack, he fell asleep in Mary Jane Kelly's bed."

"That was his last victim."

"Yes. We found him there, covered with her blood, head to toe."

"That was quite a stroke of luck for you."

"It wasn't luck." There was a long silence before March spoke again. When he did, his voice was so soft that Day could barely hear him. "We used that girl. She was bait for Jack. We were supposed to protect her and we failed."

"Your Karstphanomen make a lot of mistakes."

"What we do isn't very precise. It's not a science, you know."

Day said nothing.

"No," March said. "You're right. We failed poor Mary Jane and we failed last night. Our ideals are sound, but I'm afraid we are not all up to the task."

"So Mary Jane Kelly lured him in . . ."

"And we were meant to be waiting for him, but there was a miscommunication. Much as there was at the prison."

"You may have a traitor in your mix."

"I can't believe that."

"Then you're all incompetent and misguided. Do you believe that?"

"We are not incompetent. We thought it all out very carefully and we had Griffin inside the prison. He was our second plan, in case the first went wrong somehow."

"And what about Mary? Was there a second plan in place to protect her?"

"We learned from her. Her sacrifice was not in vain."

"Because you caught Jack?"

"We did."

"Only because he fell asleep. I've seen what he did to them. Everyone has. Jack spent so long dismembering that girl that he practically handed himself over to you, isn't that right?"

March cleared his throat as if about to respond, but then said nothing.

"And yet you didn't arrest him," Day said.

"How could we? What we had seen, we who hunted him and cleaned up his messes, it was all too much. We couldn't let him do those things and just . . ."

The images of Jack the Ripper's victims flooded Day's head. All the postmortem photographs and artists' reconstructions. It was overwhelming. Day felt dizzy and nauseated. He fought against blacking out again.

"It was wrong, what you did," Day said. "It was selfish."

"I know."

"The public still fears Jack. You left your fellow policemen to deal with the aftermath of your actions, all of the public's fears and insecurities. Everybody thinks he got away."

"Well," March said, "he did, didn't he? And now he's going to kill us if we can't get ourselves free and stop him."

"We'll get out of here. We'll catch him again and we'll turn him over to the proper authorities. And then I'm still going to place you under arrest."

March fell silent. Day concentrated on breathing. In and out, through his mouth, no deep breaths. He had threatened to arrest two people despite being shackled to a wall in a cave.

He was counting on March to get him free, but Day's mentor had no good reason to help him now. He was afraid he would die there, deep underground, his body lost forever.

But Day was a detective inspector for Scotland Yard's Murder Squad. And if he was going to die, at least he would do so with some integrity.

43

Cinderhouse dreamed that he was falling and he woke with a start. He was sitting in the upstairs hallway of the house with the red door. The first thing he noticed was the excruciating pain in his mouth, shooting through his jaw and up into his head. He put a hand to his mouth and immediately regretted it. He fished in the pockets of his trousers, no easy feat from a sitting position, and found his handkerchief, dabbed at the corners of his mouth. There was a little blood on the cloth when he pulled it back. He held it against his lips again and applied pressure, but it didn't help. The pain was deep inside.

He realized that the bedroom door was open behind him at the same time he noticed that the knife was missing from his hand. He had been waiting for the spider to wake up and unlock the bedroom door, and now the door was open and the knife was missing. He eased himself up and peered in through the open door, but the room was empty. There was the stale remnant of body odor, and dust motes swirled in the sunlight through the window opposite the big bed.

Cinderhouse blinked and sniffed and picked gunk from the corners of his eyes. He stood and staggered into the room, just to be sure no one was there, then went back to the hallway and sat at the top of the stairs, moved slowly forward and out, and bounced down each step. At the bottom of the stairs, he grabbed the post at the end of the banister and pulled himself up. He glanced in at the parlor on his way past and noted the absence of Elizabeth. The kitchen was as deserted as every other room he'd seen, but the back door was open and honeybees flitted in and out, visiting the purple blossoms in the garden and taking a wrong turn into the house before finding their way back out.

"Aaaauuoogh!"

He thought he was going to shout *hello*, but the sound that came from his tongueless mouth was some hideous howl of loneliness and pain. He winced at the sound of it.

He held perfectly still, his back to the butcher block, and listened. There was nothing. The house was empty. The echoes of silence came back to him and proved that there wasn't a sound being made anywhere except here, except by him and the honeybees.

Jack had left and he had taken Elizabeth with him.

Jack had chosen Elizabeth over Cinderhouse. Never mind

that Cinderhouse had planned to kill Jack, had been waiting for him with the biggest knife he could find in the kitchen, had fantasized about plunging that blade deep in Jack's chest and then taking it out and cutting out Jack's tongue before the spider died. Never mind any of that. Cinderhouse had helped him, and still Jack had chosen Elizabeth to be his new rock, his Peter, his fly. He had taken Elizabeth away, and Cinderhouse felt certain they would never come back for him.

He pushed away from the butcher block and turned. He opened the drawer behind him and saw a rack of silverware inside. He couldn't remember where he had found the twine he'd used to bind Elizabeth. He concentrated and crossed the kitchen and opened another drawer beside the water basin. Inside was another ball of rough string, not as thick as the stuff he'd used on Elizabeth, and a corkscrew, three pencil stubs, several thumbtacks, a pair of gloves, a shaker of salt, and a map of London, folded the wrong way round as if someone had consulted it and then been too impatient to fold it back properly.

Cinderhouse pulled out the map and one of the pencil stubs. He went to the table in the room and unfolded the map, spread it out flat across the table. He used the pencil to mark where he thought he must be, Elizabeth's house on Phoenix Street. He saw that he was still near the prison, despite the many journeys to and fro under the street, the dead dog, the ambushing of the homeowner, and the aborted attempt at friendship with the little girl across the street. None of that had taken as much time as it had seemed to take, and none of it had taken him very far from the gates of Bridewell.

He traced the pencil up along Great College Street and found Kentish Town, then west to Primrose Hill. It was nearby. He sat at the table, got his nose down so that it almost touched the map, and moved the pencil around and around and stopped at Regent's Park Road. He couldn't be sure exactly where number 184 was, but he found the rough spot where he thought it must be and he circled that spot again and again with the tip of the pencil until it began to tear through the paper and the stub broke in half.

He had a splinter under his nail from the pencil and he dug that out with a paring knife.

He was much too lonely to go on like this. He needed the companionship of someone who would not confuse him the way that Jack did. Of course, a child would be the perfect companion. Children had always made him feel big and strong and able.

The old lady had seen him and had taken away his chance with the girl. But he knew it had not been much of a chance, since he had no tongue. It wasn't the old lady's fault. And it wasn't Jack's fault for taking his tongue. Not really. Cinderhouse had earned his punishment.

What he had not earned was a prison sentence. Not when he had been so good to his last child, the lovely little boy named Fenn, who had called him Father just the way he was supposed to. He had been good to that boy. And then the policemen had come to his house and ruined everything.

He remembered that little boy, and he remembered the policeman, some of them better than others. The tall policeman in the cheap black suit. His name was Walter Day. He remembered Walter Day's wife, too. Her name was Claire.

And he remembered where they lived: 184 Regent's Park Road. In Primrose Hill.

And Primrose Hill was not far away at all.

44

H e felt a presence in the cell before he heard the voice:

"Exitus probatur."

"Is that you, Jack?"

"Hello, Walter Day."

"Let us go free."

"Hmm. Maybe. But no, probably not."

"Then are you going to kill me now?"

"Look around you, Walter Day. Oh, that's right, you can't. That hood looks silly on you, by the way. I think I carried it off a bit better. Shall I describe our surroundings for you? Let us see . . . There are chains here, dirt floors, and stone walls. There are no windows, there is no sunlight, no butterflies or chirping birds. For that matter, there is a distinct lack of shrieking and bleeding and weeping and piercing. We're not in an abattoir or some dark alley in the East End. It's quite dull here, actually. This is a dungeon, a prison, a sort of purgatory. This was a workshop for evil men, and I have taken it from them. *They* did not kill people here, and I do not mean to, either. This has become a sacred place, a birthplace. To be honest, though, I think I might have killed a man just over there on the other side of this wall. The fellow has stopped moving. I should look into that."

"Do you mean—"

"In my rambling and contradictory way, I mean to say that I'm not planning to kill you, Walter Day. Not today, I'm not."

"Why not?"

"Because I'm still thinking. I'll decide about tomorrow when tomorrow comes."

"Tomorrow?"

"Yes. Today I desire intelligent discourse and I have my hopes pinned to you. It's been such a very long time since I had a real conversation with someone who wasn't screaming."

"You said you killed someone down here. Was it Adrian March? On which side of me is the dead man?"

"Oh, I've killed so many people. Does it matter?"

"Was it March? I don't hear him."

"He's sleeping. It was the other man I killed. That is, if I killed him."

Day realized he was holding his breath and he let it out, took another breath. It sounded like a sigh.

"You can't keep us here," he said.

"I most certainly can. You don't tell me what I can and cannot do, Walter Day."

"People will be looking for us."

"But will they find you? I'm aquiver with excitement. Will the detectives solve the mystery and rescue their cohorts? I can't stand the suspense. Actually, Walter Day, I've spoken with your Inspector March, and there's little reason to think anyone will search these tunnels. Nobody even knows you're down here."

"They'll come looking for you. The Karstphanomen will. They'll come for you and find me here instead. What do you think they'll do then?"

"You're not as stupid as the rest of them, are you, Walter Day? You present a problem for me."

"And you present quite a problem for me, Jack."

Jack chuckled and patted him on the arm. Day's chains rattled with the movement.

"Yes, I suppose I do," Jack said. "Let me ask you something. Are you ready for me to ask you something?"

"I think so."

"Listen carefully now. *Exitus probatur.*"

"You said that before. What does it mean?"

"Are you being coy, Walter Day? I can't decide if you're playing a game with me. I do like games, but I'm not sure I have the patience right now."

"It sounds like Latin. What you said. Is it Latin?"

"You really don't know what it means?"

"No. I swear it."

"Fascinating."

"What *does* it mean?"

"I'm not entirely sure, Walter Day, but some of your friends do seem to know what it means."

"My friends?"

"Your man to the right of me, in the neighboring cell, Mr March. He knows what it means. And the gentleman to my left—he's to *your* right, I suppose. He knows, too. Or knew. As I said, he's stopped doing things and knowing things. Though it hardly matters. He's not important to our story anymore."

"You're mad."

"Quite probably. But that's not important just now, either. The immediate problem you pose for me arises because I believe you when you say you do not know those words, Walter Day."

"I *don't* know them."

"I already said I believe you. Don't make me repeat myself."

"But what does it mean? *Exit proboscis?*"

"You've misquoted me. I think you just told me that something's coming out of your nose. And, now you mention it, you do seem to be having some trouble breathing. *Are* you having trouble breathing?"

Day nodded. When he moved his head, he felt the rough fabric against his chin and lips and eyelids. And he felt the stab of pain in his head, but it wasn't as sharp this time. It was bearable. The fabric shifted and he felt pressure on his scalp, then the hood lifted away and cool air hit his face. He took a deep rasping breath and opened his eyes. He immediately closed them again.

"Is that better, Walter Day?"

"It is."

"You should say thank you."

"Thank you."

"You're very welcome. And I'm glad you've found your manners. Though I did have to remind you." There was a pause. "But I forgive you that because I remember how terribly stuffy this hood can be. It stifles the senses, doesn't it?"

"Yes."

Day opened his eyes again, just a little bit, kept them partially closed and ratcheted his eyelids up a bit at a time, letting them adjust to the light. When they were open far enough that he could see, he was surprised to realize that the only illumination in the cell was indirect, the glow of a lantern in another nearby alcove. He could see the light from it reflected on the tunnel wall opposite his own cell, but everything around him was black.

"It hurts, doesn't it?" Jack said. "The light, I mean. It stabs at your eyes."

The way he emphasized the word *stab* sent a shiver down Day's spine. He tried to turn his head to see Jack, but the shooting pain in his skull stopped him. The brief glimpse he had of Jack was disappointing, only a shape in the darkness.

"Do you see me, Walter Day?"

"No. I mean, you're lost in the shadows."

Jack laughed, sudden and loud, the bark of a rabid dog.

"You'll forgive me. I'm a bit giddy today. But I am indeed lost in the shadows. And gladly so. I live in them. You're merely a visitor." The humor left his voice and he leaned in closer, though Day did not turn his head. "Tell me," Jack said.

"I told you. I don't know the words. I don't know Latin."

"No, tell me something else. Do they remember me? Above, in the sunlight. Do they remember Saucy Jack, or have I truly faded into the shadows?"

"You're forgotten. No one remembers you in the slightest."

Day heard Jack move, sitting back, his body creaking like old leather and rotting wood.

"No, I don't believe you this time, Walter Day. I think they do remember me. I think I still frighten them. Am I a tale told to children to keep them in their beds? Do they see me at the back of their closets, under their beds, following them in the street at dusk?"

"Yes, if you must know. Yes. You ruined everything. You took away their trust and security. Does that make you ashamed? That you damaged the city so badly that nobody will ever feel safe again? Or does it make you happy?"

"Oh, it makes me very happy, indeed. Thank you."

"The best thing you can do for everyone in London is to die."

"If only I could. But gods don't die, Walter Day. They step back into the shadows they came from and they watch. You know, you have a lump on your head. I think perhaps I put it there when I hit you. I apologize for that. But how was I to know we'd become friends?"

"I forgive you," Day said.

This time Jack's laughter was deep and sincere, even friendly.

It rolled around the cell and boomed down the tunnel. It was the laughter of a delighted and indulgent father.

"Oh, Walter Day, you do amuse me. I think I'm going to let you keep your tongue."

Day said nothing. He was afraid to speak. He didn't know whether to take Jack literally. Did he mean that Day was free to speak? Or did he mean that he might actually cut the tongue out of his mouth?

"The tailor no longer amuses me," Jack said. "I've grown bored of him. Of course, he couldn't say anything of interest these days, even if he wanted to."

"Tailor?"

"I believe you know him."

"You mean Cinderhouse?"

"Clever boy, Walter Day. That is exactly who I mean."

"You cut out his tongue?"

"I did alter him a bit. That's a joke about tailoring. I'm sorry it's not a better one."

"Do you know where he is?"

"I do."

"Will you tell me?"

"What would you do with that information? You're here, he's there. I'm afraid it would be a useless gesture, were I to give you his location."

"I was looking for him down here. I wasn't looking for you. I didn't know you were here or even that you were still alive."

"So it was the Fates that brought us together. Do you suppose those three fine ladies speak Latin? Perhaps they could translate my phrase for me."

"How do you know him? Cinderhouse, I mean? Did he come for you? Did he help you kill those women a year ago?"

"The Fates at work again, those weird sisters. I suppose you could say the tailor works for me. Like those policemen work for you. The ones who will be coming to find you here."

"Are they coming?"

"You said they were."

"They don't work for me."

"They should. You're smarter than they are. Take the power that is yours to take, Walter Day."

"There's no power. We work together. We're the Murder Squad."

"Oh, yet another gentlemen's society. You people are so keen on those. Still, I don't see them here, the other policemen. I see you here. You were the only one smart enough to find me. You, who are wholly removed from that gentleman's club of torturers, the Karstphanomen. You, who have braved the darkness. Walter Day, you *are* the Murder Squad. At least, all of it that matters to me."

"Sergeant Hammersmith will come. He will find me."

"Hammersmith? Who is he?"

"A better policeman than I am."

"Better than the great Walter Day? This I must see. And yet he is your sergeant. You are his superior."

"I'm no one's superior."

"Someone has taught you too much humility. Who was that?

Who did that to you? You must have been a child to have learnt it so deep in your bones. Your father, was he in service?"

"He's none of your business."

"Ah, so he *was* in service. A footman, perhaps? A valet?"

"Yes."

"Well, he did you a *dis*service. That's another play on words."

"He was a good man."

"Was? He's dead now?"

"No. He's alive."

"When did you see him last?"

"I don't know."

"Hmm. Neither do I. Nor do I actually care. Let me show you something."

Jack's hands entered the soft field of light reflected from the tunnel outside. He was wearing brown leather gloves that looked almost orange in the dim glow. They didn't seem to fit him well. He was holding a black bag. He unfastened the clasp and opened it, drew out a scalpel. He held the scalpel up so that Day could see it, and Day shrank back toward the wall behind him. His chains rattled and clanked.

"I'm having . . ." Day said. "I mean, my wife's having a baby."

"That's wonderful. But why should that matter to me?"

"Don't kill me."

"Oh, this. Well, first of all, if I were to kill you, your baby would still be born. Baby doesn't care whether you're there or not, am I right? But second of all, I've already told you I'm not going to kill you. You may take me at my word. Your question should be, 'What *else* can Jack do with a scalpel?'"

"Don't."

"And the answer is . . . I can point with it. Look at this."

The sharpened tip of the scalpel moved over the outside of the bag and came to rest under a decoration stamped into the leather.

"What does this say, do you think?"

"Initials," Day said. "Someone's initials."

"Exactly. But whose?"

"Is it your bag? Are they your initials? Your real name?"

"Oh, good guess, Walter Day. But no, these are not my initials. This is my bag. But yesterday it was not my bag. And I would like to know who owned this bag yesterday, you see?"

"A doctor?"

"Well, that's a good start. A good assumption, I think. Yes, I believe, given the wonderful work he did on my own body, that he was and is a doctor. And our mystery doctor left this down here every day, which would indicate to me that this was not his primary medical bag. He must have another bag. I should be an inspector, shouldn't I? Do you need a new associate?"

"I have—"

"Ah, yes, Sergeant Hammersmith. Perhaps if I make him go away, you and I might be even better friends." The scalpel was withdrawn and disappeared in the shadows.

"No. Don't. Leave him be. Um, the initials on the bag are *MBB*. So you're looking for someone who is a doctor and has the initials . . . Oh."

"Yes?"

"I can't think."

"But you *did* think. I saw your face. You know whose bag this is. You know my doctor friend, don't you? You've met him!"

"No. I don't know him."

"Shh. We've told each other enough lies for one day."

Day heard fabric rip and felt something flutter against the calf of his left leg. There was a bright flash of pain and a burning sensation.

"What did you—"

"You lied to me just now."

"I'm sorry."

"I don't speak Latin, but I speak German well enough, Walter Day. Do you know what the word *karstphanomen* actually means?"

"My leg."

"It's bubbles of air, karstphanomen is. Pockets in the earth. These men, this doctor and that policeman in the next cell, and who knows how many others . . . they call themselves that, and they believe they mete out justice. They believe they do good work while hiding in the pockets of society. Do you believe that?"

"They were wrong to keep you here."

"Oh, most certainly. There's no question of that. But what do you think of their notions regarding justice and law?"

"It's my job to uphold the law."

"And what about justice?"

"They're the same thing."

"No, Walter Day. The Karstphanomen are right about that, right about that one little thing. They've got everything else wrong, but they're correct when they say that the law does not concern itself with justice. And yet, these men contradict their own beliefs. They hide away down here in the dark and do evil things and think themselves good men. Isn't that silly?"

Day said nothing. He could feel something warm running down his leg, trickling into his shoe.

"Perhaps we should cut the earth away and expose them, pop their bubbles, let them bleed out onto the surface. After all, if they're so convinced they're correct, why should they hide?"

"What did you do to me?"

"You won't die yet. Not of this, at any rate. I said I wouldn't kill you today and I think it will take a bit longer than that for you to bleed to death."

"Don't do this."

"I must go. But I'll be back soon to hurt your friend and to talk to you some more. Maybe I'll even stop the bleeding. I really do enjoy talking with you. I think this relationship is going to be interesting for us both, Walter Day."

"Listen, let us out of here and I'll do what I can to see that you're not hanged."

"Oh, how lovely of you. What do you think, maybe they'll let me rot in the asylum? Or maybe they'll even let me go free! I greatly appreciate your overture of friendship, but let's wait and see what tomorrow may bring. It's been a very long day for me and, despite the fun I'm having, I'd like to see the sun again. Then I'd like to visit a lady and get a good night's sleep."

"Visit a lady?"

"Yes. I haven't enjoyed the company of a woman in a very long time."

"No, please don't."

"Good night, Walter Day."

Jack stood and took a step toward him, blocking the light and casting himself in silhouette. There was a rustle of fabric and the hood was pulled roughly over Day's face. He heard Jack walk away, his boot heels clocking against the earth. Then silence rushed in and Day felt himself alone in the dark once again.

45

Another wagon was already stopped outside the gates of HM Prison Bridewell when Hammersmith's carriage arrived. Inspectors Blacker and Tiffany were at the back of the other wagon with the door open, and Blacker had his weapon drawn. They both stepped back, prepared for anything, but they relaxed visibly when they saw Hammersmith.

"We've got one of them," Blacker said. His smile was as big and guileless as a child's. "Gave us a merry chase, but he never stood a chance."

"You've got one, too?" Tiffany said.

"We caught the cannibal," Hammersmith said. "Napper."

"Good show, old boy," Blacker said.

"Which one have you got?"

"Hoffmann," Tiffany said. "The one killed his cousin's lover."

"Let's reunite these old friends," Blacker said. "I'll bet they've missed each other."

Tiffany nodded at the dark interior of their wagon, where Hammersmith could see a person waiting. "All right, all's clear," Tiffany said. "Back out slowly, now."

"Wait a minute, Nevil, and I'll help you with yours," Blacker said. "These children they've got driving the wagons today aren't of much use."

"Hey!" The driver of Hammersmith's wagon scowled down at them. His nose was dusted with freckles, a cigarette dangled from the corner of his mouth. "I didn't have to be here, you know. Got other things I could be doin' today."

"Yes, I'm sure," Hammersmith said. "No insult intended."

"All right, then."

The boy went back to reading his scandal magazine. Hammersmith stepped to the back of the other wagon and pulled the truncheon from his belt. He watched carefully as the prisoner Hoffmann moved backward to the wagon's edge and perched there awkwardly, craning his neck to see the ground three feet below him, his wrists cuffed in front of him. Hammersmith held the end of the truncheon against the back of Hoffmann's knees while Blacker and Tiffany kept their revolvers pointed at the prisoner.

"I'm right here," Hammersmith said. "There's a ledge here under the wagon's lip. You can't see it from where you are, but I'll guide your foot onto it and make sure you don't fall."

"If you do fall," Tiffany said, "or make any other movement that I don't like, I'll put a hole in you."

"He'll do it, too," Blacker said. "Inspector Tiffany's in a mood today."

Hoffmann nodded and licked his lower lip. It was hard to tell from Hammersmith's vantage point how tall the prisoner was, but he seemed abnormally thin. He was older, with a few strands of grey hair that arced up over the top of his head. He had the habitual squint of a man used to wearing spectacles, and Hammersmith wondered if he'd lost them in the escape. Hoffmann bent his knees and felt behind him with his left toe. Hammersmith used the truncheon to guide his heel, and Hoffmann found the ledge. He leaned sideways against the inside wall of the wagon and eased himself down. Hammersmith used the flat of his left hand on Hoffmann's back and helped him the rest of the way to the ground.

"Thank you," Hoffmann said.

"Don't talk to me."

"But I can . . . you know, I can help you. I know where one of the others are. I mean, where he is. One of them that escaped with me."

The three policemen looked at one another.

"You'd help us catch him?" Hammersmith said.

"I would," Hoffmann said. "I would help you if you were to put in a good word to the head warder for me."

"We don't make promises to criminals," Tiffany said.

"It's gonna . . . it's going to be harder on us this time round. In Bridewell. I mean, the head warder. He's gonna . . . he's going to hurt us, take away meals and our time outside. And he'll take away our tea. I like teatime most of all."

"You killed a man," Blacker said. "Tea seems like the least of your worries."

"Where is he?" Hammersmith said. "If you know where one of the others is, tell us."

"Promise first. Promise you'll talk to the head warder. Just a word to him. Just a good word from you, it's all I ask. A recommendation. I'm not asking for more than that. I know I've made mistakes and I don't ask for forgiveness or special favors. Tea is all. A piece of toast is all. It's not much, is it? A piece of toast? Maybe a spot of jam. But not necessarily. I didn't mean to say jam. It's too much to ask. Toast is all I need. Please, just toast." Hoffmann's voice grew more shrill as he pleaded with them. Hammersmith looked away from him at the two inspectors.

"I don't like making bargains with criminals," Tiffany said.

"And I don't like standing out here like this," Blacker said. "Let's get him inside and locked up. Then we can talk."

"Do you think he actually knows something?"

"I do," Hoffmann said. "I do know something."

"Maybe he does," Tiffany said. "But we'll find the other men without him."

Tiffany tugged on Hoffmann's elbow and led him toward the gates where a blue-uniformed warder was watching them.

"It might be worth finding out what he knows," Blacker said. "Or thinks he knows."

Hammersmith saw something move at the far corner of the high stone wall. It appeared at the periphery of his vision and moved fast toward the little cluster of policemen with Hoffmann.

"Move," Hammersmith said. "Get him through the gates."

Blacker didn't even look up. He pushed Hoffmann forward and immediately closed the gap behind him. Tiffany moved into the lane, his Webley revolver already up and aimed. Then he lowered his weapon, just as the figure resolved itself in Hammersmith's vision as a young boy on a bicycle. The two policemen looked at each other and then looked over at Blacker, who had managed to get Hoffmann through the gate and was only now turning to see if he could help the others.

"Well," Blacker said, "we know how to move fast when we have to, don't we?"

"And when we don't have to," Tiffany said. He scowled at the boy, who skidded to a halt in front of him. "Move along, son. Police business here."

"Was lookin' for police, sir." The boy gulped and took several deep breaths. He was sweating and his hair was tangled from the wind.

"Someone sent you?"

"Yes, sir. A second, please. Catchin' me breath."

"Is it the Yard?"

"No, sir. The prisoners, sir. The ones who escaped? Mrs Pye's seen two of 'em, and on my very street, sir, where I live."

"Two of the prisoners? Who's Mrs Pye?"

"Lady lives on my street, sir. Gave me a penny to ride up here and tell you."

"How did she know we were here?"

"Anybody, sir. Said to tell anybody I saw."

"Where are they?"

"Phoenix Street, sir. Not far. I'll show you. They're livin' in a house over there. They hurt Mr Michael and took his house, but Mrs Pye, she went right in like it wasn't nothin' and she untied Mr Michael and saved him, sir, but he don't got a tongue no more. They cut it out of him, if you can believe it."

Tiffany turned to Blacker. "Leave him." Then to the gate-keeper. "Can you take him from here?"

The warder nodded. "I got him, all right."

"Good. Let's go."

Blacker squeezed out through the gap in the gate and the warder swung it shut behind him with a mighty clang. Hoffmann twisted away and threw himself against the bars of the gate on the other side.

"No," he said. "I can tell you where he is. The strange one. The Harvest Man. I can tell you. I only want toast in return. That's not so much to ask! Tea and toast!"

"The hell with you and your toast," Tiffany said. "We know where the other fugitives are now. We don't need your information."

"Toast!"

Tiffany ignored him. He and Blacker hopped up into the back of the waiting wagon. The boy on the bicycle circled around so he was facing back the way he had come. He jumped on a pedal and rolled away from them down the lane.

"Follow him," Tiffany said.

The boy up top sighed. He picked up the reins and gave a

haw and the old horse out front took a tentative step and then another and the wagon began to move.

"You coming, Sergeant?"

Hammersmith nodded and allowed himself to be pulled up into the back of the wagon with the two inspectors as the horse gained momentum and chuffed along after the waiting bicyclist. Hammersmith stared out at the weeping prisoner clinging to Bridewell's gates and wondered how Inspector Day was faring.

At least, he thought, the remaining prisoners were hiding in a house on Phoenix Street while Day was safe and sound, far away from it all.

46

Is he gone?"

Day shouted at the rocks around him, not daring to hope for an answer. He knew that there were two men with him, one on either side, both shackled there by Jack. He did not know the man to his right, the one who might be dead, but Adrian March was only a few feet away, to his left. And if March was still alive . . . How long had it been since he had last heard him? An hour? Two?

"He's gone." March's voice came wavering through the rock. He sounded drugged or addled.

"Adrian?"

"I've dropped it, Walter. I dropped the lockpick."

"Were you able to—"

"No. I couldn't get the proper angle on the thing. I'm older, I suppose. I used to be able to hold those tiny things, but my fingers . . ."

"Adrian, you sound . . . Has he hurt you?"

"Of course. But he won't kill me for some time, I think. He'll keep me alive as long as he can. It's a shame I don't have my little jailer's gun with me today."

"Jailer's gun?"

"Cunning thing. I sent you one, but you don't have it here either, do you? Shaped like a key, it is. Holds a single bullet. A single bullet's all it would take, one way or another, Jack or me."

"What's he done to you?"

"He has started with the wounds he gave Annie Chapman. One of his victims. They were the last wounds we inflicted on him before he escaped."

"What kind of wounds?" He didn't know what had been done to Annie Chapman. The photographs and drawings of Jack's victims were horrible things to look at, but he had never read the autopsy reports. When Saucy Jack had committed his gruesome deeds, Day had been a country constable, riding his bicycle down winding lanes, giving warnings to children who stole apples from the market.

"He has cut my cheeks and my stomach," March said.

"Oh, God!"

"Not as bad as all that, actually. Of course, he's gone further than we ever did with him. I believe he's cut something vital in my cheek. I don't seem to be able to speak properly."

Which explained the sound of March's voice, slurred and heavy.

"Will you live?" Day said.

"For a while yet. Until he tires of me and kills me."

"Adrian, I think I may have lost my leg."

"You will lose more than that. And I will, too."

"No. Nevil will come for us. He's relentless. He's probably already looking. He'll find us, I know it."

"There are miles and miles of tunnels down here. No one will ever find us."

Day stared at the black inside of the hood and swallowed hard. He could feel icy panic in his chest. But panic didn't help. He and March needed to stay alive long enough to find some means of escape. Otherwise, Claire would be left to raise their baby with no income, no prospects. He supposed she would go back to her family. They'd take her in. They'd be delighted to. And she was lovely. She would remarry, and some other man, somebody who wasn't so afraid to be a father, would raise Walter Day's child as his own. Day could see the future without him and he saw that he would be forgotten.

Unless he could escape.

He began again to grasp at his palm with his fingertips, twisting his elbow around, trying desperately to inch the cuff of his right sleeve up his arm. If he could just reach the cufflink, he might have a chance. All he had to do was find one tiny sliver of metal and slip it into a hole somewhere above him in the dark.

47

She was tall and lanky, with big hands and blunt finger-nails. Her hair was stringy and pulled back from her wide forehead, emphasizing her eyes, which were set too far apart. She stood at the corner outside the Whistle and Flute, waiting for a man to come along and give her a coin she could spend on a bed for the night. Or on a pint of gin.

Jack watched her from across the street until he began to feel the old familiar call, that special burning sensation in his fingertips and across his shoulders. He waited for a cab to pass by, then made his unhurried way across the street. She watched him coming, and her face rearranged itself from a sullen scowl to something she apparently thought was sexy, lowering her eyelids and pouting her lips, a half smile fighting with her arched eyebrows. Jack thought she looked more *like a jester than a seductress, but he appreciated the effort. He stepped over a mound of steaming horseshit and hopped up onto the curb next to her.*

"Good evening," he said.

She affected a disinterested attitude, looking away in the other direction as if she had no idea who he might be talking to. He was amused by her attempt at subtlety. She played the game as if there were no transaction in their future, as if she were simply a woman and he a man.

He tried again. "I have sixpence here for you if you wish it."

"I don't go nowhere for less than half a crown."

He laughed out loud and was startled to hear that there was no anger in the sound of it. His laugh was genuine and robust and free of malice. He looked at the girl, this weathered, big-boned woman, and he smiled at her. And there was nothing in his smile to frighten her, nothing that gave her any indication that she was looking at a god or a monster. He was simply a man, like so many other men she had known in her unfortunate life.

"Shouldn't you be worried?"

"Worried about what, love?"

"They never caught Saucy Jack."

"You don't scare me. I know a good man when I see one, and you ain't no Saucy Jack. And you ain't gonna bargain me down."

"I thank you," he said.

"For what?" she said. "I ain't done nothin'. Not yet, at least."

"For the marvelous birthday gift you've bestowed. You have shown me something I did not know until this very moment. I suspected it, but I didn't realize it for a certainty. And I am a changed man."

"Your birthday? Well, bless you, but the price ain't changed none, birthday or no birthday. I got my standards."

"And I'm sure they're very high indeed, but I regret to inform you that I cannot afford the pleasure of your company this fine evening. Still, I believe you have earned this."

He pressed the sixpence coin into her eager hand and walked away from her. He heard her calling to him, anxious to get more money from him, but he didn't turn around. The thrill had left his bones. He had no business to conduct upon her well-worn body. No business of the kind she expected and no business of the kind he preferred.

Jack really was a changed man. A year or more of torture had given him new ideas about the world.

He was keen to begin testing those ideas.

The Devil marched off with a spring in his step, and the woman, her sixpence coin clutched tight in her fist, hurried into the Whistle and Flute. She remained blissfully ignorant about the thing she had met in the street that evening and never knew how lucky she was to be alive.

48

"Can I push? I want to push."

"Please wait a moment, Claire. Control your breathing and be calm."

Kingsley had set out his instruments on the wash table next to the door, blocking them from Claire's view with his body. He thought it probable that she had never seen a pair of forceps and he didn't want to frighten her. He took a small stack of flannels from his bag and set them beside the forceps. He picked up a small glass vial, uncorked it, and sprinkled a few drops of clear liquid onto the cloth. He turned and held the cloth up in front of Claire.

"I'm going to place this near your nose and mouth for a moment. It's ether. We talked about this before, remember?"

"Yes. Please do."

He held it up to her face and she breathed in slowly. When he removed it, she appeared to be more relaxed.

"Good," he said. "That will help with the pain."

He set the rapidly drying flannel back on the table, separate from the clean cloths. He didn't want to get them mixed up. He went back around the end of the bed and helped Claire position herself more comfortably.

"Is that better?"

"Yes," she said. "Thank you. Will there be a lot more pain?"

"Every woman is different, my dear. You'll be fine."

"Then I can push?"

"It's time."

He averted his eyes as she bore down. A moment later, she relaxed again, gasped, and began to pant quietly.

"Good," Kingsley said. "You're doing very well, Claire."

"I don't want to do this anymore. I want to stop."

"I'm afraid that isn't an option. But the baby's going to be here soon enough. Don't worry."

"I don't want the baby."

"Of course you do. You may push again when you're ready."

"I'm going to stop."

"Do you require more ether?"

"No."

"Then let's get ready to push."

"Walter doesn't want a baby."

"Nonsense."

"He doesn't. I can see it in him. He disappears at night."

"He loves you. And he loves your baby. Now I want you to stop talking about Walter and concentrate on this task right now. You're in the middle of a very difficult job and you needn't distract yourself with worry."

"I think it's his own father. Arthur Day wasn't good at being a father, and Walter thinks—"

"Few of us are good at being fathers. But we try. And eventually our children grow into men and women who make their own mistakes and blame us for them. It's the way of the world."

"He's so unhappy."

"He's nervous. I've seen this many times. He'll be fine. And you'll be fine."

"I don't know."

"Well, I do. Now I want you to push again."

"What if—"

"Claire. Push now."

She took a deep breath, closed her eyes, and pushed.

49

I can't feel my leg anymore. It's gone numb."

"That might be for the best, Walter Day."

"Am I bleeding to death?"

"Yes," Jack said. "But very slowly."

"Can you stop the bleeding?"

"Now why would I do that?"

"If I die, you won't be able to talk to me anymore."

"But of course I will. You just won't be able to talk back."

"Will you take the hood off again? It's hot and it's hard to breathe."

The hood was lifted off and Day felt cool air against his face.

"It really is beastly, this hood," Jack said. "One forgets one is a man under there."

"I thought you said you were a god, not a man."

"I was speaking of you."

"I wasn't sure you'd come back. Where do you go?"

"I've had several interesting experiences today. Any experience is interesting after a year or so under that hood, and I suppose I'm only doing my best to make the most out of life."

"Did you kill someone?"

The shape in the dark was quiet for a long moment.

"You know, I don't think I have. Aside from that fellow in the cell next to yours, of course, but that was an accident. I got overexcited. Yes, aside from him, I've killed no one. That might be the most interesting thing about today. After all, it's what I'm known for. Killing. That's not what I call it. It's a different thing for me. But your senses are not so refined as mine. Killing is the only reason you've ever heard of me and the only thing you're aware that I've ever done. And yet, here I am, a free man after all this time, and I've been . . . well, I've practically been an upstanding citizen, haven't I?"

"Did you hurt anyone else?"

"Oh, well, of course. Quite a lot of hurting. But it's not the same thing as killing, is it? Not at all."

"Maybe you're done killing. Maybe you won't kill anyone again. Maybe the Karstphanomen were correct and what they did has changed you."

Jack laughed, a deep rich baritone.

"They changed me, all right. But I don't think they'll appreciate their work when I'm done. And please, Walter Day, rest assured, I will most certainly kill someone. More than one. The day is not yet over."

There was another pause in the conversation and Day could hear Jack breathing heavily, as if he had run through the tunnels and had not yet caught his breath. Day could feel the sharp end of the cufflink pressed against his palm. He hoped Jack had not noticed that Walter's cuff was loose. The tiny pick was difficult to hold on to, and Day was having trouble maneuvering. He wished he'd been quicker and wondered if it was too late. And he was tired of wishing and wondering and he was tired of being frightened.

"Then do it," Day said. "Get it over with. I've no interest in being your plaything."

"Oh, don't be so dramatic. I wasn't talking about you. You're terribly self-absorbed, Walter Day."

"We both know you're not going to let me go."

"Do you actually want me to transform you? To kill you? You seem to be goading me."

"Of course not."

"Good. You said you have a baby on the way, didn't you? When we last spoke."

"Never mind that."

"But if I kill you now, you'll never see your baby. I wonder, would you prefer that? A baby is a terrible responsibility."

"What do you know about responsibility?"

"You know nothing about me, Walter Day. I assure you I'm

quite familiar with the concept of responsibility. I take it very seriously indeed. But we were talking about your family. Your little family. Just you and your pregnant wife, who is transforming herself, who is creating life. She's marginalizing you, isn't she? And controlling you? You're not at all ready to be a parent and you hate her for forcing you into the situation. Am I right?"

"No."

"Yes, I am. I can see it in your black beady eyes, Walter Day."

"Stop it."

"I joke. Your eyes are probably lovely. It's the lantern light that makes them look like the eyes of a rat. I should pluck one out and take it up to the sun and see how sensitive that window to your soul really is. I'm sure your wife loves your eyes. I should make her a gift of them. Put them on a silver chain for her throat. Or put them in a box for cufflinks."

Day closed his eyes and gritted his teeth and said nothing. He tried to concentrate on his leg, tried to feel something, but there was nothing there. He turned his attention to the sharp little lockpick in his hand. Perhaps he could jam it into Jack's eye, if Jack came close enough.

"Do you kiss her, Walter Day? Your wife, I mean. Isn't it fascinating how all skulls are basically the same? Just under the skin, you all look so frightfully similar. Wait here, I'll show you."

The dark shape stood and moved away, into the tunnel. The lantern light that was reflected on the wall shimmied and flowed as the shadow passed through it. Day hung his head and bunched the muscles in his shoulders, trying to alleviate the pain there. He curled the toes of his right foot and rubbed them against the inside of his shoe. He tried the same movement with his left foot, but nothing happened. Then Jack was back, standing next to Day. He held a dirty brown skull. The jawbone had fallen off. Or perhaps Jack had removed it.

"Who do you suppose he was?" Jack said. "Or she? It's hard to tell, isn't it? I'm told there are people, doctors and the like, who can tell the sex of a person based on its bones, but they're really all the same, aren't they? Bones, I mean, not doctors. There are profound differences between doctors."

Jack smacked his lips and turned the skull this way and that in his hands. "You're not being a good guest right now, Walter Day. I expect livelier conversation from you. Look at this skull, so similar to yours. But then imagine some mushy pink and brown bits on top of the bone and, voilà! A person is formed. When you kiss your wife, you're pressing against the bone, the bone is the structure, but it's the mushy bits you really like. Yes, those are the best part. People are made up entirely of the saggy flesh they carry around on their poor tired bones. How is that? Why should that be? Why is the hard part, the strong part, of a person not the best part? It's the soft gentle parts that make you different from your friends and neighbors. Isn't that awfully interesting? I think about this sort of thing a great deal."

"Is that why you cut people?"

"Well, there are so many reasons to cut people, don't you think? Really, there are too few reasons not to, when you think about it. Everyone ought to be running about cutting everyone else."

"There's decency. That's a reason not to hurt people. Do

you have any of that in you? Do you have any common human decency?"

"I don't know. Let's cut me open and take a look round for it." Jack laughed again. "Is decency something you learned from your father, Walter Day? Your father, the valet?"

"Yes."

"He taught you a great deal, didn't he? Taught you subservience and putting others before yourself. He taught you to be unhappy and unfulfilled, didn't he? What a wonderful man he must be. And what of your mother?"

Day said nothing.

"Oh, your mother's a touchy subject. I quite understand. Did you know her?"

"No."

"Why not? Did you kill her, Walter Day?"

"Yes."

"Oh, I see. May I take an educated guess? You transformed your mother even as she was creating you, am I right?"

"Yes."

"I feel very close to you right now."

"And what about you? What did your father teach you? And what about your mother? Did your mother teach you to murder women?"

Day heard Jack sniff. The atmosphere changed, like a breeze blowing in from another direction, and the tiny underground cell seemed to grow colder. Day felt fabric rustling against his right leg, the leg he could still feel. There was the sound, once more, of rending cloth, and then the feel of air against his skin.

There was another sensation that caused chills to move up his body.

"You don't mention my mother," Jack said. His voice was low and very quiet. So quiet that Day could barely hear him over the sound of blood pounding in his ears.

"You cut my other leg."

"I'm sorry. I really am, but you made me do it."

The realization that he'd had hope almost broke Day. He felt his throat close up and his eyes sting and he couldn't breathe. He'd been holding on to some belief that he might make it out of the catacombs alive, and now that belief left him in a rush and he knew the hopelessness of Jack's victims.

"This is what they felt at the end, isn't it?"

"Who? Who are you talking about, Walter Day?"

"Those women, those five women that you murdered."

"Only five? Funny how little you know, Mr Policeman."

"How many, then?"

"Oh, so very many. I'm weary. But I slept in a bed today. Did I tell you that?"

"No."

Day felt moisture trickling down his right leg and knew that he would soon lose the feeling there. Even if he managed to free himself from the shackles, he would be unable to walk back to the street above them.

"I slept, Walter Day, as men sleep. In a real bed. And I had the most interesting dream. Would you like to hear it?"

Day didn't answer. Without hope of escape, there was no reason to talk to Jack or listen to his ravings.

"In my dream, I transformed five people. I don't know whether they were men or women. I honestly don't remember that part of the dream. But they died during the transformation, as they so often do. And then I brought them back. I brought them all back from the place I'd sent them. I forgot to say, three of them were bad people and two of them were good people. The good people thought that they were going to visit a magic kingdom in the afterlife. They thought they deserved such a thing because of the entirely unimportant little decisions they'd made on this sphere. But all five people came back terrified. What they had experienced on the other side was too much for them. And do you know, the bad people became good. They thought that if they mended their ways, the next time they died they would perhaps have a better experience. But the good people gave up all hope and became indifferent. They did bad things after that. Do you see? They all experienced the same thing, but their individual perception of who they were changed everything. Their perception of what they deserved changed how they lived their lives. Those two good people learned that there was no justice or consequence."

Day raised his head and looked at the shadow next to him.

"That's why the Karstphanomen will always fail," Jack said. "Because justice is not a thing one can pursue. It is a perception."

"What did you do to Adrian March?"

"March? The policeman? Would you like to know what *he* did to *me*, what beautiful art he created on my body over the past year or so? I could show you."

"I only want to know what you have done to him."

"I think he might be alive. I've tried, at least, to keep him alive. You have to give me credit for that."

"If you've killed him . . ."

"What, Walter Day? If I've killed him, you'll be unhappy with me? What is he, your mentor? That's what he is to you, isn't he? Your father failed in certain critical ways, and so Adrian March has become important to you."

"Don't speak about my father anymore. That is not your right. If I am not to speak of your mother, then—"

"Ah. Touché, as the Froggies say. You're right about that, and I ought to allow you to cut me in return, oughtn't I? You see how I think about things? How thoughtful I am? I think it's time for you to have a new mentor. Is it too forward of me to put myself out as a possibility?"

"If I am ever free of this place," Day said. "I know it's not . . . No, but if I ever am, I will see that you are brought to justice. Then you'll see what a real thing that is. You'll see that justice is a thing to strive for, not a thing to be mocked."

"Bless your heart." The shadow was quiet again for a long time, and Day began to drift off. Then Jack spoke.

"I have an offer for you, Walter Day. A thing I will do for you, if you wish. To make up for having dragged your father and mother into our dialogue. It was wrong of me to punish you for mentioning my mother when I had already mentioned yours."

"Why me? Why do you keep talking to me? What did you do to the man in the next cell?"

"He wasn't special."

"And I am?"

"I see potential."

"You don't know me."

"Do you think you're better than the man in the next cell?"

"No."

"Do you think you're worse?"

"No."

"Believe it or not, that makes you unique. You don't judge them, those many many people out there, all of them rooting about in their own messy fleshy lives, never looking up. You try to understand them."

"Maybe you should try, too, instead of killing them."

"I don't kill them. That is only your perception. I try to help them understand themselves, to appreciate what is always there beneath the surface. I transform them. They are caterpillars, unable to see beyond the leaves they eat and shit upon. There's an entire tree waiting for them if they would only look up and see it."

"You judge them, but praise me for not judging."

"Only because I used to be like you, Walter Day. I am fascinated to watch your journey unfold. I'd like to see if it turns out like mine did."

"So you'll take these shackles off?"

"No. I think you'll free yourself without any help from me. And soon, too. Maybe not soon enough. We'll see, I suppose. Maybe you'll continue to bleed and you'll die down here after all. But that's not for me to say."

"Then what? You said you would do something for me."

"If you ask me to, I will go to your home and I will remove

your wife and your unborn child from the sphere of your responsibility."

"What does that mean?"

"You know what that means. I can free you, Walter Day, in more ways than you intend. I can do that for you."

"Don't you touch her! You stay away from my Claire!"

"Claire? What a beautiful name. She sounds lovely already. All right. I promise I'll leave her for you. You have my word. But you didn't mention the baby, and that makes me think perhaps you'd like to take me up on at least part of my offer. You don't want to follow in the footsteps of your valet father, do you? Oops, I brought him up again. Do forgive me."

"Leave them alone."

"We'll see. We'll see. I'll give it some thought and determine what might be best for you. But for now, you just rest. You're going to need your strength if you've any intention of getting out of here."

"Undo the shackles."

"No. But I have every confidence in your abilities. After all, you have a lockpick. Good-bye, Walter Day."

The shadow melted away into the gloom of the tunnels. The lantern was extinguished, and Day could not be sure whether Jack had left or had simply stepped back against the wall and was even now watching him. Nor could he be sure whether Jack had meant to leave the hood off this time. But he did his best to enjoy every breath he took of fresh air.

And he wondered which would be his last.

50

The boy led them to a section of houses on Phoenix Street. He parked his bicycle next to a black wrought-iron fence, hopped off, and waited. A door behind him opened and a girl came outside and stood in her little garden behind the boy, watching their wagon pull up in the lane. All was quiet. The horse snorted. Inspector Blacker climbed out of the wagon first and looked up and down the street. Inspector Tiffany followed and stood beside him. They looked at the boy, who shrugged back at them. When Hammersmith, in his blue uniform, hopped down from the wagon, a door opened opposite the boy and his bike. An old lady ran out and waved them over. She pointed at the next house, with a red door and an untended garden in front.

"That's where they've been," she said. "I think one of them might still be there. The bald one."

Cinderhouse, thought Hammersmith. *The bald one is Cinderhouse.*

"I'm Inspector Blacker, mum. And this is Inspector Tiffany, and this is Sergeant Hammersmith."

"I apologize," the lady said. "It's been a strange day. I'm Mrs Pye. My husband was Giles Pye." As if they should know who he was.

"What happened here?" Blacker said. He had automatically stepped into the role of communicator. Tiffany stood to one side, nervously staring at the red door.

"They've had Mr Michael in there, doing terrible things to him."

"Who's Mr Michael, mum?"

"The man who owns that house, of course." She leaned in and whispered, "They cut his tongue right out of his mouth." She drew back again and squared her shoulders, having accomplished the most distasteful bit of business she had to conduct. "I've sent for a doctor. He should be along."

"I don't suppose he can talk to us?"

"Not without a tongue, he can't."

"Of course. Can he write?"

"I think he can. One of them went out and hasn't come back. I've been watching. That one's the Devil himself."

Hammersmith supposed she must mean the Harvest Man. They didn't have a good description of him.

"But I haven't seen the other one come out again. I was away from the window for a bit and I suppose he might have left the house then, but if he didn't then he's still in there."

Blacker took a step away from Mrs Pye and looked over at Tiffany. They both drew their revolvers. Hammersmith took his truncheon from his belt and looked at the way the sun shone on its burnished black surface. He liked the weight of it in his hand and felt every bit as confident holding it as he would have felt with a gun. Maybe more so.

At that moment, a second wagon turned the corner at the end of the lane and rolled up next to their own. Both of the inspectors turned their guns toward it, but the boy up top was no older than their own driver was, and four constables piled out of the back of the new wagon before it was completely stopped.

"Name's Bentley, sir," one of the constables said. "Kett sent us. A boy came to the Yard. Said there was fugitives hereabouts somewhere."

"You're just in time," Blacker said. "It's the red door."

"We're ready, sir."

"Then let's go."

Before he could finish his sentence, Tiffany was already pushing through the gate and across the garden to the door.

"It's not latched," he said.

All seven of the policemen funneled past the red door and into the house.

51

The coverlet was ruined.

Fiona stood in the upstairs hall and spread it out over her hands, let it drape down and pool on the floor. It was covered with blood and sticky mucus. She reeled it in and ran her fingers over the names that ran all around the outside of it, sewn in red thread and passed down from one generation to the next. The names of Claire Day's female ancestors.

Margaret, Jean, Janet, Mary, another Margaret . . .

All of them had spent hours in front of their hearths sewing their daughters' names into the fabric that had been passed down to them.

There was room at one corner for Claire's daughter. If she had a daughter.

But the coverlet was ruined.

The bell rang and Fiona gathered the coverlet to her breast and hurried to the entryway. She opened the door.

"Miss Fiona, got a package here for the mister."

The postman handed it over. A small brown-paper-wrapped parcel. She nodded her thanks and closed the door on him. A corner of the coverlet fell from her arms, and as she gathered it up, the parcel fell from her hand to the floor and the paper burst open. The box inside was cardboard, a bottom and a shallow lid, which came off and flopped onto the floorboards. Fiona set the coverlet on the floor—it wasn't going to get more ruined than it already was—and snatched up the various parts: the two halves of the box, a wad of cotton, a small off-white card, and a key.

The key was large and ornate, with a filigree handle and a long barrel and a bit of metal that stuck out from the side, like a trigger. She turned it over in her hands. It was heavy, weighted at the handle end, and there was a hole in the barrel that seemed to go straight through to the handle.

She turned the card over and read the inscription: *Let's speak soon. Yours—Adrian.*

She stuck the cotton back in the big half of the box and nested the key inside. She placed the card on top, closed the lid, and stuck the whole thing in her apron pocket. She wadded the ruined brown paper and set it aside on the little occasional table in the hall. She needed to rewrap it all before presenting it to Mr Day. She wouldn't want him to think she'd opened his mail on purpose.

Fiona glanced back at the door and then gathered the cloth to her breast again and hurried down the hall. Her father had given her busywork and she knew it. He'd given her the same task he'd set for Constable Winthrop. There was something more important she could do with her time while Claire struggled with labor.

She just hoped she could get the blood out.

52

A wagon sped past Jack and around the corner onto Phoenix Street. Jack slowed down and followed it cautiously. He hung back and watched as four coppers jumped out of the wagon and joined three others who were already standing in the lane. Jack sniffed and pressed a finger to his lips. All seven of the policemen rushed through the black gate, across the garden, and in through the red door. Jack wondered what his silly little fly had done to merit the attention of so many policemen.

He stepped into the middle of the street and walked to the wagons, which were resting next to each other, front to back and back to front, blocking the lane. The two young drivers were ignoring each other. One had a deck of cards and was shuffling them repeatedly. The *other was engrossed in a tabloid of some sort. Jack caught the attention of the boy with the cards.*

"What's happening in there?" He poked his thumb in the general direction of the red door.

"Caught some dangerous murderers in there," the boy said. "Bloody-eyed madmen they are, too. You'd do well to stand back, Doctor, and let 'em do their job."

Doctor? Jack looked down at the black leather bag he was holding and smiled.

"They sent for me," he said. "Someone's been hurt?"

"Yes, sir. They cut off somebody's face, cut out his eyes, cut off his fingers, even cut out his tongue."

Well, part of that was true, at least, Jack thought. Unless that silly fly had been very busy since Jack left the house.

"I'd better go take a look, then, hadn't I?"

"You be careful and stay well back, like I say. Let them boys do their work."

"I certainly will. Thank you for your help, son."

There was an old lady talking to a little girl and a boy with a bicycle. Jack walked past them without being noticed and walked right through the door and into the house he now thought of as his own.

53

The house was empty.

Tiffany dispatched two of the constables to check the bedrooms upstairs. The other two went into the parlor, and Hammersmith went with them. Tiffany and Blacker proceeded down the hallway to the kitchen.

There was an odor of rotting meat in the parlor. A single ray of sunlight beamed through the front window, but did little to dispel the gloom. A bee buzzed lazily through the room and back out.

A chair was tipped back next to the hearth. Bits of twine curled around its legs and arms and around the cushioned back. Hammersmith knelt beside it and saw dark flecks that he was certain were blood on the brocaded seat.

"Oh, God almighty," one of the constables said. Hammersmith looked up and followed the constable's gaze to the mantelpiece. Two objects were nailed to the wood just below eye-level.

"That explains the smell in here," Hammersmith said. "But why would there be meat on the mantel?"

"It ain't just meat, Sergeant. Look at it."

Hammersmith stood and took the three steps to the fireplace. He covered his nose with the back of his hand and leaned in for a better look. It took a moment for him to realize what the things were.

"Do you suppose they're human?" the other constable said.

"Surely they're lambs' tongues," Hammersmith said. But he wasn't at all sure.

He heard the other two constables come down the stairs and clomp past the parlor door on their way to the kitchen.

"Get some more light in here, would you?" he said to the constable who had found the tongues. "And get those down from there."

"I don't wanna touch them things."

"Find a pry bar. Put them in a basin. I'll send for Dr Kingsley. He might be able to verify what sort of animal they came from."

He started out of the room, then turned back.

"No, on second thought," he said, "leave them there. Kingsley's daughter can draw this all out for us. It might be important to know where everything is."

He saw both constables relax, clearly pleased that they wouldn't have to touch the bloody tongues.

Hammersmith went out of the parlor and turned left. The

two constables who had been upstairs passed him on their way back out. One tipped his hat to Hammersmith. They went back past the parlor and out through the front door. Hammersmith watched them go, then walked down the hall and found the two inspectors in the kitchen, huddled over something on a big table. They looked up when he entered the room.

"It looks like they've gone," Blacker said. "But they left a map. It might tell us where they went."

"But it's covered with markings," Tiffany said. "They could be anywhere."

Hammersmith looked around the room, at a piece of ham on the counter, shiny and hard, at breadcrumbs on the floor. He noticed a small stub of a pencil against the bottom edge of a cabinet leg. It looked like it had rolled off the table and across the room and lodged where it was unlikely to be noticed. The honeybee from the parlor careened past his nose and bumped into the edge of the back door, then corrected its flight path and disappeared outside.

"The back door's open," Hammersmith said. "Did you check the garden?"

"Of course," Tiffany said.

"Look at this," Blacker said. He led the way out the back door and past a flowering bush where more bees were hard at work tending to bright purple blossoms. There was a high wooden fence at the back of the garden, covered with thick leafy vines. Blacker pointed at the fence. "See that? See how the vines are torn away here? And here?" He pointed. "And up there?"

"Somebody climbed over that fence," Hammersmith said.

"And they were none too neat about it. Maybe saw us coming and left in a hurry."

"What's on the other side?"

"Don't know. Just sent two of these boys around the end of the street to find out."

A voice came through the fence: "Over here now, sir!"

"That was quick," Blacker said. "Anything to see?"

Hammersmith could hear the two constables tromping about in the garden on the other side.

"There's some kind of a little tree over here," the constable said. "Branches all broken away like somebody hung on 'em. And leaves all over the ground. Somebody tipped over a table here, too."

"Is anyone at home over there?"

"Yes, sir. Got the lady of the house here with me. She seen one."

"How long ago?"

"Not sure, sir. Should I go ask?"

"Just get her inside. We'll be over to talk to her."

Blacker turned to Hammersmith, excited. "We're right be-hind them. At least one of 'em went over the fence and through the house on the other side."

They went back into the kitchen, and Blacker grabbed Tiffany by the elbow. "We've got 'em," he said. "Come on!"

Tiffany turned back as they left the kitchen. "Sergeant, why don't you take the rest of these lads and go from door to door? Talk to everybody on this street and make sure the fugitives didn't come back round. They could be hiding somewhere along here, waiting for us to leave."

Hammersmith nodded, but once the two inspectors had left, he bent and picked up the pencil from the floor. He took it to the table and stared down at the map. Some of the markings there were in ink or wax crayon, but he saw the fainter trace of graphite here and there. In one place, a pencil had been pushed down against the parchment so hard that it had torn through. Hammersmith leaned forward and stared at the rough loop made by the end of a blunt pencil. Someone had circled a spot in Primrose Hill again and again.

And Hammersmith knew all at once who had drawn the circle on the map. Cinderhouse was not on Phoenix Street or even the next street over. He was on his way to 184 Regent's Park Road. He was on his way to Walter Day's house. Day wasn't at home and Hammersmith was sure he was in no danger. But Claire would be there and she would be alone with young Fiona Kingsley. There was a constable guarding the house, but Hammersmith didn't know who it was. He couldn't believe Sir Edward would post someone very good on guard duty. Not during a manhunt.

Hammersmith ran past the parlor, where two constables were busy trying to coax the two tongues into a dirty washbasin with the tips of their truncheons. A third man was there, his back to Hammersmith, apparently supervising the removal of the tongues. He wore a tall black hat and was holding a medical bag. Hammersmith briefly wondered why the doctor hadn't gone next door to take care of the injured homeowner, why he would override Hammersmith's own orders regarding the tongues, but he didn't stop to ask. He banged out through the front door and past the two wagons, the old lady, and the children. He grabbed the bicycle out of the hands of the boy who was still standing by the gate across the street.

"I'm sorry," he said, "but I need this. I'll get it back to you straightaway. Tell the inspectors to get someone to Walter Day's house in Primrose Hill. That's where one of the fugitives has gone. Tell them Sergeant Hammersmith is going there now and to meet me there."

And before the boy could answer or protest, Hammersmith leapt on his bike and pedaled away down the street.

"Well," Eunice Pye said to the children. "Rude."

54

Fiona rooted through Claire's sewing basket, looking for a spool of red thread to match the embroidered names on the coverlet. She had found a spool of white, which she set aside on the small table next to Claire's chair in the sitting room, but all the other spools were spread across the bottom of the basket underneath fabric remnants and thimbles and cards with needles poked through, and Fiona had to be careful not to stick herself while she looked. There was no rhyme or reason to the way that Claire had stuffed her things into the basket. Fiona needed the white thread in case she had to take apart a seam in order to get the blood out. She'd have to restitch it. And she needed a pair of scissors and the needles, of course. But it was dark down in the basket and Fiona was tempted to upend it onto the table. She could sift through everything on the table-top, in the bright sunlight streaming through the window, and then shove it all back in the basket. Claire would probably never even know. It was very clear that Claire didn't spend a lot of time mending things.

Fiona found the scissors just as Rupert Winthrop entered the room behind her. She turned around and saw him staring at the bloody coverlet on the table behind her.

"Took up some water and things," he said.

"Good."

"He didn't say much, the doctor didn't. Do you think she's all right?"

"Mrs Day, you mean?"

"Yes."

"My father's an excellent doctor. I have every confidence that she'll be just fine."

"I do hope so. That don't look good, though."

"The coverlet?"

"I mean, is that blood on it?"

"Yes."

"Is she supposed to bleed?"

"I think a little blood's okay." But she didn't feel at all certain, despite her father's assurances.

"Your dad's gonna take care of her?"

"There's nobody better."

"Wanted to help her somehow, but didn't want to intrude during this time, you know. Didn't know what to do."

"I'm sure she understands that."

"I feel useless just sitting there in the hall."

"Well, you've made us all feel safe and protected. So no time wasted."

"Good of you to say."

It *was* good of her to say. In fact, she had nearly forgotten he was in the house. She certainly didn't need him underfoot. She wanted to get the coverlet cleaned and hung up to dry as quickly as possible so she would be able to stitch Claire's baby's name in along the edge of it and present it to her as a gift. Claire would be so pleased.

"I put some more water on to boil," Rupert said. "And I've found all the basins there is in the house, as far as I can tell, miss. It's really not much. Is there anything I can help you do?"

Fiona looked down at the scissors in her hand and smiled. "As a matter of fact," she said, "would you be a dear and look through this basket? I need a spool of thread."

"There's one right there on the table."

"That's white thread, which I do need. But I also need red thread."

"Are you sure there's any in that basket?"

"Not at all. But there might be, and I'd like to find it if it's there."

"Well, I'll take a look."

"That would be wonderful."

He smiled. "Happy to do it, if it helps."

"It does. Now I can go clean this up before it sets."

"Will the blood come out?"

"I certainly hope so."

"Me, too."

Fiona picked up the spool of white thread and the coverlet, careful not to perforate it with the tip of the scissors, and went to the door. She peeked back over her shoulder just in time to see the constable pick up the basket and scatter its contents over the tabletop. She sighed and hurried away down the hall to the kitchen.

55

Jack heard someone rush past in the hallway behind him and turned around too late. All he saw was the blue-uniformed back of a policeman. Then the front door banged shut.

"What do we do with these when we get 'em off of here?" one of the constables said.

Jack contemplated the tongues, sagging from their iron nails, dried and no longer vital. He felt a lack of connection to them that surprised him. His trophies had always meant so much.

"Take them back to Scotland Yard," he said. "Leave them on the desk of Detective Inspector Walter Day. Do you know who that is?"

"Sure," the other constable said. "I know him. He'll know what to do with them?"

"Tell him they're a gift from a new friend."

The older of the two constables sniffed and rubbed his nose with his thumb. He squinted at Jack, trying to determine whether he was the butt of a joke, whether he ought to laugh.

"The inspector's probably not at his desk right now," the younger one said. "Out looking for the escaped prisoners, same as everybody else."

"Oh, I imagine he's busy escaping, too. He should be returning to the Yard soon, if he doesn't lose his leg."

"Lose his leg?"

"Well, it was dark and I'm not completely sure about the depth of that incision. Still, I'm reasonably confident he'll be back and in one piece. Please tender my apologies and tell him I hope these offerings will cement our friendship."

Jack turned and walked away, out of the parlor and out of the house. He heard the constables behind him yelling questions, but paid no attention to them. They were simpletons. He ran his fingers over the bloodred surface of Elizabeth's door one last time as he passed it. He knew he would not return, but felt little regret. He was done with this place.

There were two wagons in the lane and Jack lingered next to one of them, stroking the horse's nose, as the old woman who lived next door hurried past and into her own house, leaving her front door standing open.

"How much to take me away from here?" Jack said to the young boy who sat up top, reading a magazine and chewing on the butt of a cigarette.

"Working for the police, mister. This's their wagon. Can't go nowhere but where they tell me to go."

"I'll give you a quid."

The boy put down his magazine and squinted at Jack. He straightened the front of his jacket and tossed the cigarette butt into the street. "Where you wanna go, sir?"

"Just a moment, please."

Jack went around behind the wagon and walked over to the children standing against the short black fence along the opposite side of the street.

"You had a bicycle," *he said to the boy.* "Where did it go?"

"Some copper just stole it away from me."

"He did?"

"Just took it right out of me hands. Didn't ask or nuffin'."

"Oh, my. How dreadful."

"You don't know how much. That bicycle's dear. Can't afford a new one."

"I'm sure he'll give it back. He's a policeman, after all. What was his name?"

"Said it was Hammersmith. Like the place."

"You don't say."

"I do say! Never heard of anybody with that name before."

"I have. Earlier this very day. It's a small world, isn't it?"

"Looks big enough to me."

"Sergeant Hammersmith didn't happen to tell you where he was going, did he?"

The boy looked Jack up and down. "He said to tell it to the police, not to any doctors."

"Oh, but I'm a police doctor."

"That's different, then. He said he was going to an inspector's house. Walter somebody. Walter Dew, maybe."

"Could it have been Walter Day?"

"Yeah, that's the name. In Primrose Hill."

"Oh, my, but it is a very small world indeed. Thank you, young man."

"You're gonna get my bike back?"

"I doubt very much that I shall remember you by the end of the day. You should look after yourself and get your own bike back. How else will you learn self-reliance?"

Jack turned back to the wagon and climbed in. He patted the side of it with his palm and shouted up to the driver.

"We're going to Primrose Hill, young man."

"Where to in Primrose Hill?"

"Just get me to the area and I'll sort it out from there. Do hurry. I promised a friend I would look in on his wife."

56

Cinderhouse was careful about his approach. He did not go right up to the front door of the Day house. Instead, he left the road just after he crossed the bridge and traveled through the back gardens of the terrace houses connected to number 184. It was the same way he had left the house with the red door. When he had escaped that house, he'd been worried that Jack might be waiting outside for him. Here, he simply wanted the element of surprise. Day wasn't as tall as the bald man, but he looked stronger, and Cinderhouse didn't want to confront him head-on.

He had to climb a fence at the end of the row of homes, and when he fell down on the other side, his jaw bumped against his upper molars and the fresh wound in his mouth sent pain shooting up behind his eyes. He spit blood, wiped his lips on the sleeve of his jacket, and sat for a moment until the pain became bearable. Then he stood and straightened his collar and fixed his resolve. He needed to show Jack that he was capable, that he could follow through with a task. He needed Jack to respect him. And so he needed to kill Walter Day and his wife. It was the logical move to make.

He crept up to the back of number 184 and peered through the small window next to the door. There was a girl in the kitchen whom Cinderhouse took to be the housekeeper. She was filling a basin with water from a big pail. She struggled with the pail because it was heavy and she was quite petite, but she managed to get the water into the basin without spilling much. She added salt to the water and dunked a mass of fabric into the mixture.

Cinderhouse opened his lips and tried to lick them before remembering that his tongue now adorned the mantelpiece in Elizabeth's home. The girl in the kitchen before him was perhaps a trifle old for his tastes, but she was nearly young enough and she was pretty, and it had been so long for him. She had straw-colored hair and quick little hands, and he imagined sitting by the fire with her after a day at the shop. They wouldn't talk. He couldn't talk, not anymore. But she would perhaps mend a sock with her clever little hands and he would read the paper and they would be happy together.

He blinked away a tear and smiled. And, after a moment's further reflection, he turned the doorknob and entered the kitchen.

57

Fiona looked up when she heard the door open. The coverlet was soaking in a basin, and she hoped salt water would lift most of the worst of the stains. Her mind had already turned to her father and Claire upstairs, thinking about what they would need, and so she assumed that it was Constable Winthrop entering the kitchen with water, even though she knew that he was in the parlor rooting through Claire's sewing basket for a spool of red-colored thread.

Of course, it was not Rupert Winthrop at the door. The man who entered the kitchen was thin and bald and he was wearing a very nice suit. But his jaw was badly bruised, purple and green, and his lips were puffy, and his eyes were wide and staring. Fiona glanced at the card of sewing needles on the table in front of her, then she saw the scissors and she grabbed them, but the bald man was already moving across the kitchen. He took hold of her arm just above the elbow and snatched the scissors out of her hand. He dragged her to the pantry—only four or five steps, there was no time for her to break free of his grip—and he shoved her inside.

It all happened so quickly that Fiona was still stunned. Later, she thought of several things she might have done: stomped on the stranger's foot or clawed at his wide, madly rolling eyes, perhaps even slapped his tender bruised jaw or grabbed the scissors back from him. But she did none of these things in the moment.

As the pantry door closed on her, she did manage to scream: "Rupert!"

Then she was alone in the dark.

58

Cinderhouse heard a commotion down the hall, like someone dropping something. He kept the fist that held the scissors tight against the pantry door, holding it shut, and reached with his other hand for a low chair that was just within arm's reach. It had a basket-weave seat and an embroidered back, all bright yellow and shiny blue, and he tipped it up and shoved it under the pantry's doorknob.

Footsteps outside in the hallway, someone answering the girl's scream for help. Cinderhouse opened the scissors, looking over the blades with an experienced eye. They were very much like the scissors he was accustomed to using, nice and sharp, hardly used and never dulled.

A man in a constable's uniform, presumably Rupert, a policeman in another policeman's house, lurched through the kitchen door as Cinderhouse swept his right arm through the air in front of him, left to right, a magnificent gleaming arc. One of the scissors' twin blades sliced through the flesh of Rupert's throat and a gout of blood erupted across Cinderhouse's face and chest. It leapt from Rupert to him as if it had been waiting for him, longing for him. He smiled and bared his teeth and felt the warmth of the other man's blood on his lips.

Rupert clapped a hand against his throat and stopped its joyous rush. The blood bubbled out and over and through his fingers like a rill over its rocky bed. It flowed down the constable's arm, soaking his cuffs and shirtsleeves and jacket. His other arm hung down at his side, his fist clenched tight around some small thing.

But young Rupert was still able to talk. The scissor blade hadn't severed his vocal cords and he still had a tongue, lucky devil. And, as he talked, he continued to move forward, pushing Cinderhouse back against the long wooden table in the center of the room.

"Miss Fiona?"

The girl was banging on the pantry door, but the chair held. Rupert began to turn toward the noise, but his free arm was still held out at an angle, forcing Cinderhouse down and back, his spine bending at an uncomfortable angle against the table's edge. He fumbled for the scissors, but his hands were wet with blood, and he felt the blade, possibly the same blade that had snicker-snacked through Rupert's throat, slice into his right index finger. He couldn't see how deep the cut was, but he dropped the scissors on the table. He fumbled with them in the sticky pool already growing there and found the loop at the end of one blade. He stuck his first two fingers through the loop, ratcheted the blades apart, and drove one of them into Rupert's thigh.

Rupert didn't seem to notice. He continued through his turn and staggered toward the pantry. One arm still hung down at his side, the other bent up, his hand loose at his throat, his blood pumping sluggishly now, as if it had lost interest in the whole affair and was preparing for sleep. Rupert put one leg forward . . .

"Fiona?"

As if he had forgotten who Fiona was or why he should care.

He put out the other leg, that side of his trousers sopping with whatever blood had been left over for the lower half of his body, the cheap fabric there puckering and clammy. His foot hit the floor without the force of his body behind it and he stumbled and caught himself, one hand, the fist still bunched, against the pantry door.

The banging against the other side of the door stopped.

"Constable?" Her voice was muffled and distant.

"I'm . . . Fiona . . . I'll do that."

And Rupert fell forward toward the door and bounced off of it, reeled away into the kitchen. Cinderhouse, free from the table, leapt upon the constable's back and drove him to the floor and stabbed him in the back. And stabbed him again and again, and his teeth gnashed and ground against one another, and he brought the scissors down again and through the thin fabric of the constable's uniform.

And again.

Rupert stopped moving, stopped trying to crawl across the slimy red kitchen floor with Cinderhouse on his back. His hands scrabbled one last time in the syrupy blood, and then he let go of his last breath. Cinderhouse felt it go, felt himself sink down against Rupert's rib cage. Rupert's fist opened up and a spool of red thread rolled away from him, red against red, leaving a lopsided trail until it bumped up against a table leg and stopped.

The banging on the other side of the pantry door started up again, but Cinderhouse ignored the noise. He stood and set the blood-slick scissors on the tabletop. He listened for any other sound in the house, for anyone else who might be coming to see what had happened. He heard a woman scream, once, and felt a moment of blind panic, thinking that Jack had somehow followed him here, but the scream had sounded far off, and no one was approaching down the hall beyond the kitchen. He and the girl and the body of the policeman seemed to be alone.

He examined his finger where it was cut. The two edges of skin and flesh gaped apart, smooth and even down the middle of the finger, all the way to the first knuckle. He could see blood welling up and out, but couldn't tell how bad it was. The finger was already covered with blood, dripping with it, some his, some Rupert's.

He pulled the sopping white coverlet out of the basin of water on the table and wrapped it around his hand and gasped. He had forgotten that the little bitch was soaking the thing in salt water! He sat heavily on the chair against the pantry door and felt it creak beneath him. Salt water in the basin. A trap for him. She was a crafty girl, and comely. A valuable prize to be had. After he had finished his business.

"What did you do?" Her voice soft and frightened behind the door. "Where's Constable Winthrop?"

Cinderhouse pursed his lips and looked around the kitchen. Perhaps there was notepaper and a pencil somewhere in a drawer or a cabinet. But even if he found it, even if he wrote a note to the little girl and pushed it under the door to her, she wouldn't be able to read it in the dark. Still, he stood and paced about, twisting the balls of his feet so as not to slip when he walked through the smeared and pooling blood. There was no notepaper, but he did find a key on a shelf in the cupboard closest to the kitchen window. It was tucked up against the side and he took it out and looked it over. He walked back to the pantry door and tried the key in the keyhole under the knob. It was a perfect fit.

"Rupert! Rupert!"

I should be very surprised if he answered you, Cinderhouse thought. He chuckled, a rasping sound in the back of his throat, and wished he could share this joke with his new girl.

"You've made a mistake, sir! This is the house of Detective Inspector Walter Day. Whatever you're doing here, this is the wrong house. He will find you and arrest you."

Cinderhouse nodded at the closed door and smiled again. It wasn't the wrong house at all. He turned the key and heard a confident snick as the lock slid into place.

"No! You can't do this!" And then louder: "Father! Father!"

He pulled the chair out from under the knob. *Father? Who might that be? Walter Day?*

He picked up the spool of thread and grabbed the card of needles from the table and carried the chair over to the body on the floor. He sat down again, poked at the body with the toe of his boot. It was as dead as a person could get. He used his foot to roll the constable over. Rupert's eyes were open, staring blankly at the ceiling.

Mustn't have that.

Cinderhouse slipped off the chair onto his knees. There was no point in worrying about the blood. He was covered with it, head to feet; it was dripping from his chin whiskers. He broke off a length of bloody red thread with his teeth, wet the end of it with his lips, and poked it through the eye of a needle. He tied a knot in the thread's hanging end, then bent over the body and stuck the needle through Rupert's left eyelid. He pulled it through and around and hummed to himself as he began the work of quieting Rupert's accusing eyes for good and all.

59

"I t's not time to rest," Kingsley said. "Push again."

"I can't," Claire said. "I won't. I'm tired."

"Well, you may be tired, but nature hasn't given you a choice. You'll push or you'll die."

"Just take it out."

"If I do, you'll surely die."

"Please stop saying that I'll die."

"I'm sorry. It's my hope that I might motivate you to avoid death."

"Well, you're scaring me."

"Yes."

"No more."

"Once more."

"Only once?"

"I think once might be enough. I know you can do it. Just one more time."

She didn't answer. Instead, she leaned forward, her hands tight around the bedposts behind her, and she screamed and she bore down.

Kingsley held his breath as he saw the furry crown come into view. He did not consider childbirth to be a miracle. It was a natural animal occurrence, and he would prefer that a midwife be in attendance.

Where was Fiona? He had heard a racket downstairs and assumed that the clumsy constable—what was his name?—was tripping over himself in an effort to collect basins and heat water at the fireplace. He hoped the boy hadn't burned himself.

The baby emerged amid a slurry of fluid and Kingsley caught it, felt her body pushing it toward him. He snipped the cord and expertly tied off the end. He turned with the infant girl in his hands, but there was no towel ready, no basin of fresh water, nobody to help.

Fiona should have stopped in by now to check on Claire.

Claire slumped, exhausted, back against the bed, and Kingsley used a face flannel from the washbasin on the table to wipe the baby down as well as he could and warm her, and she made the same tentative movements that he had seen from dozens of healthy newborns. She gurgled and tested her new voice, and he came around the side of the bed and rested her in her mother's arms. Claire managed a weak smile and touched the baby's face with her fingertip.

Kingsley went to the bedroom door and opened it, poked his head out hoping to see Fiona, but the hall was dark and empty. He went to the top of the stairs and heard the doorbell ring below him just as Claire called out to him from the bedroom.

"Doctor! I think something's wrong."

60

Jack asked the driver to stop as soon as they reached Primrose Hill. He got out and strolled away from the two-wheeler with no destination in mind and a clear sense of anticipation. Fate would provide. Fate and the city.

And so, when he turned the corner, he was not surprised to see a man standing at a door at the end of the street ahead. The man was very tall and very thin and, Jack thought, quite beautiful. But he was dressed in a shabby blue uniform that appeared to have dirt pressed into its many creases. The jacket might have been taken from a corpse. Lying on the footpath behind the man was a boy's bicycle, cast hastily aside. This could be no one but Sergeant Hammersmith.

Hammersmith was pounding on the door of the last house and took no notice as Jack passed behind him in the lane.

"Claire!" Hammersmith said to the door. "Fiona! Someone answer!" No one did, and Hammersmith began to frantically pull the bell cord.

Jack turned the corner and passed out of sight of the agitated policeman. There was a low fence behind the house, just above waist level, and Jack hopped it, landing neatly on the other side of a nettle bush. The instruments in his medical bag clattered against one another, but the clasp held tight.

Jack strolled across the garden, staying as close as possible to the house's rear wall without snagging his trousers on the nettles, and peered around the edge of an open door. He was looking into a kitchen, which seemed to have been decorated in the fashion of an abattoir. The floor was pooled with congealing blood, and a fine red spray had coated most of the vertical surfaces that Jack could see. A pair of legs belonging to a prostrate man extended out of sight behind a long wooden table that was too large for the room. There was another door at the far side of the room, and another man was passing through that door now, walking away from Jack down a hallway. Even from behind, Jack had no trouble recognizing his foolish little fly. He shook his head and clucked his tongue and carefully sidled into the room.

Cinderhouse did not hear him or turn around. The fly was hurrying toward the front door, directly in front of him along the hallway. The doorbell was pealing in the most annoying way, and Jack could faintly hear Hammersmith's voice on the other side of the house, still calling out women's names.

It occurred to him that he might very well have saved Walter Day from a bit of trouble by detaining him belowground on this fine spring afternoon.

Jack stepped over the largest plash of blood and around to the other side of the table. He looked down at the dead man who had decorated the room with his blood. The man didn't look familiar. He was young, but it was difficult to tell more than that because his throat had been torn open and his mouth and eyes stitched shut. Jack frowned at the dead man. He had been transformed, that was certain. But there was no artistry in this. It was savagery for the sake of savagery. A waste of sticky blood.

A thumping noise distracted Jack and he turned toward yet another door, next to the one leading out into the hall. This second door, which Jack presumed separated the pantry from the rest of the kitchen, was closed, and someone was pounding on it as if in response to Sergeant Hammersmith's attack on the front door. Jack stepped closer to the closed door.

"Hello?"

"Hello?" said a girl on the other side of the door. "Is someone there?"

Oh, little fly, *Jack thought,* I told you to leave the children alone.

"Your back door was open," he said. "There's a terrible mess out here. What's happened?"

"Be careful. There's a very dangerous man out there."

"Oh, I'm sure you're right."

"He locked the door. Can you open it?"

Jack shrugged and glanced around for a key, but he didn't care very much whether the girl stayed in the pantry.

"I don't see a key," he said.

He set his black leather bag down in a relatively clean space on the table and opened it. He leaned to one side and looked down the hallway. The tailor was still there, hesitating, his hand on the latch, while Hammersmith battered at the other side of the front door.

KINGSLEY HAD ALREADY STARTED to turn back toward the bedroom when he saw a bald man appear at the bottom of the stairs, facing the door. The man was covered in blood and he was twitching. Kingsley felt torn for a moment, then hurried back to the room. Claire was clutching the bedsheets with one hand, her face pale, her baby squirming in the crook of her other elbow.

"Claire," he said, "what you undoubtedly feel is the placenta coming. It will not be difficult to deliver."

"It feels just like before. Not easy at all."

Kingsley found a scalpel in his bag. He didn't want to tell Claire that there was an intruder in the house. She might panic. And he couldn't move her. She needed to remain calm.

"You'll be fine for a moment, Claire. Just breathe slowly and evenly and I'll be right back."

"Don't leave me!"

He went to the bedroom door, swallowed hard, and ran to the staircase. Fiona was somewhere below and the stranger had an awful lot of blood on his suit.

Behind him, the baby began to cry.

. . .

"Who are you?" the girl in the pantry said. "I don't recognize your voice."

"I'm . . ." Jack hesitated, then glanced at the black bag on the table. "I'm a doctor."

"Can you see . . . Is there a constable out there somewhere?"

"Oh, I see him."

Jack looked through the bag and found what he was looking for. He removed a flannel the size of a handkerchief and a small glass vial. He unstoppered the vial and poured a bit of the colorless liquid onto the cloth, careful to keep it far away from his face. The fumes were powerful. He set the vial back on the table and stepped out of the kitchen just as someone ran down the stairs ahead of him at the far end of the hall.

"Who are you?" Kingsley said.

But he didn't wait for an answer. He was afraid he might lose his nerve if he hesitated, so he barreled straight at the bloody bald man and knocked him back against the wall next to the front door.

"Don't move," he said. Then: "Fiona!"

He looked around wildly, hoping he would not see her body on the floor, shouting as loud as he could, and hoping she was able to respond.

"Fiona, are you all right?"

He had the scalpel in his hand, kept it near the bald man's throat while he reached over with his free hand and unlatched the door. Sergeant Hammersmith immediately burst into the room, but stopped cold when he saw the bald man, who glared at Hammersmith with fear and rage in his eyes.

"Hongermiff!" the bald man said. "Gie!"

The bald man wrenched himself away from Kingsley as Hammersmith lunged toward them. Too late, Kingsley realized the stranger was holding a pair of sewing scissors. Kingsley brought the scalpel down, trying to stop the bald man's forward motion or even cut the scissors out of his hand. He sliced through the tendons of the man's arm as it swept around, and the scissors buried themselves in Hammersmith's chest.

All three men stopped moving and stared at the handles of the scissors, miraculously stuck to the front of Hammersmith's shirt, a black enameled double loop magnetized to his body. Then a red stain crept outward from a buttonhole and a thin tributary made its way down the shirt, toward Hammersmith's belly. The sergeant looked up at Kingsley with a reverential expression. He opened his mouth and a bubble of blood burst against his lips.

Hammersmith fell to his knees and toppled backward against the doorjamb.

Upstairs, Claire screamed and broke the silence.

Dr Kingsley realized that someone was standing behind him and began to turn just as a pair of rough hands grabbed him and stuck a cloth over his mouth and nose. There was a sharp odor and then the room was washed away and he felt himself falling as if he were watching someone else at a great distance.

He thought perhaps he heard Claire scream again, but she was also far away and he couldn't move and he floated off into a dark and dreamless ocean.

61

⚜

Cinderhouse was frozen to the spot. Jack had come for him. The spider had found his fly. Had he followed Cinderhouse? Had he seen everything? Did he know what his fly was thinking, had been thinking? Or was he genuinely a god, anywhere and everywhere according to His whims?

The front door was still partially open, and Jack nudged Hammersmith's body aside with the toe of his shoe so that he could get the door closed. He was still holding the handkerchief and Cinderhouse could smell ether on it, even from several feet away. In Jack's other hand, he held his black medical bag by its handle.

The older man was crumpled against the bottom of the staircase, breathing strong and steady, in a deep drug-induced sleep.

Upstairs, a woman moaned, but nobody moved to investigate the noise.

When the door was closed and Jack had turned silently toward him, Cinderhouse heard a faint plopping sound, something splashing nearby. He looked down and realized his arm was bleeding. Blood ran swiftly down and around his knuckles and leapt free of him to the floor, where a dark puddle was forming. The edges of the gash were separated and rubbery, and Cinderhouse thought he could see bone down there at the bottom of that elastic red canyon. As he stared at his arm, it suddenly began to hurt. It hurt very much.

"I told you no more children," Jack said.

"Ngo," Cinderhouse said. *No.* Without a tongue, his *n* sounds came out as *g* sounds. But even those were strange and different, like a choking bird. "Ngo, I wag't gong-ga . . ." *No, I wasn't going to . . .*

"Don't be afraid." Jack stepped over Hammersmith's legs and around the dozing body of the older man and took Cinderhouse by the arm, just above his elbow. Panicked, Cinderhouse batted at him with his other hand, but the muscle wasn't responsive and his hand flopped about, flicking blood against the walls. Jack smiled, but angled backward so as to avoid the worst of the blood spatter.

"Be calm," Jack said. "You've disobeyed me and you must be punished again. But you did me a great service in freeing me and I do not forget. I am fully aware of what I owe you."

He smiled again and Cinderhouse looked at his eyes, saw

affection and gentleness, and he relaxed, began to refocus his attention on his injured arm.

"Come," Jack said. "Let's take a look at that. You're bleeding a great deal."

There was now a hungry glint in Jack's eye. He turned Cinderhouse around and guided him toward the parlor on the other side of the hall. Cinderhouse was amazed by the strength in Jack's fingers. He hadn't moved in more than a year. How strong must he have been before his imprisonment?

He walked ahead of Jack into the front room, with its well-used but comfortable-looking chesterfield, the fireplace, and the mismatched chairs. He felt a sharp pain at the back of his neck, like a bee sting, and tried to lift his hand to touch his neck, but his hand didn't respond. Neither of his arms would move. His knees buckled under him and he fell straight down, collapsing in on himself. He would have hit his face on the floor if Jack hadn't caught him.

"A scalpel between the vertebrae," Jack said. "I've only done that once before, so I'm quite excited to see how well it works for you." He rolled Cinderhouse over and arranged his arms and legs so that the bald man was lying flat on his back with his limbs spread slightly away from his body. "Can you move at all?"

Cinderhouse tried to shake his head, but could not.

"I think that means no," Jack said. "Can you still feel anything?"

He poked Cinderhouse in the cheek with the tip of his scalpel. The bald man shouted and Jack clamped a hand over his mouth.

"Oh, good," Jack said. "It's a delicate thing, cutting off your body from your head and yet allowing the sensation to remain. I'm afraid I didn't do it quite right the last time, but I'm delighted that today's operation seems to be a complete success. Hold still."

Jack chuckled at his own joke. He sat on Cinderhouse's chest and used his free hand, the one holding the scalpel, to cut away the sleeve of the bald man's jacket. Really it was Elizabeth's jacket, but to the victor go the spoils. Cinderhouse rolled his eyes to the side and watched Jack work the sleeve down his arm and off. Jack took his hand away, but before Cinderhouse could make a sound, the jacket sleeve was in his mouth. Jack lifted the bald man's head and tied the ends of the sleeve together at the back of his neck. Jack pulled at the makeshift gag, testing it.

"There," he said. "Nice and tight. Can you talk?"

Cinderhouse shouted, but the sound was muffled and remote.

"I think that will do. Now, I don't have a lot of time. There's a woman upstairs who is screaming for me. But I will try to honor you as well as I'm able."

Cinderhouse lay helpless while Jack undressed him. Saucy Jack was quick and efficient. Cinderhouse was completely nude in no time at all.

Jack knelt beside him and smoothed the worried furrows from Cinderhouse's forehead. He bent and kissed Cinderhouse lightly on the mouth, pulled back, and smiled. His expression was loving and gentle, a father tucking his son in at bedtime. Cinderhouse did his best to smile back, but the gag was in the way.

Then Jack held up the scalpel, regarded it curiously in the half-light from the parlor window, and went to work.

Cinderhouse felt nothing until the scalpel began to cut into his face.

62

Walter heard the soft *snick* of the shackle's lock and then his arm swung free and the heavy chain dropped to the ground. He held his breath, listened, and watched the darkness, waiting to see if Jack was still nearby, if he would hear and return.

After a long moment, he got to work on the shackle around his other wrist. It took only seconds. A little freedom of movement made all the difference. The chains fell away and he slumped back against the rocky wall behind him. He waited until he had caught his breath again, then bent to work on the restraints at his ankles. When he was completely free, he took a step forward.

And fell.

He rolled over and leaned forward, massaged the circulation back into his legs. His left trouser leg was damp and sticky and the feeling did not return to that leg. His right leg seemed much better, although it was painful to the touch.

He pulled himself to the opening at the front of his cell. He felt his way to the next cell and ran his hands along the wall until he found a wooden cube, a box that had been upended to make a table. He eased himself up and rested against it. The lantern Jack had used was still there, along with a box of tapers. When the lamp was lit, he held it up and looked around the tiny space. Adrian March hung from the wall above a gleaming black puddle in the dirt. The odor in the enclosed space was overwhelmingly foul. There was a long branding iron propped against the box, shiny and never used. Day used it as a cane, limped across to March and set the lantern down on the ground. He put his ear to March's mouth and heard the faint rasp of breath.

His lockpick was bent and so it took him a little longer to get March out of his chains. He eased March down to the ground and left him there.

He picked up the lantern and leaned on his iron, went out of March's cell and past his own into the cell on the other side. A man—or rather most of a man—hung there, tangled in his chains as if he had struggled with them. March had called him Griffin, but his name hardly mattered anymore.

Day looked around the cell. There was another box here, like the one in March's cell. On top of the box, Day saw his own jacket, his flask, and his handcuffs. He picked them up and put them away in his jacket pocket, then put the jacket on. He looked for his revolver, but it wasn't there. Which meant that Jack was armed.

Day took a deep breath and went to the back wall of the cell and freed Griffin's corpse from the chains. He was tired, and it took a great deal of effort to unwrap the heavy links from Griffin's tattered flesh. He mistook a loop of intestines for a chain and, when he realized what he was holding, he panicked and began to sob.

When the body was finally extricated from its fetters, Day laid it down against the wall. He closed Griffin's wide staring eyes and limped away, left it there in the dark. He would send people for it. He could barely walk, and March would need help. The living came first.

He sat on the box in March's cell and drained his flask, felt the honey-colored liquid warm him from his chest out in a radiant spreading wave. When the flask was empty, he corked it and put it away. He used the branding iron and stood as well as he was able, went to March, and woke the elder inspector.

March was weak, but he could stand. The two of them leaned on each other and made their way out through the tunnel. They passed the ancient ruined city and the underground wilderness where few humans had ever set foot. They saw a pack of wild dogs from a distance, but the dogs were chasing a deer that bounded through the darkness and they showed no interest in the two men.

At last they found a ladder sunk into the wall. They pushed and pulled each other up the ancient wooden rungs and shoved against the ceiling at the top. They came up through a trapdoor in the floor of a small room that was filled with religious artifacts. They crossed the room slowly and quietly, picked a lock on a door, and stepped outside into the waning sun.

They were in yet another churchyard and, far across the grass, under the trees, they saw a lane where people walked and carriages rolled past. Day drew the handcuffs from his pocket and turned and snapped them shut around Adrian March's wrists.

"I told you I would place you under arrest when we were free," he said.

"You are as good as your word. And I don't have the strength to fight you, Walter."

The sound of March's voice sickened Day. He didn't want to talk to his mentor. He wanted to make sure his wife was all right. He wanted to collapse into bed and hold her. But he knew that once he left Adrian March in a cell, he would never go back to see him. And there were things he needed to know.

"Tell me who the others are. Tell me where to find the rest of your Karstphanomen."

"So you can arrest them, too?"

"Yes."

"I won't do that."

"No matter. I'll find them."

"I believe you might. But I won't help you do it."

Day nodded and held March's arm above the elbow, and together they staggered across the churchyard.

Day kept his eyes wide open and focused on that distant thoroughfare. He prayed that it wasn't a dream or a mirage.

63

Claire shut her eyes tight and pushed. She wanted Dr Kingsley to come back, to come and take her new baby away from her so that she could concentrate properly on whatever was happening now. She was afraid that if she pushed too hard she might let the baby fall from the crook of her arm, that her daughter would roll off the bed and be injured.

She had given birth already. Why was it happening again? Why hadn't it stopped? She was helpless. She wanted to rest and her body wasn't allowing it.

Above the sound of her own hard breathing, she heard footsteps on the stairs. Someone moved past the foot of the bed, and then the light from the bedroom window was blocked.

"I heard noises," Claire said. "A lot of them. From down-stairs. What's happening?"

"Nothing that need concern you, Claire."

It was not Dr Kingsley's voice.

She opened her eyes and saw the dark shape of a man silhou-etted against the window. He had long wavy hair, and the light haloed around him, making it seem as if he were glowing. She shut her eyes again.

"You're not Dr Kingsley! Get out! Leave at once!"

She wrapped her arm around her crying daughter and used her free hand to rearrange the sheets on the bed, trying to cover herself, but the man chuckled. It was a warm sound, sympa-thetic and caring.

"Your baby is perfect," he said. "What a transformation you have wrought."

"Leave this room."

"Dr Kingsley is very tired and I'm afraid he's fallen asleep. But I'm . . . Well, Claire, you could say I'm a good friend of your husband's. Walter Day and I were just talking a short while ago, and he asked me to stop and look in on you."

"Walter's all right?"

"I should imagine he's on his way here by now."

"You're a doctor?"

"I must be. Else why would I be carrying this black bag?" He looked down at her diary on the bedside table. "Is this yours? How delicious."

He flipped it open and riffled through it from back to front. He stopped at the first page that wasn't blank.

"It hurts," Claire said.

"It's a poem."

"Why does it hurt when the baby's already come?"

"May I read this? Do you mind?"

"Please help."

He began to read out loud, and Claire was quiet. The urge to push subsided for a moment and the baby stopped crying. The new doctor's voice was deep and pleasant as he read:

"Baby hears a sound at night:
A silent footstep in the hall.
Something moves, but nothing's there.
It's just a shadow on the wall.

Baby pulls her blanket tight
And she reaches for her doll.
''Tisn't very nice to stare,'
Remarks the shadow on the wall.

Shadow's voice is soft and slight,
But evil lurks where shadows fall.
Listen to it if you dare,
To that dark shadow on the wall.

Baby says, 'I think you're right,
But, as you see, I'm awfully small.
Just now you gave me quite a scare,
You wicked shadow on the wall.'

Shadow moves, that evil sprite.
It starts to creep; it starts to crawl.
It stops to perch upon a chair.
It waits, that shadow on the wall.

Shadow grows to its full height.
It's ample, dark, and terribly tall.
Oh, Baby, Baby, please beware
Of that black shadow on the wall!

Baby says, 'I'll make a light
And then you won't exist at all.
You'll disappear into the air,
You silly shadow on the wall.'

Candles fill the room with light
For brightness is the shadow's pall.
Baby sleeps without a care.
There are no shadows on the wall."

When he had finished, he closed the covers of the diary and held it clasped in his hands.

"I quite like it," he said. "It appears you were expecting me, after all. May I keep this?"

"Keep it?"

"Consider it your gift to me. You ought to give me something for the occasion, don't you think?"

Claire felt a new wave of pain ripple out from her abdomen. "I don't . . . Can't you help me? Tell me what's happening?"

"You haven't finished what's begun, Mrs Day. Say please."

"Please."

"You had only to ask properly."

She felt the weight of her daughter lifted from her and she opened her eyes again, too late to see the new doctor as he passed beyond her sight near the foot of the bed.

"You know," he said, "this little one and I have something in common." There was a gentle singsong quality to his voice, perhaps left over from reading the nursery rhyme. "We share a birthday. Did you know that? Although in my case, I suppose you'd call it a *re*birthday."

"My baby . . ."

"She'll be fine here with me," he said. "Don't you worry about her. You've got quite enough to do right now."

"Who are you? I don't know your name."

"My special friends call me Jack. And I think we're going to be very special friends indeed."

"Please tell me what's happening," she said again.

"You're having another baby. Twins."

"No. That's not possible. I already had my baby."

"Softly now. Stop your worries. Jack is here."

"Jack?"

"You have given me so many lovely gifts today. A poem to treasure for always and secrets still to read. And you have given me the best thing of all. A party and guests to celebrate with. I have never had a special birthday friend, and now I have two.

Isn't that marvelous? We shall be close, your babies and I, and I think we shall have a party every year on this day."

"Nnnggg!" Claire bore down. She couldn't stop what was happening, couldn't listen anymore to the strange doctor. She couldn't make sense of his words, and so she let him disappear back into the darkness that fuzzed the edges of her vision.

"Yes," said the shadow on the wall. "By all means, let us welcome our final guest."

64

Fiona had stopped banging on the pantry door quite some time ago. She'd heard a struggle happening in the kitchen, just outside her door, then the strange doctor had wandered through. There had come the sound of yet another struggle from somewhere else in the house, but nothing since. Everything was quiet except for an occasional creaking floorboard upstairs.

She felt around on the shelves in the pantry and eventually found a pair of tea candles. She lit them and used the light to look for something to help her get the door open, but there was nothing she thought might be useful.

She turned around, sat down facing the door, and resigned herself to a long wait. At least, she thought, she wouldn't starve to death in the pantry. She folded her hands in her lap and was surprised to feel the shape of a small box in her apron pocket. She drew it out and blinked at it.

The package that had come in the post for Inspector Day. The giant key. In all the excitement she had forgotten to rewrap it.

She opened the box again and took out the key. It was worth a shot. She stood and went to the door and, already grimacing in anticipation of disappointment, she tried to put it in the lock. Of course it was much too large to fit, and she let out a big sigh. She hadn't even realized she was holding her breath.

She looked the key over, not because it was particularly interesting, but it was something to do, a new thing to look at. There was a hole in the end of the key and she put her eye to it, but in the flickering candlelight she couldn't see down the barrel. It had a small curved protuberance near the intricately looped handle. She held the key this way and that and frowned at it. It actually looked a bit like a pistol. She pointed it at the lock on the pantry door and said "bang" under her breath and pulled on the little trigger-thing below the handle.

The explosion was deafening in the confines of the small room, and the key flipped up and back and hit her in the chin. She dropped it to the floor and screamed.

HAMMERSMITH HEARD AN EXPLOSION somewhere in the house and he struggled to open his eyes. Light streamed over him from somewhere nearby and the backs of his eyelids were red. His chest hurt more than anything had ever hurt before.

"Shh." The voice was unfamiliar, deep and gentle. "Lie still. It's not your time to change yet. That stupid buzzing fly. He's missed your heart completely. But he has nicked one of your lungs."

"Can't . . ."

"I know. You can barely breathe, much less talk. So be quiet and let me finish this. A mutual friend would not like you to leave him just yet."

Hammersmith felt something piercing him, pulling on him. Whoever was talking to him was also sewing his wound. No, sewing something beyond his wound, something inside him.

"Don't . . ."

Hammersmith's mouth was forced open and salty fingers clamped onto his tongue. "I said to be quiet." This time the voice was stern and there was something dry beneath it, like metal. "Hush now, or I'll take this from you. It's been a very long day and I'm in no mood."

Hammersmith tried to breathe in, tried to maneuver himself upright, but the effort was too much for him to bear, and he felt the world recede.

"That's better," the voice said.

Hammersmith passed out again.

THE PANTRY WAS FULL of smoke. Fiona coughed and waved her hand in front of her face. Then she noticed the door. The entire doorknob plate hung loose, the knob was on the floor, and a crack of light showed between the jamb and the door. She grabbed up the tiny gun and pushed against the door and ran out into the kitchen.

The floor was a swamp of blood and gore, and Constable Rupert Winthrop was directly in front of the pantry, part of the way under the table. Fiona gasped and put her hand up to her mouth. She felt her gorge rise and swallowed hard against it, forcing it back down. She had seen many corpses while assisting her father, but never the body of someone she knew. Always before she had approached bodies as artistic things, tragic forms to capture in charcoal. This one had a name. This one had been sweet and stupid and caring.

When she had recovered, she pulled up the end of her apron and wiped her mouth. She did not look at the mutilated body of poor Rupert Winthrop again. She went to the kitchen door and out, the key gun held straight out from her body, her finger on the mini-trigger.

Far down the hall, just inside the entryway, someone knelt over the body of a man. She raised her strange pistol.

"Get away from him!"

The man kneeling over the body on the floor stood and picked up a black bag and walked to the door. He didn't turn toward her when he spoke.

"There is still time," he said. "You may save him yet, if you want to."

"Stop!" Fiona pulled the trigger, but nothing happened. She pulled it again. *Click.* She realized too late that the gun was too small to hold more than a single bullet, and she had used that bullet to escape the pantry.

The man with the black bag was already out the door. When he reached Regent's Park Road, he turned and passed out of sight. Fiona dropped the jailer's gun at her feet and ran down the hall. She slowed and looked in through the parlor door as she passed that room. What she saw would come back to her in her dreams for the rest of her life, but she looked away and kept moving. Her father was stretched out at the bottom of the stairs. A few feet away from him, blocking the open front door, Sergeant Nevil Hammersmith lay in a pool of blood. He looked dead.

She checked on her father first. His pulse was strong and he was breathing evenly, but she couldn't wake him. She left him there and went to Hammersmith, knelt down beside him. His pulse was faint, but regular. His shirt was torn open and a wound in his chest leaked a steady trickle of blood, down under his left armpit and into the spreading pool beneath him. A spool of red thread and a card of needles that she recognized from Claire's sewing basket rested on the floor next to Hammersmith's body, and she knew what the stranger had meant when he told her that she could save him.

One of the needles was already threaded, as if she had interrupted the stranger in his work. She picked it up and burst into tears. She recovered quickly and wiped her eyes on her sleeve and began to sew the man she loved back together.

65

Inspector Michael Blacker was the first through the door, and Inspector James Tiffany was right behind him. Both of them had their revolvers out, at the ready. The front door stood open and there was a girl passed out across the threshold, cradling Sergeant Hammersmith's head in her lap. Hammersmith was covered in blood. Blacker recognized the girl as Dr Kingsley's daughter. She helped sometimes, sketching out crime scenes. He couldn't remember her name. Beyond Hammersmith's outstretched feet, they could see Dr Kingsley himself, lying with one foot on the bottom step of the staircase. His chest was moving gently up and down.

"Good Lord," Tiffany said.

"What do you suppose happened here?"

"As long as nothing else happens . . ."

They stepped carefully past the girl and Hammersmith, both of the inspectors alert for any sound in the house. Blacker checked on Kingsley and his daughter, then moved them into more comfortable positions. Tiffany bent over Hammersmith and felt for a pulse.

"He's alive," he said. "Do you believe that?"

Blacker shook his head. "I really don't," he said. Hammersmith's shirt was torn open and his chest was a railroad switchyard of red and black stitches.

Constable Jones followed them through the door. Inspector Day was behind them, but he was barely upright. Sir Edward had sent him to hospital, but Day had ignored his orders. Neither Blacker nor Tiffany could blame him. They had only asked that he stay well back until they could look through his house to make sure it was safe.

Day stopped and bent unsteadily over Fiona, filled with guilt and shame and fear for the girl. What had she seen?

Tiffany waved Jones past them down the hall to the kitchen. Blacker started up the stairs, but turned and hurried back down when he heard Jones gagging. He and Tiffany came up behind Jones and looked into the parlor.

The man on the floor was spread-eagle, a horizontal Vitruvian Man. He was bald and naked, and his torso had been cut straight up the middle, the flaps of skin and slabs of muscle folded to either side. His rib cage was broken, the bones pointed up at the ceiling. His major internal organs had been removed, but were still attached, their veins and arteries spun like fishing line to various points around the body. The intestines had also been removed and had been spooled out to the farthest corner of the room, then arranged along the baseboards like an elaborate red and grey glistening picture frame, made to show off the artistry of the killer. The bald man's hands had been cut off and lay several inches away from the stumps of his wrists, as if they had flown off his arms in surprise. The same had been done to his feet. His eyes had been removed and laid on his cheeks, each of them looking away in a different direction. His genitals were entirely missing. Neither Blacker nor Tiffany nor any of the policemen or coroners who followed them would find those particular anatomical items.

His clothes were neatly folded on a nearby chair.

Three or four fat houseflies lazily circled the body, darting away and then back after bumping into the big window at the front of the house.

Tiffany left the house and went to the street, where he vomited. He spat and wiped his mouth, then instructed the watching carriage driver to send for more wagons and for as many doctors as could be found. Meanwhile, Constable Jones walked away from Cinderhouse to the kitchen, and so had the dubious honor of having discovered both of the corpses in Day's house. Jones had come up at the Yard with Rupert Winthrop, and the sight of the body caused him to lose himself. Tiffany found him sitting at the kitchen table, softly crying and squeezing a damp coverlet.

Blacker accompanied Day up the stairs. They went as quickly

as Day could manage. Halfway up, they could hear an odd mewling sound, and Blacker left Day there on the staircase. He ran ahead, while Day called out his wife's name.

He was relieved beyond words to hear her answer him.

By the time Day got to their bedroom, Blacker was already coming back out. Blacker nodded at him and went to check the other rooms on that floor.

Day stood in the doorway and held on to the wall. Claire smiled at him from the bed. She looked sleepy, but relaxed. In her arms, she held two tiny babies.

"Walter," she said, "would you like to come say hello to your daughters?"

Day smiled and let go of the wall. He took a step forward.

And fainted.

66

Jack stopped outside and knelt by the curb. He took Griffin's blue chalk from his pocket and drew a large zero on the footpath. Above it, he drew an arrow pointing toward the house. He stood and put the chalk back in his pocket and went to the door, pulled the bell.

He had been busy in the two days since saving Sergeant Hammersmith's life. He had a lot of time to make up. When the housekeeper came to the door, he handed her Inspector Day's card, lifted from the occasional table in Day's hall, and was ushered into a reception room. He sat in a chair next to the door so that he wouldn't be immediately noticed by anyone entering the room, and he waited. There was a large portrait above the fireplace of a jowly man with thinning hair.

Jack stared at the portrait and folded his hands in his lap and felt utterly at peace.

Some fifteen minutes later, a man was preceded into the room by his voice: "So, Day, you've decided to join us, have you?"

A stout man stopped just inside the door and looked around, confused. He didn't see Jack until it was too late. Jack rose and stepped into the doorway and grabbed the man about the throat from behind. With his free hand, he closed the reception room door, pushing it gently until the latch clicked.

The stout man resembled the jowly man above the fire. Jack wondered how they were related.

"Dr Martin Bickford-Buckley?"

"I'm Dr Bickford-Buckley. Who are you?" His voice was strangled and hoarse.

Jack let go of the man's throat and allowed him to turn. As soon as the doctor saw him, he gasped.

"It's you," he said.

"You weren't expecting me?"

"How did you . . ."

"I thought I'd take the time to return your bag," Jack said. He held up the black medical bag with the initials MBB stamped into the side. "And now that I have, perhaps there is a thing or two we might discuss."

"I'll discuss nothing with you."

There was a knock at the door.

Jack whispered, "If you say a word that I don't like, I'll kill her, too. You have a last opportunity to be a noble man. Do you understand?"

Bickford-Buckley nodded, and Jack opened the door. The house-

keeper entered with a silver tray. She set it on the table, curtsied, and left again without ever looking up at them. Jack closed the door behind her and latched it.

He smiled at the doctor. "How do you take your tea?"

"You've come to kill me. I regret nothing, so get on with it."

"Gladly. But first, I hope you'll give me the names of our mutual Karstphanomen friends. Not too soon, mind you. I have some sharp clinky metal things here I'd like to show you. Tell me, have you ever heard the phrase 'divine retribution'?"

"Oh, good Lord!"

"Yes. That's exactly right. I'm glad you understand."

Jack barely caught the man again before he screamed, and after that he ensured that Dr Bickford-Buckley made no loud noises during their long visit. He didn't want to disturb the housekeeper. She seemed like a nice lady.

He left a gift for her on the mantel before he let himself out.

67

Dr Kingsley had made special arrangements at University College Hospital, and a large sitting room had been refashioned into a private convalescence ward for two special patients. Day and Hammersmith lay side by side in clean white beds while nurses bustled about and patients in the nearby public wards cried out. Most of the time, the two policemen slept. When they were awake, they rarely spoke. Day's legs were heavily wrapped in layers of gauze, and he was sedated for the first two days and nights of his stay. Hammersmith required more attention. One of his lungs was perforated, but the wound had been sewn shut in time to save his life. Dr Kingsley inspected the stitches and declared them to be adequate. It was clearly the work of an amateur, but a talented amateur, and there was no reason to submit Hammersmith to the trauma of reopening that wound. His chest posed a different problem. Fiona had kept him from bleeding to death, but her stitchwork was clumsy. Kingsley had removed the stitches from his chest and sewn him back up. He informed both Hammersmith and Fiona that there would be significant scarring, but that he had every reason to expect a full recovery. This did not comfort Hammersmith, who felt he should not have allowed himself to be stabbed in the first place.

Cinderhouse's body had been put back together and examined. In addition to the missing genitals, Kingsley was unable to find the left kidney or the tongue. Mr Michael, owner of the house on Phoenix Street, eventually verified that one of the tongues found on his chimneypiece had come from Cinderhouse's mouth, but there was no way to determine which one, and so both tongues were cremated along with the tailor's remains.

The same day that Cinderhouse was burned and discarded, Claire Day finally visited the hospital. She pushed a pram that had been modified to fit two babies. A young nurse cooed over the infants and led Claire to the private room where Day had been awakened and dressed for the occasion. He lay atop his starched white sheets and smiled at Claire when she entered. She ran to him and they hugged, carefully, and she showered his lips and eyes and forehead with kisses.

"I've been so worried," she said. "Dr Kingsley wouldn't let me come."

They whispered to each other, careful not to wake Hammer-smith, whose ravaged chest rose and fell rhythmically, miraculously.

"How are you?"

"How am *I*? How are *you*? Walter, you almost died."

"Nonsense. A rough day on the job, that's all."

"You didn't really get a chance to see the girls."

She went to the pram and wheeled it to the bed. Day looked down at his daughters, who slept curled up around each other like kittens.

"They're lovely," he said. "Did it . . . I'm sorry I wasn't there for you."

"Well, you've got a wonderful excuse."

Day laughed. "Yes, I suppose I do. You're all right now?"

"I haven't slept much."

"I've slept entirely too much."

"Tell me about your legs," Claire said.

"I've kept them both."

"Well, that's a good start. Will you walk?"

"I'm told I will, in time. There was tissue damage to the left leg. He didn't do much to the right, and I should make a full recovery there. But I'll walk with a cane."

"It will make you look dignified."

"It will make me look old."

"I don't care how old you look."

Day pointed at the pram. "I wasn't expecting two."

"Imagine my surprise."

"They're so tiny."

"They came early. But they're healthy."

"They'll live?"

"I told you, they're healthy."

"What about you? Are you all right?"

"I'm fine. Dr Kingsley has given me a clean bill of health. Only I don't like to be at home by myself anymore. Not even with Fiona there. I can't go into the kitchen. I certainly can't go into the parlor."

"I heard about what happened."

"Poor Constable Winthrop. I can't even look in that room now. The parlor, either. Our house is ruined."

"Nonsense. Give it a little time. We'll make new memories there."

"I spend a lot of time with our girls at the park. I make up little rhymes for them and they love it. They smile when I sing."

"Of course they do. They know they've got the best mother in London. In the world."

"Would you like to hear one of my rhymes?"

"Perhaps later. Maybe once I'm home again."

"Oh, Walter, I know you've had second thoughts about having a child. And now there are two. Please don't—"

"What are you talking about?"

"I know."

He shook his head. "Not second thoughts. Not really. I was worried about you. After what happened to my mother . . ."

"I'm fine. I'm not sad like your mother was. And you are not your father."

"And you are not yours, thank God."

She laughed. "Thank God. We really ought to name them. The babies."

"That can wait."

"When will you come home?"

"That's a question for the doctor, but I should think no later than tomorrow."

"And what about Nevil?"

"His recovery will take a good bit longer, I think."

"Not so," Hammersmith said. They looked at him and saw that his eyes were open and he was smiling at them. His face was very pale, and the nurses had not done a good job of shaving his chin. "If you leave tomorrow, I leave tomorrow."

"Nevil," Claire said, "you'll do what Dr Kingsley tells you to or you'll answer to me, sir."

She stood and went to Hammersmith's bedside, put a hand on his forehead. His hair was sweaty, but his skin was cool to the touch.

"How are you, Mrs Day?"

"Better than you are, Nevil."

"I'm just fine."

"Of course you are. I begin to think you're indestructible."

"I do wish people would stop testing that theory."

"Yes."

"What about Fiona Kingsley? I'd like to thank her. I'm told she saved my life."

Claire looked away. "She'll visit soon." In fact, Fiona had declared that she could not bear to see Hammersmith again. She felt she was doomed to remember him always at death's door.

They all turned at the sound of someone clearing his throat. Sir Edward Bradford stood at the door, a gift-wrapped package in his hand.

"Good," he said. "You're both awake. Mrs Day, good morning to you."

"Please come in," Claire said.

He stepped over the threshold and held the package out to her.

"I brought this," he said, "thinking I'd give it to the inspector. I didn't want to disturb you at home so soon after the . . ." He glanced nervously at the pram.

"Oh, thank you, sir. Would you like to see them?"

"I can't stay long. There's still a prisoner on the loose."

She took the package and turned the pram around so that he could look down into it. He nodded at the sleeping babies and smiled back up at Claire.

"They're perfect, aren't they?" he said.

"Very much so," Claire said.

"Well done, mum."

"Thank you."

"That's, um . . ." He pointed to the package. "It's a toy. I didn't think to get two of them. I'll send another one."

"They can share, I'm sure."

"It's the sort of thing you wind up and the puppet pops up at the end."

"How thoughtful."

"They may have to wait to play with it. It might be frightening for babies that small. I'd forgotten how small they can be."

"I'll put it aside for them," Claire said. "For when they're ready."

Sir Edward nodded and looked over at the men in their beds. Claire followed his gaze and hurried over to her husband, kissed his cheek.

"Well," she said, "I suppose you men have business to discuss. I'd better go and feed these young ladies."

"It was good to see you, Mrs Day."

"And you, sir."

Sir Edward watched as she covered the babies with a white coverlet and wheeled the pram out of the room. He looked down the hall after her, then closed the door and turned to his men.

"Very kind of you, sir," Day said.

"Don't give it a thought."

"Well, thank you anyway. Tell me . . . the Harvest Man, have they caught him yet?"

"There's been no sign. An apothecary was broken into the night before last. Ether was stolen. And an old mask they kept as decoration. It might have been him, but we've got nowhere with it. Blacker and Tiffany especially are beside themselves. Haven't slept since you two went down."

"And what about Jack? Have you found him?"

"I'm charging Adrian March with the crimes against you."

Day swung his legs off the bed and stood, balanced carefully on his right foot. He tried to take a step toward the commissioner, but fell backward and sat on the edge of his bed.

"Sir, it wasn't Adrian March."

"You were under considerable duress and those tunnels are filled with pockets of gas, Inspector Day. Your mind was not your own. I imagine you saw a great many spectacular things."

"It was no gas. Jack the Ripper is on the loose again, and we've got to track him before he does something worse than he already has."

Sir Edward gave him a long, sad look. "Don't . . . Inspector Day, I have already made my report. In it, I state that you were instrumental in stopping the murderer Cinderhouse, who invaded your home and killed poor Constable Winthrop. You found and apprehended both Napper and Griffin. You're a hero. There's only one convict still out there, and the public believes, largely because of what they've read about you in the tabloids, that we will capture the Harvest Man any day now. What do you think it would do to London, to the people in this city, if you told them that Saucy Jack was still out there among them?"

"It doesn't matter," Hammersmith said. Day and Sir Edward both turned to the sergeant, who had not spoken to this point. "It doesn't matter what anyone thinks. There's a madman about and he will kill more people unless we stop him."

"Ah, Sergeant, your attitude is what I've actually come here to discuss," Sir Edward said.

"Sir?" Hammersmith's expression was grim, and Day wondered how much pain he was experiencing. His own wounds hurt much more than they had two days earlier in the underground cell. In some ways the healing process was worse than the injury.

"Sergeant, you almost died," Sir Edward said.

"I'll be right as rain by tomorrow," Hammersmith said.

"No, you won't. But knowing you, you'll attempt to come back to work anyway."

"Sir, I—"

"Let me say it, Sergeant. Since I've known you, you've been beaten, poisoned at least twice, nearly frozen to death, and now you've been stabbed, cut open, and sewn back together. You rarely seem to eat or sleep. You regularly push yourself past the limits of your body."

"I try to do my job, sir."

"But I believe your job is killing you, Mr Hammersmith."

"Sir, I respectfully—"

"I can't let you do this anymore. For your own good—"

"Sir," Day said. "You can't."

"I think I have to."

"If you dismiss him, I'll go, too."

"You have two new babies, Inspector. Think about what you're saying."

"I stand by Nevil. We need him on the Murder Squad."

"Well," Sir Edward said, "I need him to live. And I firmly believe he will die if he continues at this pace. I am dismissing him from his duties. And you as well, Mr Day, if that is what you choose. In fact, that makes things a bit easier for me. It has crossed my mind that you might be mad." He looked away from them toward the small window in the far wall. "I mean no ill will toward either of you, but I have given this a great deal of thought and I believe it's the only responsible decision I can make."

He went to the door and stopped there, but did not turn back around, didn't look at them. "I wish you both a speedy recovery and a very long life," he said.

And he left them there.

68

Claire pushed the pram away from the hospital. The sun was warm on her face, but she stopped on the path and tucked the coverlet in around her daughters. She ran her fingers along its seams, where her ancestors' names were embroidered. There was a faint pink stain left there in the shape of a hand. She tried not to think about what it was. One of the babies, the quiet one who always seemed to be deep in thought, opened her eyes and smiled. Claire didn't know whether it was a genuine smile or the effect of gas, but she smiled back.

"Would you like to hear a rhyme, Baby Day?"

She wiped a bit of moisture from the baby's cheek and smoothed its fine dark hair and stood back up. A stranger tipped his hat to her and she nodded back at him, went around to the other side of the pram, and pushed it across the path to a bench. She sat where she could see her children's faces and she leaned forward and very softly recited the poem she had written that morning:

"I have two hands to clap and pray, two feet to skip and run.
I have two ears to hear you with, I have two eyes to see.

But of the most important things, the Lord just gave me one:
One head, one heart, and one thing more: One sister just like me."

The thoughtful baby rocked and cooed and woke up her sleeping sister. Both girls stared up at her expectantly, and so she began to tell them another verse, something she had read in a book once. She had only written two or three rhymes of her own so far, but she liked thinking them up and she liked telling them to the babies. Perhaps one day she might even write them all down somewhere in one place so that the girls could keep them and tell them to their own children when they grew up.

She sat on the bench and talked to her babies and was in no hurry to return home, where she felt certain that blood had soaked between the cracks in the floor and deep into the wood. She did not think she would ever feel safe in that house again, but the sun was warm on her face and her babies were smiling and her husband was healing.

69

W ell," Day said, "at least my wife wasn't in the room. Now I have some time to figure out what to tell her."

"There's nothing to tell," Hammersmith said. "You'll go back to work."

"I said I'd stand by you and I meant it."

"I know. And I thank you. But the commissioner will accept you back without a word about it if you simply appear at your desk in the morning. I'd wager he never brings the subject up again."

"Nevil . . ."

"No, Mr Day, you have two new babies to provide for. I have nothing."

Day opened his mouth to respond, but didn't know how. He

had no intention of returning to the Murder Squad without his friend, but he didn't want to argue about it. When Nevil Hammersmith said he had nothing, he was literally correct. His work was his life, and vice versa. He was a policeman through and through, and Day couldn't imagine him doing anything else. He turned his head and looked at Hammersmith on the other bed. His throat, from just above his collarbone down to the loose collar of his hospital blouse, was bright pink, inflamed and irritated after all that had been done to him.

"I will go back," Day said, "but only to talk to Sir Edward again. He's a reasonable man."

Hammersmith waved a weak dismissive hand in his direction. "I'd rather not talk about this anymore, if it's all right with you," he said. "I'm quite tired."

"Yes, of course. Sorry."

"After all, I've been awake for most of half an hour now."

"You are insufferably lazy."

"It comes naturally."

Day smiled and did his best to relax. He stared up at the ceiling, at a water stain that had spread from one corner and had advanced in stages, darker at its origin and increasingly fainter as it worked out toward the center of the room. He rehearsed in his mind the sorts of arguments he might make with Sir Edward, looking for the one logical thing he could say to change the commissioner's mind. Of course, Sir Edward wasn't incorrect: Hammersmith was often careless, he jumped forward into every battle, he pushed himself seemingly beyond the limits of human endurance . . . None of that helped his case. Perhaps, Day thought, if he promised to look after Hammersmith, keep him out of future danger . . .

"I don't need permission," Hammersmith said. His voice startled Day, who had thought the sergeant was asleep. "There's a murderer walking around out there, more than one, and I don't need to ask anyone what I can and can't do. I'm going to find that missing prisoner. And I'm going to find Jack for you, even if nobody else wants to do it."

"I believe this is exactly what Sir Edward is talking about. You almost died, Nevil."

"But I *didn't* die. Here I am and there they are, and I am going to catch them."

"No, you're not."

"Yes, I am. I really am, you know."

Day sighed. "Yes, I know. But would you please rest first? Would you wait until you're able to breathe properly and move without pain?"

"I tell you, I'm fine."

"You won't wait? Won't rest and let me try to talk to Sir Edward for you?"

"How many people will they kill while I lie in bed?"

"You can't wait even a week?"

"Tomorrow. I'm going to find them tomorrow."

"Then I'm going to help you."

"You can't walk."

"With you around, I hardly need to," Day said. "I could never keep up with you anyway."

"Then tomorrow."

"Perhaps. But today, will you please just lie there and think about pleasant things and let your body mend?"

"What kind of pleasant things?"

"I have no idea," Day said.

"Your babies are healthy. That's profoundly pleasant."

"It is." Day shook his head at the water stain on the ceiling. "That's really the only thing that matters, isn't it? And you're right."

"Of course I am," Hammersmith said. "Which part am I right about?"

"I have new responsibilities. I should go back to work."

"Yes, of course you should."

"I will."

"Good."

"After tomorrow."

"Yes. We've got one hell of a busy day ahead of us."

EPILOGUE

———✦———

Once upon a time, he knew, there had been other children. There had been friends and playmates for him, and they had probably called him by name. They had probably known who he was and maybe they had shouted at him across a public square or chased him round and round in the lane outside his home. But he couldn't remember those children, couldn't bring their faces to mind when he tried to think about them. He didn't know what words they had shouted, what name they had used to get his attention. For as long as he could remember, he had simply been called the Harvest Man.

He didn't mind it when the police and the doctors called him that. He had no other name he preferred. In fact, he didn't think of himself by any name at all. He simply was.

But he knew that someday he would find his family again and they would open their arms to him and gather him up, and they would lean in close to him and whisper his true name in his ear. And then he would remember everything that had been good before they died and left him alone.

Finding them was the trick. He had tried many times with no success. But his father had always said (and these were words he did remember), "If at first you don't succeed, try, try again."

And so the Harvest Man did try again.

He had his ether and he had his plague mask, to protect himself from the spirits, and he had his blade. It was long and curved and sharp. He had found it in a little store next to the apothecary where he had taken the ether and the mask. It was not as long or as curved as his old blade, the blade the policemen had taken away from him, but it was just as sharp and he liked it.

He crept to the attic door, opened it a crack, and listened. The family downstairs was still eating their evening meal. They were talking and laughing just exactly the way a family should. He couldn't hear what they were saying, but he could hear the love in their voices. He had chosen a good house. They were a good family.

He wondered what their names were.

He pushed the attic door shut again, careful not to make a sound, and crept back over to the wall. He sat down and crossed his legs and rested his back against the wall. He closed his eyes. There was nothing to look at, only the same dusty joists and cobwebs and dark corners that he had seen in other attics, in different houses.

But this time would be different. He could feel it.

All he had to do was wait until they fell asleep, and then he would go downstairs and use the ether and take his time. He would use the blade on their faces, he would carve away what didn't belong, and this time he was confident that he would find his family under those unfamiliar features.

He imagined the faces of his family smiling at him and he smiled back at them. The Harvest Man crossed his legs and relaxed and waited in the attic for the people downstairs to stop making noise.

He was a patient boy.

ACKNOWLEDGMENTS

Many thanks to my long-suffering agent, Seth Fishman, and my *very* patient editor, Neil Nyren. And to Ivan Held, for his continued faith in me and in the Murder Squad series.

Thanks to Emily Walters and Kristy Blomquist for helping me understand Claire's experience. And to Benito Cereno for his help with the Karstphanomen's Latin phrases.

My Bad Karma mates, B. Clay Moore, Jeremy Haun, and Seth Peck, helped keep me going, offering many helpful suggestions and contact information. (Seth found the jailer's gun used by the Karstphanomen.) Thanks, fellas!

My early readers, Roxane White, Alison Clayton, Ande Parks, and Brandy Schillace, helped enormously with their enthusiasm, expertise, and eagle eyes.

ACKNOWLEDGMENTS

Richard Walters provided the haunting sound track I listened to while writing this book.

As much as I've enjoyed getting to know my shadow on the wall, the real-life Jack the Ripper killed at least five innocent women: Mary Ann Nichols, Annie Chapman, Elizabeth Stride, Catherine Eddowes, and Mary Jane Kelly. I do not wish to minimize their lives or their tragic deaths in any way.

And, finally, many thanks for ever and always to my wonderful wife and son.